Can't Let You Go

Jenny B. Jones

Can't Let You Go

An old love whose kisses make her weak, but whose secrets threaten to destroy all she holds dear . . .

Fresh out of college, Katie Parker had it all—a charming romance, a role in a famous stage production, and an idyllic life in London. *Until* she found her boyfriend cheating and got herself fired from the play. Leaving everything behind, Katie hops a plane home, only to run into her first love, Charlie Benson. As the couple returns to In Between, Katie questions everything she ever thought she wanted—including a renewed romance with her high school flame.

While she attempts to rebuild her life, Katie's plan to manage the family's theater meets a devastating obstacle, dragging her into a legal battle that will rock her small town. And the boy who once broke her heart seems to have the power to do it again. As Charlie's secrets unravel, Katie must make a choice. Can she overcome her past and trust Charlie with her heart again?

Cover Design: Kelli Standish

For information contact:
jen@jennybjones.com

Follow Jenny on Facebook:
https://www.facebook.com/jennybjones

Follow Jenny on Twitter:
https://twitter.com/JenBJones

Sign up for Jenny's Book News Blasts
http://www.jennybjones.com/news/

Dedicated to Dana Tanner

Rock star of positivity, inspiration to all, beautiful inside and out, day-maker, light-giver, anointed one, overcomer, friend

Chapter One

"WHAT DO YOU mean my bags aren't here?" I leaned over the counter at the O'Hare airport, fresh out of patience and smiles. The TSA employee's fingers clickity-clacked on his keyboard, his generous brows knit together like an escaped wooly worm.

"I'm sorry, Miss Parker. Something apparently went very wrong, and your luggage seems to be on a flight to Reykjavik."

"This is unacceptable. Who goes to Iceland?"

"Apparently your bags do. Look ma'am, I'm just the gate agent. You'll have to talk to the folks in baggage."

"I already did that." I wanted to slap my hand on the counter and yell until Mr. Brows made this all okay, and I knew it wasn't his job. But I just couldn't handle one more catastrophe. My bottom lip quivered, and I heard the pitiful words tumble from my lips. "My whole life is in those bags."

"Surely not everything," said a voice behind me.

That voice.

One I hadn't heard in years, except in my dreams of home and heartache.

I turned around, pushing my tired, limp hair from my flushed cheek. Suddenly all the exhaustion of a ten hour flight evaporated, the weeks without sleep, the homesickness. All that I'd left behind in London.

"Charlie Benson." His name came out of my mouth like a sacred whisper as he stood there smiling.

I immediately burst into tears.

"Hey." Strong arms wrapped around me, and I was taken right back. My head pressed to Charlie's chest, I inhaled his achingly familiar scent, and I was no longer this broken, exhausted twenty-three year old, who'd just spent a year studying abroad, the pieces of my heart the only luggage that followed. I was sixteen, back in my hometown of In Between, dancing with one sweet Charlie Benson on my back porch underneath the Texas stars.

"How are you here?" I dashed at the tears and took a much-needed step back. I let my eyes roam over the boy before me. Could I even call him a boy? He stood tall and broad shouldered, as if now carrying not just muscle, but some of the world's responsibilities. With his dark dress pants, white button down, and navy tie, Charlie looked all man. And a professional one at that. "Are you headed home?"

"Yes. Got out of a meeting only minutes ago." Charlie now lived and worked in the Windy City. "So my big brother and your best friend getting married. Crazy, huh?"

"Crazy that Frances and Joey got together, or that they're pulling this quickie wedding business?"

His smile told me he didn't share in my concern over Frances Vega and Joey Benson going from first date to wedding date in less than ninety days.

"I mean, three months?" I held up an appropriate number of fingers as a stunning visual aid. "Who does that? What's their rush?" Frances swore to me she wasn't pregnant, brainwashed, or trying to avoid testifying on Joey's behalf, but this was not like my neurotic, nerdy, logic-ruled best friend.

"I guess they just know it's right," Charlie said, as we both began to walk toward our gate. "I've never seen my brother so happy."

"It's called lust."

"Is it?" Charlie laughed. "That's just sad, Katie. When did you get so cynical?" He didn't bother to let me answer. "So trouble with your last flight?"

"It's been the longest day. A flight cancellation, a lot of waiting and stress-eating, then the new plane got delayed, and for my finale, a little scrap with customs. It's so good to be finally headed home." To my mom and dad, my crazy grandmother, to people who loved me. My gosh, I'd missed them.

"How was living in London?"

Don't think about it. Don't think about it. "Very nice."

"My mom keeps me updated on In Between. She said you were in some great plays on the West End." At my nod he smiled. "She says you're kind of a big deal."

Glad someone thought so. "Just lucked into some good roles, I guess."

"*Flight 247 for Houston will now begin boarding our first class passengers. . .*"

Rain pelted the wall of windows at the gate, and I wondered if the crew had noticed.

"Are you on this flight?" Charlie asked.

"Yes, you?"

"Yep. I'm going home until the wedding. A little working vacation." He reached out, ran his hand down my arm, his head tilted just so. "Are you sure you're okay?"

"What, me? This?" I gestured to my mess of a face. "Jet lag, you know? And then the airline losing my stuff." I gave a laugh so genuine, the Academy should've FexExed me an Oscar. "I'm sorry. I'm a little homesick, and when I saw you—" I shook my head and smiled. "I guess you were just a sight for sore eyes. So how are your folks?" I knew exactly how they were, but it was time to divert the focus from my crazy.

"Mom stays busy with my little sister. And Dad. . ." Charlie adjusted the strap of his laptop bag. "He's ambitious as ever. Yours?"

"James and Millie are actually scheduled to leave on a mission trip to Haiti a few days after I arrive." My foster parents had adopted me when I was seventeen, and I couldn't have asked for a better mom and dad. I had taken their last name, officially becoming Katie Parker Scott, but Katie Parker was my stage name. And the only thing Charlie had ever called me.

It had been over five months since I'd seen my parents when they'd visited me at Christmas, and I was dying for a Scott family reunion.

The garbled voice came across the speakers again.

"Time for me to board," Charlie said. "Where are you sitting?" He held out a hand for my ticket, and I fumbled in my bag to find it.

"It's here somewhere." I dug through the outer-pocket, coming up with a nail file, half a Snickers, two pieces of gum, and ten wads of semi-used Kleenex.

"Hey." He stepped nearer. "You're shaking."

I waved it off. "Fatigue."

He took my worn leather messenger bag, searched the middle compartment, and pulled out my ticket. "You're still afraid of flying, aren't you?"

The things people remembered. One senior class trip to Miami Beach in which I tried to storm the cockpit demanding two forms of identification from the pilots, and everyone labels you a full-blown nut job.

Please. I had grown up since then.

"Final boarding call . . ."

"It's been incredible seeing you today." Charlie pulled me in for a hug, and I just breathed him in. The warm, the familiar, the safe. "We have more catching up to do." His voice was a caress near my ear. "Are you going to be okay?"

"Definitely. I haven't had a flying meltdown in such a long time."

It had been at least three hours.

Clutching a water bottle and my wrinkled ticket, I followed Charlie as we boarded the sparsely populated plane. He stopped off in row seven, while I schlepped to the very back of the cabin. Next to the bathroom. How these odiferous seats didn't come with a discount was beyond me.

I squeezed my bag in the bin above me, then settled into the window seat, hoping the two empty seats on my right remained that way. Buckling in, I checked my phone one last time. I quickly responded to a text from my mom, two from my dad, and five from my grandma that consisted of nothing more than her fish-lipped selfies with the message, "My face misses yours!"

And then there were those voicemails I'd immediately deleted.

Fifteen minutes later, we taxied down the runway. I sat in my blissfully empty row, pushed my breath in and out, and prayed to the Lord Jesus to spare me one more day. I wasn't afraid of what came after death. I was just a little terrified of the actual dying process. Especially if it involved crashing, flames, and wasted drink carts.

I was just promising the Holy Father my favorite mascara and first born when a shoulder bumped mine, as someone threw himself into the seat beside me. I continued to whisper my beggar's prayer when a hand covered my clenched fingers.

I looked up.

Charlie smiled. He brushed my damp hair from my face like he'd done it a million times before. He pulled my hand from my lap and just held it in his.

"I'm not afraid to fly," I said.

"Of course not." He gave my fingers a squeeze. "It's the fatigue."

Thunder cracked outside. "Do you think it's safe to be in the air?"

"I do."

"But I read this report that when it storms, your statistical chances of—"

"It's perfectly safe."

"But sometimes lightning can strike the plane—"

"Nearly impossible."

"And then there's the possibility of—"

"Katie?"

My heart beat wildly, and my bones ached with exhaustion. "Yes?"

His gray eyes held mine. "I won't let anything happen to us."

"Promise?"

With a smile as safe as church and sweet as sun tea, he slowly nodded. "Always."

Chapter Two

I WAS PRACTICALLY raised on the streets. By twelve, I had a rap sheet, knew how to steal to eat, could pick a lock with just paper clips and Trident, and could deflect the advances of my druggie mom's boyfriends with one well-placed knee.

I was fearless.

And now here I sat in my worn, cramped plane seat two hours into the ride, shaking like a weed in a tornado, and noticing I was still clutching Charlie Benson's hand like it was all that held us upright.

I let go and gave a small laugh. "Sorry." Nothing like reuniting with an old friend by welcoming them into your neurotic phobia. "Takeoffs make me nervous." And the part that comes after—the whole driving in the sky thing, hanging by clouds, winds, and various gravitational whims. "Takes me a while to wind down afterward."

His eyes softened, and I remembered all the times as a teenager I'd stared into them, sure there was a God, and He had baptized Charlie with a benevolence of genetic blessings that resulted in one beautiful, intelligent boy who had routinely taken my breath away.

"I love to fly." Charlie rested his head against the seat and smiled. "I've put in a lot of miles in the last year. I love the rocking of the plane, the hum of the engine. Some of the best sleeping conditions."

"Right." I would have to be drugged unconscious. "So tell me about your job." Charlie had gone to college in Chicago, leaving the town of In Between, while I had stayed behind, doing junior college, then moving on to a state university in South Texas.

His gaze left mine, and he looked down the aisle toward the flight attendant pushing a cart. "Nothing exciting. I interned for this company my senior year. They hired me right after graduation."

"What do you do?"

"I'm very entry level," he said. "I'm kind of a glorified paper pusher right now."

"I know that won't last long. What company did you say you're with?"

"Would you like a beverage?" The flight attendant brought her silver cart to a stop by us, her red lips smiling.

I requested a soda, and the woman popped the top on the can and poured it over ice.

"You probably want to give her the whole can," Charlie said. "I think Katie here could use the stiff drink."

"Would you like me to pour in some complimentary tequila?" the flight attendant asked.

I nodded vigorously. "Yes, please."

"I was just kidding." She laughed and pushed her cart down the aisle.

More cruelty delivered mid-air. Thanks, lady.

"You're fine," Charlie said. "The hard part is over."

"Maybe you could keep talking." I snuggled my side into the chair, facing my old friend. My old boyfriend. "Keep my mind off our imminent doom."

He laughed. "Tell me about you. You haven't been too present on Facebook the last year. Hard to tell what you've been up to."

Images of the last six years flashed through my mind. Some of them amazing. Some of them . . . not worth thinking on. "I finally graduated." I took a bolstering swig of soda, enjoying the way it burned going down. "Then I got selected to go work in London." Had that been a blessing or a curse?

"My mom said you were in some pretty impressive productions."

I'd forgotten how intense his gray eyes could be. So focused, like I was the only person he wanted to be talking to. Those eyes were older now, still full of mischief, always reflecting an intimidating intelligence, but now there was something more looking back at me. Something darker, maybe a little bit heavy. Like Charlie Benson might have had some sadness and secrets of his own.

"It was an unforgettable experience," I finally said.

"How long are you staying?"

"A while." I left it at that, clutching my arm rest as we hit a few bumps of turbulence. "What about you?"

He lifted his drink and absently swirled it, studying the dark contents. "I'm staying until the wedding at least. Spend some time with my family." Charlie had his brother Joey, who was four years older than us, but he also had a very young sister who had come along our junior year of high school, a late surprise to his parents.

The wedding was still almost a month away. "So you could be in In Between for quite a while."

"My job is pretty flexible right now. I can work from anywhere. I never get to spend any time with Sadie. Skype is great, but I think we need some brother-sister time."

"That's really sweet." I didn't know Joey well, but I hoped he was just as thoughtful. Frances deserved the best.

The plane made a sharp jerk to the right, and I slapped my hand on Charlie's. I frantically looked around, but neither of the flight attendants seemed concerned. The person across from us read a *People*, while the couple a row ahead amiably chatted away.

Lightning cracked outside, and I jumped.

Charlie's fingers slid back and forth over mine. "We're fine," he said as the plane dipped, sending my stomach to my feet. "Just a storm."

And just how many more of those did I have to endure?

I looked at my hand captured in his, and I knew Charlie was just being nice. That's just who he was. But the rhythmic strokes of his fingers calmed my frayed nerves as nothing else had on this long voyage home.

The plane began to shake and rattle like the busted glove compartment on my old Toyota. Only I couldn't turn up the radio, sing my car solos, and drown out the noisy vibrations.

"Why do you think we didn't work out?" I asked.

Charlie didn't startle. Merely lifted a dark brow as he inclined his head closer to mine. "Where did that come from?"

"Was it me?"

"I—"

"Is there something about me that pushes guys away? That asks to be dumped?"

His hand on mine stilled just as a flight attendant gave a staticky report. "Ladies and gentlemen, we will be preparing for landing soon, and the captain has turned on the seat belt sign a bit early. We're hitting a brief patch of turbulence with this storm, but we'll be out of it in no time and getting you on the ground."

"She sounded worried didn't she? Did you hear that tension?" I sat up as straight as my seatbelt would let me, frantically taking in every detail around me—the location of the flight attendants, the body language of fellow passengers, the reassuring presence of the wings that still seem to be blessedly attached.

Charlie poured more drink into my icy cup. He was probably regretting sitting by me. He probably wished I'd drink my diet soda and happily pass out in a carbonated coma, so he could go back to his own seat and read his *Wall Street Journal* or whatever it was a calm, *normal* professional would read.

I needed medication.

"Here, eat some of these." Charlie reached into the leather bag at his feet and pulled out a box of M&Ms.

I snatched them out of his grip and downed a handful. I chewed vigorously, savoring the sugar and chocolate on my tongue. What if this was the last time I tasted such heaven?

The plane, deciding the shaking was just its opening act, brought on the full-on quaking, jumping up and down like a Pentecostal at a Holy Ghost revival. My butt gained some air, and I turned my frightened gaze to Charlie. "What's happening?"

"Turbulence." He lifted a shoulder in such a lazy fashion, you'd have thought he hadn't noticed the way his hair bounced on his head from the aeronautical shenanigan. "You were asking me why we didn't work out."

"I was?" Those overhead bins were vibrating loud enough to crack something. Like a wall.

His smile was a slow lifting of the lips. "Why do you think we didn't make it?"

I tightened my seatbelt, trying not to wonder at the age and durability of it. "Because you had your eye on some blonde Barbie who I could never compete with."

"That's not true."

"That you didn't have your eye on Chelsea Blake?" My high school nemesis.

He had the decency to look guilty. "That you couldn't compare. You were prettier and smarter than her any day."

Men in shimmy-shaky planes will say anything. "But you dumped me to go after her."

"Geez, that was high school. And I believe it was a mutual break-up. What was that guy's name you started dating that summer?"

"Tate." Sweet boy, but we had made better friends than a romantic duo. When he had dumped me he'd said, "*Katie, your heart's just somewhere else. And it's not with me.*"

"I got smart our senior year," Charlie said. "Finally worked up the nerve to ask you to prom." He squeezed the hand he was still holding and gave me a look that zinged right to my weary core. "And you and I spent most of the night camping on a blanket under the stars."

"At the lake." I'd been in a wreck that week, missing school for five days. With my leg in a cast, prom had been too much for me, and

Charlie had come to my rescue, taking me out to the lake. He'd built me a fire, made a pallet on the rocky ground, tucked me into the crook of his arm, and pointed out every constellation he could find in that April sky while I rested my head on his chest and listened to the crickets and the cadence of his heart.

Then we graduated. And Charlie Benson, of the lingering kisses and spell-binding astronomy, had moved away.

Rain and wind battled outside my window, and I uttered a quick litany of prayers. Prayers that begged for calm skies and fifty more years of life.

"Guys don't stick around though." I watched bolt of lightning slash the sky. "Eventually they find someone else, something better."

He leaned close. "Is that what you really think? That you weren't good enough?"

"It's hard to argue with history." I held up a hand to stop him from interrupting. "I'm not trying to be pitiful. I just want to get to the bottom of it. I'm tired of making mistakes, wasting my time." Being tossed out, left behind.

The plane took a leap north then dipped back down. My breath caught in my throat. "I want off this thing," I said. "I want off this thing right now."

"Please put your seats in the upright position," announced the flight attendant. "Return your tray to its proper place."

The pilot took his turn next, giving instructions and saying God only knew what—probably Last Rites. But I couldn't hear a thing for the rising noise around me. Somewhere up front a baby wailed. Nervous chatter swelled within the cabin.

"What's the pilot saying?" My heart beat a crazed staccato, and I wanted to both cry and laugh at the insanity of it all.

"He said to stay calm, that we'd be out of this storm soon." Charlie took quick stock of the situation around us, then turned his attention back to me. "You were telling me why you broke my heart when we saw each other last."

"I did not."

I expected him to smile, to follow up with a joke.

But Charlie said nothing.

He captured my other hand, prying my fingers off the armrest, then pulled me closer, laying his forehead against mine. "I don't think you remember the events of those last few months accurately. Katie, I—"

His words died as light and fury exploded around us.

The flash of lightning.

Screaming.

Falling.

Plummeting.

Spinning.

Fear clawed within me as Charlie threw his body over mine. "Hang on," he yelled in my ear. "Just hang on to me."

I couldn't breathe. Couldn't drag in enough breath.

Please, God, save us.

I uttered the plea silently.

Then aloud.

It wasn't that I didn't want to go to heaven. It was just that I didn't want to clock-in at the age of twenty-three. I'd always known flying through the sky was a bad idea. Always.

"Charlie?"

"I'm right here. I'm not letting you go."

His arms encircled me and held my tight. He mumbled words of assurance, broken prayers, and other utterances the terror swallowed whole.

I couldn't go like this. I couldn't let the words I'd held for so long die with me.

With all my strength I pushed Charlie off of me, only to grab his face, his stubbly cheeks in the palms of my hands. His wide, dilated eyes searched mine.

"I love you, Charlie." I pulled his face closer, blocking out the shrieks around us and the spin and tilt of death. "Do you hear me? I never stopped loving you."

"Katie, I—"

Then I pressed my mouth to his, holding Charlie Benson to me, knowing these lips would soon draw their last breath.

And I didn't want to waste those seconds.

Then Charlie Benson was kissing me back. His lips covered mine. His hands cradled my head. Hot tears slipped down my cheeks, and I thought of my family. The foster parents who had taken me in when I'd been a broken, rough sixteen years old. Mad Maxine, the crazy old lady who'd become not just my grandmother, but my best friend. They'd changed me. Given me a new life, rewritten my future.

The world spun.

The plane fell.

And I just held on.

"I've got you," I heard him say again. "I'm not letting you go."

And after all these years, I believed him.

Just when it was too late.

And with Charlie's kiss consuming me, my world went dark.

Chapter Three

HEAVEN WAS. . . UNEXPECTEDLY noisy.

Eyes still shut, I listened to the beeps and clicks around me. I expected angel choirs, a hallelujah chorus, maybe some cheering at my arrival.

And *ow*.

My body ached like I'd been hit by a train.

What happened to being pain-free? Was that just a line to get us to drop more in the collection plate?

I struggled to lift open my eyelids, but nothing seemed to be working. If I was in a new body, clearly Jesus owed me a refund.

"Katie?"

At least someone knew my name.

"Katie, can you hear me?"

I tried to answer, but my lips wouldn't work, my tongue somehow stuck to the roof of my mouth. So thirsty. So tired.

"Squeeze my hand if you can hear me."

That voice. It was so familiar.

Millie?

"She squeezed my hand. Did you see that, James?"

"I did. Can you open your eyes, sweetheart?"

The light.

"Turn it off." Jesus needed to turn his high beams down. Glory was painfully bright.

"Come on, girl. Talk to us."

I blinked with hangover-heavy eyelids, and the scene slowly came into focus, one blurry pixel at a time.

"Millie?" I swallowed past the dry, copper taste on my tongue. "James?" I was surely alive. Beeps and voices sounded in the hall outside, and the walls around me told me I was in a hospital room. A very ugly one.

"What happened?" I asked.

"Oh, geez. She doesn't remember anything." My grandma hip-bumped Millie and scooted her way to my bed. "This happened on *Days of Our Lives*." She grabbed my hands and leaned down inches from my face. "You're Katie Parker Scott." Her volume could've lifted the ceiling. "This is your mom, Millie and your dad . . ." She looked at James then shrugged. "I don't remember his name, but they've been legally bound for at least a few years. And I'm Millie's younger sister Maxine."

"I know who you are."

"If you recall, I had an illustrious movie career, everyone back home adores me, and in polite company, we do not talk about my torrid affair with Brad Pitt."

It hurt to smile. "Stop yelling," I whispered. "I remember every-thing."

Maxine arched an artfully plucked brow. "You do?"

I nodded. "And we all know you've never even met Brad Pitt."

She sniffed. "It could happen."

Millie sat on the white-blanketed bed. "You've been out for about six hours. Do you remember what happened?"

I shot straight up from my pillow. "Millie—all those people!" Dear God, we had crashed. "Charlie. Where's Charlie?" Was I the lone survivor? I didn't want to be! They would put me on *Good Morning America* and expect me to write a book and do some made-for-TV movie starring some down-and-out Disney actress.

"He's fine. You're all fine." Millie held me down with gentle arms.

"There was no crash."

My heart raced. "He's okay?"

"He's been right by your side the whole time," James said. "We just sent him to get coffee downstairs."

My body shook with the relief, and I deflated in exhaustion. "But I don't understand. We were going down. It was awful. I just knew we were going to—"

"You hit a pretty bad storm," James said. "We still don't have much information, but it appears the plane lost control for a bit. The pilot made an emergency landing."

"In a cornfield." Maxine gripped my hands harder. "Did you see any crop circles while you were landing?"

"She didn't see anything," Millie said. "It got so rough anything not belted down went airborne. A few of the overhead bins flew open and a bag hit you on the head. Knocked you out cold."

"Charlie scooped you into his strong, manly arms, held you to him, slid with you down the emergency thingie, then carried you to safety." Maxine hid her lips behind her hand. "You should've used your feminine wiles and held out for mouth-to-mouth."

"I was a little busy being unconscious."

"You should sue the airline and get tons of money," Maxine said. "I'll represent you. I've watched a lot of court shows. I bet that pilot was sexting."

"How do you feel?" Millie ran her hand over my hair. "You got some stitches on your forehead."

Maxine eyed my wound. "And even though it's puffy and ugly, and you could be deformed for life, we want you to know we're still gonna try and love you anyway."

"Noble of you." I lifted my hand to my head, my fingers sliding over the bandage.

The door eased open and in walked Charlie Benson, carrying a burrito, three candy bars, and a YooHoo. His gaze landed on me, his eyes softening. "You're awake."

I smiled. "Near death experiences make you a little hungry?"

"They really do." Maxine snatched every bit of the food from Charlie's full hands. "You forgot the hot dog."

"Sorry," he said. "I was halfway through your order in the cafeteria when a doctor started lecturing me on my food choices. Said this was a heart attack waiting to happen."

Maxine shrugged. "I got a defibrillator in my purse."

I had so much to say to Charlie. My mind filled with thousands of words, all of them spinning and careening like falling stars.

"Why don't we step out for a bit and get some coffee?" James put his hand at Millie's back and guided her toward the door. "Maxine, let's go to the cafeteria."

"Nah." Her lips surrounded an oozing burrito. "I got all I need."

James held open the oak door. "I'm buying."

Maxine patted my blanket-covered feet. "See ya, tootsie."

My family escaped into the hall, leaving me with my old friend.

The boy who had saved me.

The one I had declared my love to.

"Charlie—"

"Katie—"

Our words overlapped, crashing like cymbals, then fell to the ground, leaving us with a silence so heavy, I sank deeper into the pillows.

"The doctor says you're going to be released soon." Charlie settled on my bed, his hip nestled against my calves.

"I feel fine." I tried to focus on his eyes, but his lips captured my attention. I had kissed those lips. Those lips had kissed me. "They, um. . ." What were we talking about? "They should let me go home now."

He scooted closer, his hand gently reaching out, then slowly tracing across my bandage. "We've had quite a day, Parker."

My old last name always sounded like an endearment from him. "I hear I have you to thank."

"That's what friends are for."

"Exactly," I said. "Friends."

Somehow he had moved even nearer. Charlie's lips did a slow curve while he rested his hands on either bed rail, leaning in, so close I could smell the remains of his morning after shave. "You took a pretty hard knock to the head."

"I did." His eyes were as silver as a stormy ocean.

"The doctor said you might have some temporary memory loss."

"Understandable."

"How much do you remember?"

Plane diving. Passengers screaming. Charlie and I kissing.

"Bits and pieces."

"Is that so?" His voice was a low rumble in his chest, a mere hush in the room. "Tell me what you recall."

"Maxine said you carried me to safety. I wanted to thank you for—"

"Answer the question."

I nibbled on my bottom lip, feeling a flush climb up my skin under his intense scrutiny. "I'm sure it will all come back to me eventually."

"How about I fill you in? I'll start at the beginning—"

"No!" My flailing hand covered his. "No need for that."

"Because you recall every second on that plane."

I did.

It was the type of memory you carried with you the rest of your days, one you thought about on sleepless nights and still held close to your heart when your hair was white and your steps were feeble. Charlie and I had kissed before, but never at the gates of life or death, never with that kind of desperation. He had kissed me back, but that didn't mean a thing.

Or did it?

"I think I remember most of it." I reached for my water cup and took my sweet time drinking from the straw. "You came and sat by me on the plane. We talked for a few hours. The plane started to drop and. . .I blacked out."

"That's all you got?"

"Seems that way."

"You don't remember anything else?"

There was no need to revisit the kiss or my errant, crazy declaration. Charlie was still out of my league, and I had left what was left of my beating heart in London. All I wanted was to return to In Between, settle in, and clear my head. Without the interference of any member of the male species. They could not be trusted. Even if they carried your limp form off weather-beaten planes.

"Thank you," I said again. "You were wonderful to me today."

My eyes widened as Charlie shifted, his face an inch from mine. His fingers slipped into my hair, his thumbs grazing my cheeks.

"Charlie?" I breathed. "What are you doing?"

He smiled as his mouth descended. "Jogging your memory."

Chapter Four

I WOKE THE next morning to an old woman standing over me, a mirror in my face, and the realization that I had not dreamed the last thirty-six hours.

I had indeed quit the show in London and hopped on a plane three weeks early. That plane had done the watoosie in the sky, and I had thrown myself at my teenage love. It was a lot to pack into seventy-two hours.

I blinked against the sun filtering through my old bedroom window. "Maxine, what exactly are you doing?"

"Checking to see if you were still breathing." She removed the pink handheld mirror. "For a moment there it was iffy."

"Is that my Hermes scarf around your neck? Were you even going to wait until my body was cold?"

"It's twelve-thirty in the flippin' afternoon. Who sleeps that late except werewolves and dead folk?"

"People with jet lag? People who nearly crashed in an airplane and have a concussion?"

"You're boring me." She plopped herself on the bed and flopped to her side, her blue eyes assessing me like a hanging judge. "You gonna tell me what's wrong?"

I sat up, feeling slightly underdressed in my worn In Between High School t-shirt, while Mad Maxine wore canary yellow skinny pants, a white button-down, and layers of turquoise beads artfully wrapped around her slender and surgically smoothed neck.

She kicked off her black patent spike heels and leaned her chin into a propped hand. "I'm waiting."

"Nothing's wrong. I'm exhausted, and I have a headache."

"Please. I've dated two former presidents. I know a lie when I see it."

I scrubbed a hand over my face and wondered how a woman who had to surely be from her own planet could be this intuitive. I'd never been able to get away with anything with her—from little white lies to sneaking candy from the secret liner in her purse.

"I have no idea what you're talking about." Sitting up, I swung my feet over the edge of the bed, the room tilting a little to the left.

"You know what I think?"

I grabbed Maxine's mirror and inspected my bandage, as well as the bruise covering my forehead.

"I think something happened in London." Maxine's hands mimed an explosion, complete with sound effects. *Pow!* "Something big."

"I was homesick."

"Oh, yeah? One of your college friends from your drama program has been calling here for days. Said she was sorry about what happened, but she knew a director in New York who wanted you to give him a ring-a-ding."

My head ached for caffeine and a room without prying conversation. "I'm taking a break."

"From what?"

Life. Love. Airplanes. "The theater."

A knock interrupted my grandmother's next comment as Millie poked her blonde, curly head in the room. Her familiar smile had me blinking back tears, and for a moment I longed for the days when she'd slip her arm around me, kiss the top of my head, and talk me off some adolescent ledge of drama. "There's my girl. How are you feeling?"

"A little gassy." Maxine patted her tummy. "I think it was that sixth piece of bacon."

"I meant Katie."

Maxine rolled her eyes. "Attention hog."

"I'm okay," I said as Millie padded across the floor in her bare feet. Since she'd conquered breast cancer seven years ago, Millie had taken up yoga, even teaching it at a studio downtown, and she now moved with an enviable grace I would never possess.

"Why don't you get dressed and come downstairs? I'll whip you up something to eat, and we can all talk." Millie leaned down and kissed my cheek.

But as I shuffled to the bathroom and freshened up, I knew it wouldn't be chit-chat that awaited me downstairs. You didn't suddenly come back from your Chance-of-a-Lifetime-Part, in a Chance-of-a-Lifetime-Play in Chance-of-a-Lifetime-London just because you were missing home. My family wanted answers.

But did I have them?

MILLIE STOOD AT the stove and stirred something I hoped was edible. "We were kind of limited on groceries, so I ran to the store and stocked the fridge this morning. Do you want breakfast or lunch?"

What I wanted was to go back to bed, pull the covers over my head, and not resurface until sometime next year. "Lunch is fine."

"Good." She smiled and stood on tiptoe to get some bowls. "We're having tomato soup and gluten free grilled cheese."

"Sounds delightful."

Maxine snorted as she pulled out a chair and sat down. "It's better than the vegan burgers she fed my honey and me last week. Not only were there beans in those things, but spinach. Who puts spinach in burgers?" She took a sip of tea from a sweating glass. "Weirdos, that's who."

James walked into the kitchen, unfolding a newspaper. "You made the In Between front page today." He held it out for me to see, pointing a finger at the headline in all caps. "Local Woman Injured in Plane Incident. Saved by Former Beau." He leaned down and kissed my cheek. "You guys are famous."

"That's one for the scrapbook." I slid my tired body into a seat, folding one leg beneath me.

"Still think we ought to sue the airlines," Maxine said. "Your pilots were probably having a little drinkie poo."

I ignored this. Again.

My grandmother was not deterred. "Stuff like this usually involves mental anguish."

James grinned. "I'm familiar with that."

Maxine cut her eyes at her son-in-law. "I mean Katie could turn straight-up crazy from this. She could end up unable to work, roaming the streets, talking to the voices in her head."

Millie set a platter of grilled cheese sandwiches on the table. "Come fill your bowls with soup."

"Speaking of work, I do need to find a job." The room halted like someone had pressed *pause*. Millie held a ladle over a pot, her eyes round. James's hand hovered toward the newspaper, and Maxine just stared, her collagen-filled lips pursed.

"But you're. . ." Millie didn't seem to know where to start. "You're an actress. All that training. Surely—"

"I'm taking a break."

"For how long?" James asked.

"Not sure. Six months. A few years." I tore the crust away from my sandwich. "Forever."

Maxine shook her angled bob. "The crazy has done set in."

Millie put a bowl of soup before me, then sat down. "Katie, what's going on?"

"I just need some time. London was great." In the beginning. "But lately I realized . . . it's not what I want."

"Did something happen?" Millie asks. "You weren't supposed to be here for weeks."

"I missed home." I took a bite, and the cheese slid against my tongue. Knowing Millie, it wasn't really cheese, but I didn't even want to think about what veggie product had been sacrificed in its place.

"You've wanted to be an actress since you were sixteen," James said. "All those plays, all that training. You get handed this amazing opportunity right out of college, and now you're done? When we talked to you last week, everything seemed fine."

I'd barely been holding it together. When Ian, my ex-boyfriend *and* director, had replaced me in the show that had been the last straw. I'd packed my bags and jumped on the first flight out.

"Tell us what happened, hon." Millie's voice was so gentle, aching with concern, and I considered pouring it all out, telling them every detail. "Did you and Ian break up?"

I pushed aside my soup, not the least bit hungry. "Yes."

"I knew I didn't like him," Maxine said. "You cannot trust a man with an accent. One time I dated this chap named Jean Luc and—"

"You seemed pretty serious," James said. "I thought he was coming back with you at Thanksgiving."

"I don't want to talk about him." Or think about him, or hear his name, or see his face. "We broke up. There's really nothing to it. It didn't work out."

"Who dumped whom?" Maxine asked.

"I dumped him." Technically.

"Atta girl."

"So you break up with a boy, then hop on the next flight to Houston?" Millie asked. "Switching that plane ticket had to be astronomical."

It had completely depleted my checking and savings. I had about fifty dollars to my name, and most of that was in foreign currency. "So, know anyone who's hiring?"

Their unanswered questions hung over us, thick and sweltering. I knew I was disappointing them. But I just wasn't ready to talk. I'd yet to process it all myself. In one year of living in London, I'd gone from being "woman number seven" in Shakespeare's *Much Ado About Nothing* to finally getting a small speaking part, to being the understudy for the lead, grateful to fill in every few weeks. When the lead quit, I had the insane opportunity to stand in the spotlight as the permanent Beatrice, only *the* best character in the history of literature. One whirlwind year.

"Verla May's son runs the funeral parlor." Maxine patted my hand. "He could use an assistant."

"In the office?" I asked.

"Nope." She smiled. "The makeup department."

"Katie, we hate to leave you like this," Millie said. "I could stay here while you—"

"I'll be fine." Though the thought of staying in this home all alone for the rest of the month my parents would be gone did not sound the least bit enticing. "I'll keep an eye on the house. Hold down the fort."

Millie enfolded me in a warm hug. "We just want you happy, sweetie."

"Being here makes me happy." I put on my best smile and felt the sting behind my eyes. "I've missed you guys so much."

"When you're ready to talk, we're here," James said. "But know one thing."

I dashed a tear and sniffed. "Yes?"

"You can run from your troubles." He watched me over the rim of his glasses. "But those troubles will find you no matter where you live."

Chapter Five

MY HEAD WAS as muddled as it was achy. Despite the protests of my family, I got in my car and drove across town to Frances Vega's parents' house. My best friend and I had gone different directions after high school. Frances had chosen a fancy Ivy League college where she could attempt to improve upon her science genius, and I had attended a plain Jane smaller school a few hours away. Even though Frances and I had taken radically different paths, we had remained close, visiting one another at least twice a year.

"Katie!" Frances opened the door, and I was immediately swallowed into a mighty hug. "Thank God you're alive! I've missed you!" She pulled me inside to the kitchen, our old hangout. Like the rest of the house, the kitchen was a home decorator's nightmare of two cultures that were supposed to be blended, but looked to be more at war. Frances's father was a first generation Mexican-American, and her mother's family was Chinese. They were each very proud of their cultures and believed their home should show it, from the food they ate to the art on the wall. Frances still hated every bit of it and resented the years of cultural tug-of-war.

"So," I said, taking a glass of tea from Frances. "What's new?"

"I'm getting married! I'm getting married! I'm marrying Joey Benson!"

I smiled at my friend's crazy enthusiasm and bragged appropriately when she shoved her engagement ring in my face. "Frances . . ." I sat down on a stool at the bar. "You've barely dated this guy. What's the rush?"

"We've been together three glorious months. And when it's right, it's right. Besides, I've known Joey all my life."

"Yeah, knew him, but not as in friends with him." Joey was four years older than us and had rarely been around when we'd hung out with Charlie. The couple had connected through Facebook, both of them being "friends" of Charlie. "You probably hadn't ever spoken to him before he asked you out."

"I know!" She sipped her own tea. "Isn't it the coolest story?"

Apparently it was a rhetorical question, as Frances didn't give me a second to respond.

"We have so much to do. I still have to find a dress, find you a dress, order the flowers, write my vows, get some shoes that look pretty but don't make me hate the world, and finish finding us an apartment in Massachusetts. It's so much fun!"

Frances seemed to speak in never-ending exclamation points and sentences whose theme were all "yay!" How could either one of us be old enough to be college graduates, let alone old enough to get married?

Some days I just wanted to be sixteen again—going to high school, no rent payments, no major boy wounds, when every dream was still shiny, polished, and possible. Sure, we had worries, but nothing like the ones in adulthood. Nothing like the ones lodged in my brain like a splinter I couldn't extract.

"You know I'm happy for you, right?" How to approach this? I didn't want to burst any happy balloons here.

"Of course you are. You're my best friend. Were you thinking strapless for your dress or is that just a bra nightmare?"

"But have you considered slowing it down? Wait to get married until you get settled at school?" While Joey had chosen the technical route, becoming a mechanic and doing something with some fancy form of auto painting, Frances had already earned her masters and was now on her way to Harvard for a PhD in nuclear physics.

While I played dress-up for a living.

"A Christmas wedding might be fun," I suggested.

"You sound just like my dad." Frances had inherited her father's thick, wavy black hair and her mother's porcelain skin. Her nerdy glasses did nothing to hide her enviable exotic looks. Joey was getting a total cover model. "We know what we're doing, and we want to get married now."

"You're such a planner, though. You and that scientific brain of yours. You like to pore over every detail. Wouldn't you feel better if you had time to really plan this ceremony? That way you could make it just how you wanted it instead of whatever's available last minute."

"The important elements are available." Frances smiled. "Joey, his family, my family, and our closest friends." She pulled me to her for another breath-restricting squeeze. "Thank you so much for coming in all the way from London. It means so much to me."

"Anything for you."

"Here, sit." Frances patted a bar stool covered in the colors of the Mexican flag as she reached for her iPad. "It's going to be a small wedding, so you're my only bridesmaid. Do you like the navy for your dress or maybe the coral? Because those are my two colors. Aren't they so pretty together? The guys are going to wear gray suits with pink bow ties. . ."

The rest of the details rolled past me like a fog, and I traced my finger across the bubbles meandering down my glass. I had kissed Charlie Benson.

Panic was one crazy lady. She made you do things you didn't know you wanted to do. My last moments of life, and I chose to lock lips with Charlie. And when he'd kissed me again in the hospital, my heart rate had more than spiked the monitor beside me. He'd kissed me senseless, only stopping when my parents had returned. As my family had chattered around us, Charlie had given me a slow wink, then disappeared. Disappeared like a hot specter of sexy.

One I had no business getting involved with.

Frances cleared her throat, drawing me back to the present. From behind a pair of hot pink glasses, she studied my face. "Are you okay? How's your head?"

"I'm, fine. Just a slight headache. Jet lag."

"Anything else?"

"Maybe a little concern for you."

"Katie, this is the right thing. I have never felt such peace about something in my entire life."

"Last Tuesday I felt a great peace about a sushi bar. I spent the whole night clutching the toilet and begging for death."

Frances laughed. "I know what I'm doing. Be happy for me."

Acting happy for her was one of my jobs as maid-of-honor. I could do this. "I just want the best for you. I don't want to see you hurt."

"Is that what happened to you in London? With Ian? Did he hurt you?"

I twisted in my seat, searching for that cookie jar that Mrs. Vega always kept on her counter. "Where's Pancho Villa?" When you lifted his sombrero, a mountain of chocolate chip cookies would usually be inside.

"First, you're dodging my question. And second, Mom got rid of him. My parents no longer eat cookies. They keep carrot sticks and Greek yogurt in the fridge."

Too many changes at once! My leaving the theater. Frances getting married. Mr. And Mrs. Vega going sugar free. My head throbbed with it all.

"So you were telling me about your breakup with Ian."

I propped my chin into my hand and sighed. I had said very little to my best friend about Ian. "Ian cheated on me, and I broke up with him. That's pretty much all there is to it. I thought I knew him, but I found out I didn't."

"I'm sorry Ian broke your heart. And if I didn't have a quickie wedding to plan, I'd hop on a plane and punch him in the man parts."

I'd already done that, but it was nice to hear.

"You'll find love," Frances said like an age-old sage who had it all figured out. "And when you do, it will make every old hurt fade away. One day you won't even think about Ian."

Funny, I seemed to already have arrived at the point of forgetting Ian. Maybe it was the hard bump to the head. But all I could think about was Charlie.

"When do your parents leave for Haiti?" Frances asked.

"Monday. I miss them already."

"I wish James could perform my ceremony."

I bit my lip on further helpful comments. We chatted and planned for another two hours, then I hugged the future Mrs. Benson and walked to my car.

"Thanks for flying in for my wedding, Katie," Frances said as she stood by my Toyota. "It means a lot to me that you'd come in for a long visit."

"Oh, I'm not here to visit." I settled in behind the wheel. "I'm here to stay."

ALL THE MARRIAGE talk had left me more than a little depressed. Frances was getting married, fully stepping into the adult world. And where was I? In some alternate universe, caught between the college years and whatever came next.

My car seemed to have a mind of its own, and before I knew it, I was on Maple Street, pulling into the parking lot of the Valiant Theater. Between college and church, I had gotten to travel abroad in the last five or six years—France, Ireland, London. I had seen the Eiffel Tower at sunset, sitting on a blanket with a crusty loaf of bread and a chilled bottle of wine. I had done mission work in the wet, raw wilds of a Panamanian rain forest. I had stood on a bridge overlooking the Thames, as well as watched the changing of the guard at Buckingham Palace.

But no place was as lovely to me as the Valiant Theater.

James and Millie had purchased the 1930s remnant, lovingly restoring it 'til it was a reborn architectural masterpiece. The crown jewel of In Between, the Valiant was the place where I had first given my heart away, finding my soul and purpose on the wooden planks of the stage. The theater had a history, every inch of it holding a story. My own tale was within these walls.

As I opened the doors, the familiar smell greeted me. Popcorn, wood polish, and a magical scent that slipped from the dressing rooms, swirled around the spotlights, and flew in the air with all the boldness that accompanied hopes, dreams, and what-ifs.

It was easy to believe anything was possible here.

"Well, aren't you a sight for these old, tired eyes."

Sam Dayberry, caretaker of the Valiant, and my grandmother's sainted husband, intercepted me in the lobby, arms outstretched, smile wide.

"Hi, Sam." I hugged him tight, grinning at his ever-present ball cap and overalls. Happy that some things, at least, would never change.

He held me at arm's length and gave my face a grandfatherly inspection. "I wanted to come with the others to Houston, but some stuff came up and someone had to stay here. Prayed like crazy for you."

"I know you did."

"That's quite a bruise you got going there."

"Just a little bump on the head." I glanced at a production poster hanging on the wall behind him. "*Sound of Music*, huh? Pretty ambitious. I'm impressed."

"Don't be." He wiped his brow with a handkerchief. "Our Captain Von Trapp towers at five-foot-three, and Maria sings like a howling coyote."

"Save me a front row seat."

He chuckled, the lines around his eyes a gathering of creases and folds. "Your grandma sure is glad to have her little buddy back. How long are you staying?"

"Oh, probably indefinitely."

Sam blinked. "What do you mean?"

"I'm not going back to London."

"Well, of course you are. You're the pride of this family. The pride of this town."

I laughed at the ridiculousness of the very thought. "This town needs to raise the bar a bit. It was time to come back home. The theater life was nice for a while, but I can't live like that forever."

"What are you going to do?"

Wasn't that just the question of the moment. "Not sure. Kind of limited with a drama degree. I was hoping the manager job was still an option here." In fact, I was counting on it.

"Delores still says she's retiring in six months," Sam said. "You know your parents would give you that job in a heartbeat. Well, that is if the theater's—" Sam startled at the beeping of his phone. "Drat. Five minutes late for lunch, and that woman's sending me snippy texts." He slipped the phone back in his overall pocket. "I better get home. I promised Maxine I'd take her to a nice lunch."

"The Burger Barn?"

He nodded. "Your grandma wants a triple scoop." His worn, strong hands cupped my shoulders in gentle pats. "No matter what you decide, we're all proud of you, dear."

With a final hug for Sam, I flung open the doors and stepped into the theater. Following the carpeted runner, I walked the slight decline, my breath easing the closer I got to that stage.

And by the time I laid down on the old, restored wood floor, staring up at the lights, I almost felt like my old self. Lights hummed above me, the cool of the stage seeped into my palms, and I closed my eyes and just slowly inhaled.

"Hello, Parker."

My eyes popped open as Charlie Benson stood at the foot of the stage.

"I thought I might find you here." His rascal grin still devastated, sending a sonar ping straight to my lost heart. He wore a white button down, pressed khakis, and hair that was almost in need of a trim. Almost.

"Come on up," I said.

And he did. In seconds, he settled in beside me, his shoulder pressed to mine. I tried to focus on the dreamy scent of my theater and not Charlie's cologne that promised manly things I'd absolutely sworn off.

We stayed that way for a while, just lying on the stage floor, our breaths eventually synchronizing, our thoughts going in their own directions.

"What are you doing here?" My hushed voice broke the lengthy silence.

"I came to see you." He turned his face toward mine, and our lips were so close, if I just leaned in the slightest—

"I'm not going to fall for you again, Charlie." I didn't know if I said this for him—or for me.

His smile lit those pretty gray eyes. "I used to find you here just like this when we were in high school. I always knew it meant you had something big to work out." He ran his finger down my temple and across my cheek. "You want to talk about it?"

I sighed, the sound coming from the pit of my stomach and echoing in the space. "I thought I had it all figured out. I was one of the lucky ones. I knew who I was, and I certainly knew who I wanted to be. And everything just magically fell into place. It was just this big confirmation that I was on the right track."

"Who says you were wrong?"

"I can't go back to London. I don't think I can ever get on the stage again."

"I've seen you in action. You were born for this."

I shrugged. "Maybe it was just a season."

"I don't believe that. You know what I do believe in?" His pinkie latched onto mine. "You."

Lightning zinged from the top of my head straight to my toes.

Dear Lord, I was just like my bio-mother. She fell in love weekly with a different man. I would not be her. I was not going to be that stupid.

"I've made a lot of mistakes," I said. If mistakes were raindrops, I'd flood this whole town.

"Was declaring your never-ending love for me at twenty-thousand feet one of them?"

"I didn't mean it."

He smiled. "No?"

"I thought we were about to die."

"So the deal is null and void in the event of our unfortunate survival?"

"I was overtaken by adrenaline."

"Not crashing can really mess things up."

"Are you laughing at me?"

His eyes darkened and he stilled. "I find myself very serious when it comes to you, Parker."

I ran my hand over my face, regretting my bandage, my lack of makeup. "My life's a mess, Charlie. You do not want to get mixed up in that."

"None of us have uncomplicated lives. Maybe I want to be mixed up in yours."

"No."

He squeezed my hand. "How messy are we talking?"

"More than my usual fare. I've stepped it up in my adult years."

"Katie?" Charlie turned on his side, leaning over me. "You said you loved me."

So I had. But I could not have meant it. I couldn't have. "I meant that in a universal way. Not romantic at all." My gosh, his eyes were hypnotic.

Charlie thought about this. "So if the guy in the next aisle had been sitting by you—the four-hundred pound man with excessive body hair—"

"The really sweaty one?"

"If he would've been sitting next to you, then you would've declared your undying love to him?"

"Everyone needs a solid send-off to glory."

Charlie smiled. "You're lying."

"A side-hug at the very least."

Charlie just watched me for a moment. A handful of painfully long seconds. "We need to discuss this," he said at last.

I sat up, needing some distance between me and the invisible lasso Charlie seemed to be whirling in my general direction. "You and I are long over. You've moved on. I've moved on."

He rose to his feet, held out his hand, then pulled me up. My body collided with his. "What I recall moving," he said, "was your lips on mine."

"I've already forgotten it. You should too."

His head dipped, his gaze hot on mine. "I don't want to."

"Charlie."

His thumb traced across my cheek. "Stop talking."

"I'm a mess."

He kissed the corner of my mouth. "Be my mess."

And I was lost.

Later I would blame my concussion. The mystical energy of the theater. The weird cheesy substance Millie fed me for lunch.

But now?

Now I just leaned into Charlie Benson, wrapped my arms around his back, and pretended like I wasn't making another giant mistake.

Chapter Six

"**I** HAVE TO stop kissing Charlie Benson."

Maxine did a whiplash double-take in the passenger side of my Corolla, flung off her Hollywood sunglasses, then pointed her red-nailed finger right at me. "I knew it! I knew you'd never gotten that boy out of your system." She fanned herself with both hands. "Who could blame you? You have quite the history, and he is a dish."

"I'm through with men."

After a sleepless night, tossing and turning with thoughts of Charlie Benson, London, and Ian the Loser Ex, I woke up this morning, determined to get at least a temporary job until I figured out my career plan. Maxine's friend Loretta owned Micky's Diner, and they were looking for a waitress. I had zero experience with waiting tables, but in last year's summer touring production, I had been a serial-killing drag queen, and I'd had no experience with that line of work either. Minus a few sprained ankles and one glitter eye shadow incident, that had turned out okay. I'd just *act* like a waitress.

"When have you been kissing Charlie?"

On a plane. On a stage. "It doesn't matter. It's not going to happen again. I have a life to figure out."

"Making out is much more fun."

"Guys are stupid."

"But necessary." She slid her big, black sunglasses back on her face. "How did this Ian break your heart?"

I turned the car left onto Maple Street. "He just wasn't who I thought he was."

"That happened to me once. Harvey Dillerbink." She flipped down the visor and used the mirror to apply glossy pink lipstick. "Said it wasn't a toupee, but these fingers know the difference between real hair and a synthetic mop."

"Our stories are so similar, it's eerie."

She blotted her lips on a tissue. "I hear that sass. You wait 'til you're fifty like me. Men come up with all new ways to be Satan's ambassadors of deceit."

The gravel crunched beneath the tires of the car as I pulled into the parking lot of Micky's Diner. It was an aqua blue stucco with a flashing neon sign, promising the best cup of coffee in town. It sat three driveways down from the Valiant, and I had spent many a morning in the vinyl-covered booths eating hotcakes and bacon with James. Initially it had been forced together-time between a foster dad and his rebellious young charge. But James never gave up on me, feeding me pancakes and conversation until one Saturday I put my fork down and looked across the table at the man who was no longer my guardian, but my father.

A bell clanged as we walked inside, and we weaved through the tables of hungry In Between locals to find an empty table. I peeled open a menu that was sticky with years of syrup drips, and let the din of cafe chatter lull me away from my relentless thoughts.

"Coffee?" Our waitress set down two water glasses and nodded at a neighboring couple in need of refills. Her name was Kourtney with a K, and she had graduated the year after me at In Between High School. Last I'd heard, she already had two babies. How different our lives were. Did our choices lock us into paths we couldn't get out of?

"I'll have hot tea, please." I said.

Maxine closed her menu. "Yes, bring the Queen here a cup of tea and me a black coffee and creamer. None of that low fat stuff, sweetie."

"Coming right up."

"Good morning to you, Maxine." Loretta Parsons, with hair so flat black it could only come from a drugstore bottle and jeans that declared she did not give two hoots about fashion, swaggered her way to our table. The owner of Micky's always carried a coffee pot and the latest in In Between gossip. "This your granddaughter?"

"Hello, Loretta. This is my Katie."

My Katie. For a girl who had been discarded by her mom at fifteen and in the system for over a year, these moments of unfiltered love and belonging were still like Christmas and birthdays all rolled into one powerful gift of joy. These words would be added to the collection tattooed on the walls of my heart.

"You've grown up since I last saw you. My sister taught you in school. Mary Hall."

"My drama teacher." I had loved that woman. Crazy enough to have her own reality show, but she had taught me how to dig deep and bring all I had to a role. "Tell her I said hello."

"Your grandma says you want a job."

"I do."

"You got a college degree?"

"Yes, ma'am."

"You're overqualified."

My new credit card balance didn't care about details such as this, and I needed something to keep me busy until the Valiant could be all mine. "I'm a good worker. Great with people." Except for the kind you dated.

Loretta pulled the pen from the perch above her ear and twirled it in fingers that had served the breakfast crowd faithfully for forty years. "Can you cook?"

I thought of the Ramen and canned soup I had lived on since leaving home. "Not exactly."

"Ever been a waitress?"

"No."

"Can you balance three plates of chicken fried steak on one arm while refilling sweet teas with the other?"

"Doubtful."

A crash sounded behind us, and all heads in the room turned as Kourtney with a K stared at the ruined coffee pot now lying in glass shards on the floor.

Loretta turned her gaze back to me. "You'll fit right in."

"When do you want me to start?"

"This time next week. With all these meetings I got, I won't have time to train you 'til then. Work begins at five."

"In the morning?"

"Them eggs don't scramble themselves."

"Five a.m. will be just fine."

"Kourtney, get over here and get these ladies' order," Loretta barked before walking away.

"I still think you should wait to get a job," Maxine said. "Take some time and just rest. You're whining about Frances rushing into things, and you're doing the exact same thing."

"I'm broke."

"Not broke enough to take me up on the job *I* offered you."

"Daily foot rubs and pedis is not an acceptable job offer." A familiar flash of blue caught my eye, the blur resembling my dad. "Was that James?"

"Huh?" Maxine held out her coffee cup as Kourtney finally came to fill it. "No, he's not here. Probably his doppelganger. We all have one." She took the creamer from the waitress. "Mine goes by the name of Gisele Bündchen."

"I swear that was him. I'd know that church polo shirt anywhere." I thanked Kourtney for my tea. "I'm going to go say hi."

"No!" Maxine said a little too strongly.

"Why?"

"Because I'm starving, and we need to order. Old ladies can't go too long without food. Messes with our blood sugar. I don't want to get the diabeedus."

"For dinner last night you had Reese's Pieces." I removed the napkin from my lap and returned it to the table. "I'll be right back."

"Wait—he's in a meeting."

Something wasn't right. "For what?"

"Some pastor thing. Boring stuff. Involves lots of praying, Bible reading, sharing the latest joke they've stolen from the internet, that sort of thing." Maxine gave her order to the harried waitress, and judging by the five course breakfast she requested, I didn't think she was too concerned with her glucose levels.

The table James sat at was not filled with local pastors, but with various members of the community. There was Evan, one of the night cops who'd given me a ride home my junior year when my car had broken down at midnight on the one lane bridge. Randall Foster, owner of the hardware store, sat to his right. Across from James was Dana Lou Tanner, who had the best bakery this side of Dixie, and whose husband kept the liquor store across the county line in business. Six or seven more filled the large table, each leaning in, intent on the conversation. Dana spoke to the group, her hands animated, a ringed finger jabbing the air.

"Looks pretty heated over there," I said.

"It's inter-denominational." Maxine darted her eyes to the gathering, then gave me a reassuring smile. "When you put the Baptists and Methodists together, it's like Southside L.A. The Bloods and the Crips. The Sharks and the Jets. Avon ladies and Mary Kay."

"You're hiding something, Mad Maxine."

"Moi?"

"I'm going to go talk to James."

"No, Katie! Sit!" Maxine's manicured fingers latched onto my wrist. Then her eyes looked past me, and her smile broadened. "Well, hello, Charlie."

I turned around, and like a predictable soap opera, there stood

Charlie. Any woman with estrogen left in her body would appreciate the sight. The handsome man stood over six-feet tall, the contours of hard muscles visible beneath his dark denim shirt. His khaki shorts stopped at his knees, revealing tanned legs that had carried him through years of high school and college football. But the heart-clincher, the part that had a table of white-headed ladies audibly sighing beside us, was the way he held his little sister's hand. The way she stared adoringly at her handsome big brother like he was her Prince Charming.

Maybe I did need something stronger than tea.

"Charlie!" Maxine glowed like a spotlight. "And Miss Sadie, don't you look cute as a puppy nose. Do join us."

"What do you think, Sadie?" Charlie twirled his sister beneath his arm, sending the white haired hens a twittering. "Want to sit with Mrs. Dayberry and Katie?"

"Okay."

Charlie's eyes never left mine as he helped his sister into her seat, then lowered himself into the chair beside me. His warm arm settled against mine, clearly crossing my table boundary line.

"Breakfast is on me," Maxine said. "It's the least I can do for your saving my granddaughter."

"I didn't save her," Charlie said. "Just helped her get off the plane."

"Why, my dear boy, I disagree." Maxine turned to little Sadie. "He carried my Katie like she was Sleeping Beauty. She was wounded and unconscious, bleeding from the head. He threw his own body over her to shield her from further damage, then when the plane finally touched down, your brother lifted her in his big strong arms and brought her to safety. Isn't it just the most romantic thing you've ever heard?"

"Romantic is probably not the word I'd use," I said.

Sadie turned her wide eyes to me. "Are you going to marry my brother?"

"What? No!" I searched frantically for our waitress. "Can we get some crayons over here?"

The little girl was as ruthless as Maxine. "If you were in a Disney movie, it would end with you two getting married."

I forced my teeth to unclench. "Your brother and I are old friends."

"Right." Charlie took a drink from my water glass. "Friends."

"Charlie," Maxine cooed. "How long are you in town?"

"Until after the wedding."

He was going back to Chicago soon. I had no business even considering getting tangled up with him or any form of long-distance relationship. Soon he would be back in his high-rise apartment sitting behind his desk doing whatever important businessy things he did.

"Your company must really think a lot of you to let you have that much time off," Maxine said.

"Charlie's working while he's here," I said as Kourtney flittered over and secured Charlie and Sadie's order.

Maxine blew on her coffee. "Doing what?"

"A very important project." Sadie leaned her blonde head into her brother. "Right?"

Charlie straightened in his seat. "I don't want to bore anyone with business talk."

I took a sip of tea. "Bore away."

Charlie opened his mouth, only to be interrupted by the reappearance of Loretta. "Here's the job application." She plopped it beside my saucer. "Bring this back with you next week so I can pretend to check your references. And here's your uniform." She thrust a wad of extra-extra-large t-shirts into my hands.

I held one up. "They're a little roomie."

"You get a discount on my pies," Loretta said. "Maybe you'll grow into them."

Wouldn't that just be the cherry on top of my life?

"Loretta, I had a few questions about the job—"

"Sorry, hon. I'm wanted in a meeting. Dang corporation thinks they can take my diner? They got another thing coming."

"Someone's trying to buy you out?" This was the first I'd heard of it.

"Where's that waitress?" Maxine said. "I'm ready for my food."

"Buy me out is putting it politely." Loretta propped a hand at her hip. "What Thrifty Co. is doing is corporate terrorism."

Maxine clanged her fork to her glass. "What does it take to get a short stack around here?"

"Did you know about this?" I asked my grandmother.

"Who can keep up with a big metropolis like this?" Maxine's laugh was a little too forced. "Loretta, I think they're calling you in the kitchen. She's coming!"

"Thrifty Co. is wanting to build one of their discount stores right here," Loretta said.

"But your diner's not for sale." I glanced at Charlie. "Can you believe this?"

He slowly shook his head. "It's a tough situation."

"The mayor said it doesn't matter that my diner's not for sale. Said the city can sell the land right out from under me. Eminent domain. But I'm getting myself a lawyer."

"Loretta, that's terrible." I had so many memories at this diner. Charlie and I had shared many a banana split in booth number twelve my senior year.

"I gotta get back to the meeting." Loretta gestured her spiky head to the large table in the back of the restaurant.

The one where James now sat. "Is my dad helping you?"

"Helping?" Loretta huffed. "Honey, Thrifty Co. doesn't just want my restaurant. The want almost the whole block."

Maxine stood to her feet. "I want eggs, and I want them now!"

But I ignored the outburst.

As the cold blood drained from my body, and I stood eye to eye with my grandmother.

"Is there something you'd like to tell me?"

She eyed my print blouse. "You really shouldn't wear orange. Clashes with your hair."

"How. . ." I breathed maple-scented air through my nostrils. "How could you keep this from me?"

"Now, Sweet Pea, we didn't want to upset you."

"When were you going to tell me?"

"When your head healed. Or if it didn't, when we got you settled in the institution."

"Did you know about this?" I asked Charlie again.

His face tensed in sympathy. "I'm sorry, Katie."

"Exactly what properties does Jiffy Co. want, Maxine?"

She wrung her hands, the gold bangles on her wrist clanging like a gypsy. "It's not a done deal."

"Which ones?"

She pressed her pink lips together. "Micky's Diner. Betty's Hair Salon—but that's no loss. The old bird only knows bowl cuts and poodle perms. I forget the rest."

A hammer pummeled my head. "Spit it out."

"The Valiant." Maxine reached for my hand and held it tight. "Katie, they're going to tear down the Valiant."

Chapter Seven

THERE COMES A point where the dark overtakes you, and a girl just has to give into the sinking pull of despair.

I was at that point.

I had spent the last three days locked in my bedroom with unwashed hair, season four of *Friday Night Lights*, *People* magazine on my iPad, and the empty carcasses of two jars of peanut butter.

I had received three voice mails from some director in New York, one from another theater friend with an audition lead, and two from Ian the Ex. I didn't want to talk to any of them. I wouldn't spit on Ian if he were on fire, and as for the director, I didn't know what he was looking for, but I was certain I wasn't it. I was a screw-up of an actress. You didn't just bolt on a play. Like any job, you gave notice. I would probably be blacklisted, but that really didn't matter anyway. I wasn't going back to the stage.

James and Millie had tried to coax me out with ice cream, offers of shopping, even invitations to a big concert in Houston. But I remained in my room. Just me, my comfy bed, and Coach Taylor. Clear eyes, full heart, total loser.

I had no career, no direction, no love life, and now my beloved Valiant was going to be destroyed.

And I was out of peanut butter.

I loved the Valiant for a million reasons, but if I lost it, that was the end of my job plans.

I clutched my pillow to my chest and sat up as someone knocked at my door.

"Go away."

Maxine bravely walked in. "How much longer is this pitiful display going to last?"

I reached for the remote and upped the volume. "I've only just started. I haven't even moved on to the sleep days on end and cry uncontrollably portion yet."

She plopped herself on my bed. "Let me know when that is. I'll want to snap photos for my blog."

"What are you all dressed up for?"

Maxine wore black cropped pants, shiny red flats, and a sweater that accentuated the curves she still had at whatever mysterious age she was. "It's First Friday Festival. The whole town is going. You should join us."

"Give me one reason I should."

"Food trailers."

If anything could tempt me, that would be it. On the first Friday of the month, the town gathered on the square. They showed a movie on a giant screen, food vendors sold all varieties of gourmet and deep-fried delights, and a local band sang deep into the night.

"You guys have a good time."

Maxine sighed heavy enough for me to smell the spearmint of her gum. "Katie, this is ridiculous and totally unlike you. Quit your moping and get out of this room."

"My life is crap."

"Your hair is crap."

I touched my frizzy strands.

"Look, I know things are bad. And we should've told you about the Valiant, but you had your London issues, and then we didn't know how wackadoodle you'd be when you woke up from getting brained by the luggage."

"How can that company just tear down parts of this town like it means nothing?"

"There's another town hall meeting Tuesday night. Maybe the mayor will see reason. Thrifty offered everyone a payout, but nobody's taking it. You know James isn't going to go down without a fight." She gave me a loud, smacky kiss on my cheek. "Now get up and go with us."

"Another time." After all, I was back in town to stay.

"Fine. Have it your way." She leapt from the bed and all but skipped out. "Oh, I almost forgot." Maxine pulled the door halfway closed. "That handsome Charlie fellow is downstairs."

What? "Tell him I'm not here."

"He'll be up in five minutes. Fix that hair. Oh, and one more teensy, tiny thing."

I jumped up from my bed, scrambling for a bra. "What?"

"That New York director called the house. Said your friend gave him the number."

"He called here? Did he leave a message?"

"Um, sorta."

I looked under my bed, my hands patting around for anything that felt small and padded. "What does that mean?"

"I talked to him myself. I might've told him you were interested in the audition."

My hands stilled. "Why would you do that?"

"Because you need to get back on the horse. So you fell off. So what?"

"Because the horse kicked me between the eyeballs. I'm not getting back on."

"Well, you have an audition next Thursday at two. I can drive you myself."

"You haven't been behind the wheel since you took out a chicken truck nearly a decade ago. And you sure aren't driving across country. I'm not going to any audition."

"You're clearly angry and irrational right now. I'll just leave you to your grouchiness before this turns ugly and you're sobbing for my forgiveness."

Maxine got one look at my menacing face and backed herself out of my bedroom.

I took the world's fastest shower, fueled by anger and some twisted desire for Charlie not to see me at my absolute worst. But what did it matter?

My hair wrapped in a towel, I stepped out of the bathroom, and just as promised, there was Charlie. He sat on my bed like he had a right to be there, a right to my throne of self-pity.

There was something toe-curling about the way his eyes slowly traveled the length of me, from the tops of my bare feet to my face.

"I've called you for three days," he finally said.

"Sometimes concussions make you forget things like voicemail."

"What about texts? You ignoring those too?"

"I've been very busy." I pulled the pink fuzzy towel from my head and let my hair fall in waves across my shoulders. My hair was naturally strawberry blonde, and Ian had preferred my stylist to highlight out any traces of red. The day after our breakup, I'd shown up for the performance with hair as fiery red as my temper. The color had calmed down some, but apparently I had not.

I leaned against the bathroom doorway, sort of regretting my lack of thought to my clothing choice. The gray tank top and running shorts had been within quick reach, and surely it was better than the pizza-stained t-shirt that said, *"Get out of my spotlight."*

"So this is your room." Charlie walked to my desk and looked at some of the framed black and white photos hanging on the wall. Pictures of me in various productions, snapshots of family vacations, a few of me and my best friend Frances acting silly and wild before the adult cares of bills, bad relationships, and taking wrong turns in the roadmap of life.

He moved on to inspect my bulletin board of old play bills. "Your parents would never let me up here in high school."

"The life of a preacher's kid. Plus James probably knew you couldn't be trusted."

His white teeth flashed with his quick grin. "He would've been right about that."

"I'm surprised they let you up even now."

"I think they're desperate." Charlie smiled over his shoulder. "Said you were in a pretty bad way."

I resumed my seat on the bed, curling my legs beneath me. "What are you doing here, Charlie?"

He crossed the room and stood before me, his storm cloud eyes searching mine. "I'm worried about you."

"Don't be."

"You need to get out of this house."

"I will."

"Preferably before dry rot sets in."

"I'm not molding in here. I'm eating and bathing." Mostly eating.

"Come out with me tonight."

"That's a really bad idea."

He lifted an empty jar of Skippy from the floor. "And this lockdown's a good one?"

"Maybe I just need some thinking time."

"It's a nice evening. Stars will be out soon."

"So will the humidity and mosquitoes."

Charlie's hand traced the edge of the bandage on my forehead. "Right now you're running from more things than you're running toward." He leaned close, so close I could feel his breath brush my cheek. His lips hovered near my ear. "Meet me downstairs in five minutes."

"I don't want to," I whispered.

"Go out with me tonight, Katie Parker."

I expected to see that flash of heat and mischief in his eyes. And, oh, it was there. But so was something else.

Just like the day we met in the airport, there was something faintly lurking in his gaze. Something troubled, heavy.

Like I wasn't the only one swimming in the depths.

"Charlie?"

"Yes?"

"You're gonna buy me a funnel cake."

THE TOWN SQUARE was a Hallmark movie come to life. As the sun slipped away, the good folks of In Between came out, happy to be done with the work week and ready for a little celebrating. In the very center of downtown was a grassy park, decorated with various botanical and floral landscaping courtesy of the In Between Garden Club. Food trailers and vendors circled the area like modern day wagons, and to the east was a flatbed trailer brought in once a month that served as a stage for the featured band. Tonight it was Denny Vinson and the Doo-Wops, a group of middle-aged men who wore black leather jackets and slicked-back hair and sang songs from the Fifties.

As I walked down the sidewalk next to Charlie, I said hello to a dozen people I knew. While we exchanged greetings, I moved on before they asked the questions I knew they wanted to know. Like how long was I in town? How was London? What play was I in now?

"All right, Parker," Charlie said, a blanket under his arm. "Let's see if we can put a smile on that face." He stopped at a trailer painted like the American flag and got us two cheeseburger meals and drinks.

"I wanted dessert first."

He stuck a French fry in my mouth. "Later. Come on." Charlie's hand reached for mine, and he led me to an empty spot at the edge of the lawn. "Best seat in the house. Within earshot of the band, but far away from the crowd." He smoothed the blanket over the ground and gestured for me to sit.

"Do you always keep a blanket in your car?"

He handed me a burger. "Just one of the tools in my arsenal of charm."

"I think I'm all through with charm."

"Now that is too bad. I was just about to turn mine on." He took a drink of his iced tea. "This Ian guy really did a number on you, didn't he?"

I dug in my brown paper bag, knowing at the bottom were hand cut, homemade fries. "I don't want to talk about him."

"I'm a good listener."

"You didn't used to be."

He propped up a knee and rested his arm on it. "People change."

I smiled. "So you're saying you're more sensitive now."

"I'm ready to watch Lifetime movies and discuss our feelings any time."

I laughed for the first time in days. "And why this change? What's your life been like the last few years?"

He dipped a fry in ketchup. "Now it's mostly work. It's pretty much all I do."

"Just like your dad." His father had been the bank president for years, not even stopping when, like Millie, he'd had a bout with cancer.

"*Nothing* like my father." The warmth left Charlie's tone, and he looked out into the swarm of people. "And I recall being your crying shoulder a time or two."

"Your dad's a good man. He's helped this community a lot."

His dark head slowly nodded. "He was never home when I was growing up. At the end of the day, work was more important. Getting ahead. Money. Those were the things that really mattered."

"I think the older we get, the more we'll see traces of our parents in us." And wasn't that just a frightening thought.

"James and Millie are amazing people," Charlie said. Had I noticed how close he was sitting? His leg touched mine on the blanket; his skin heated against mine. "It can't be a bad thing to hear yourself sound like them."

"I mean my bio-mom. Lately when I look in the mirror. . . I see her."

"She's a part of you, a big part of your history."

"I don't want to be like her."

"You're not."

"Oh, yeah? My mom had horrible judgment in friends, boy-friends, bosses, drug dealers. When I saw Ian for who he really was, I realized I was no better at picking a good man than she was."

"Maybe he was just really good at being someone else."

"But how do you know?" I pushed my food aside. "How do you really know if someone is honest, genuine, the person they project to the world?"

Charlie's serious eyes held mine. "It's a chance you take."

"It's not worth it."

"Isn't it?"

"How could I not know he was a loser? That he was lying to me?"

"He was cheating on you?"

I swallowed past the lump in my throat. "There was definitely another woman. And then when I broke it off, he put me on two weeks paid leave. He gave my understudy the role." I swiped at a rogue tear. "They were right. The things they had said about me, had whispered behind my back. They were right all along."

Charlie reached out and brushed another tear from my cheek. "Who?"

"Some of the cast. All along there had been murmurings that I only had the role because I was dating Ian. That I wasn't talented enough or experienced nearly enough to get the lead." My voice quivered. "How could I have been so stupid?"

"Katie, you're crazy talented. I'm sure you had the role because—"

"Because I was snogging the director?"

Charlie stilled. "Are pants worn in this snogging?"

"All those people were right. I don't have the talent for London or Broadway."

His hand ran up my arm, gently rubbing, as if trying to ease the dark right out of me. "That's what all of this is about, isn't it? You're back because you think your acting career was a lie?"

"It was."

"Your jerk boyfriend was a lie, but your gift on the stage is something you can't just throw away. Katie, I don't even like plays. I like baseball, football, soccer. Guy stuff where people win or lose, get hurt, yell at the ref. But when you're in a play, I can't look away. You're. . .amazing."

His words spun around me, pulling me in like a trance. I wanted to believe him. But what did I know? My truth-meter was so broken these days.

"You can't give up on your dream. Or the Valiant."

"Both seem pretty hopeless."

"It's not like you to just pack it up and walk away. The Katie Parker I know is a fiery force to be reckoned with. She'd never just quit."

"The things they said about me." I shut my eyes against the memory, their whispered voices so fresh in my mind. "And then Ian took me out of the play. He just confirmed what they said."

"So some of the cast said you weren't talented enough to land the part and you believed them."

"I'm just a girl from a small town in Texas. Home of the fighting Chihuahuas."

Charlie smiled, his lips turning up on a face that had an adorable light stubble. "You're still the girl with incredible talent, who once had the confidence and drive to take on the world."

"Sometimes the confidence runs out and reality sets in."

"Fight for this, Katie. Believe in you." His eyes searched mine, and I wondered what he saw. "I believe in you."

"And what if they tear the Valiant down? Maybe it's this big symbolic gesture from God to give up acting."

"If you want the Valiant to survive, then fight for that, too. But if Jiffy Co. takes it, it doesn't change who you are."

"How can that company just bulldoze part of our town?"

"I guess they call it progress. It happens all the time."

"At what cost? At the cost of Loretta losing her diner? It's as much a part of In Between as Friday night football games. Loretta still feeds the team cheeseburgers and shakes after every win. And the Valiant? Did you know in World War II, they had plays and dances as fundraisers, giving the money to war widows and families? An unknown singer named Janis Joplin sang there. Presidents have spoken there. And—"

"Our first kiss was there."

My next words died mid-sentence. "You remember that?"

He planted his arm beside me and leaned in. "I think about it. A lot."

"It was a long time ago."

"Remind me how it went."

I laughed and put my hands on his chest to push him away, but those hands seemed to have a mind of their own and stayed right there on the curves of his muscles. Someone clearly visited the gym in Chicago. "I don't want to like you again, Charlie."

"What we had has never been resolved. There will always be something between us." He reached for one of my hands and pressed his lips to the tops of my fingers. "You know I'm right."

"And what if you're just another bad decision on my part? What if you're not who I think you are."

He studied our joined hands. "We all make mistakes. I've made bad choices, too."

"I don't want to be one of them."

He shook his head, then kissed my temple. "Right now you're all that's right in my life."

"Charlie—" As his mouth moved to my cheek, trailing a tingling path, I struggled to recall all that I had wanted to ask him. "We should. . .we should talk about what's going on with you."

But his arms pulled me in close, and his hands cradled my face. "You." His lips hovered. "Just you."

"Katie! Charlie!"

A bucket of cold water could not have startled me more, so deep was I in Charlie's trance. Red-faced, I jumped up from the blanket and turned toward the sound of Frances's call.

"Do you think she saw that?" I asked Charlie between stiff lips.

"The whole town just saw that." He stood way too close behind me.

"Hey, guys!" Frances all but skipped to us, a giant ice cream cone in hand, a knowing grin on her face. "What's going on here?"

"Katie won't keep her hands off me." Charlie had the nerve to throw a chummy arm around my shoulders. "Her attempts at seduction would weaken a lesser man, but so far I'm staying strong."

Frances hid her laugh behind her uneaten double scoop. "Very gallant of you." Her phone chirped, and Frances extracted it from her purse. "Joey's here! Katie, I'm so excited you can hang out with him!" With dreamy-eyes, she fired a text in response that probably included lots of X's and O's, some "No, I love you mores," and little kissy emojis.

"I haven't seen him in weeks. This long-distance thing is really hard, you know?" Without waiting for a response, Frances turned on her heel and began scanning the town square. "We should all do dinner tomorrow night. What do you say?"

"I think I have this—"

"We'd love to." Charlie sent me a slow wink.

"Aw, that will be great, won't it?"

I shot an elbow into Charlie's ribs. "Just terrific."

"There he is!" She waved her free hand like she was bringing in a 747. "Joey!"

My friend handed me her ice cream, then with a girly squeal, tore off in Joey's direction. Charlie and I stood there and watched the reunion like two people viewing a car wreck—slightly dismayed, but unable to look away. As if in a synchronized ballet, Frances ran into Joey's waiting arms, laughing as he spun her around, her short floral skirt twirling.

"Ah, young love," Charlie said dryly as his brother kissed my best friend silly. "Want to show them how it's really done?"

I took a lick of Frances's dripping ice cream and mumbled something barely civil.

"I've never seen my brother like this." Charlie's fingers snaked around my wrist, and he brought the cone to his lips. I watched him take a slow, generous bite.

Little electric currents whipped from Charlie's hand through my system, and I struggled to focus. "Joey hasn't won me over."

"Why so cynical, Parker? You don't think they can make it?"

"Your brother's a player. Do you know how many times I saw his name scribbled on the bathroom wall in high school?"

His lips curved upward in a rake's grin. "Was my name ever on there?"

"Are you even listening to what I'm saying?"

Whatever Charlie was about to say would have to wait, as Frances returned with her fiancé, her face lit up brighter than the performance stage.

"Katie, you remember Joey." Frances leaned into his shoulder. Joey stood a few inches shorter than Charlie, but still towered over his petite fiancée. His hair was darker than Charlie's, and he had his father's brown eyes. Like his brother, Joey made jeans and a t-shirt look good, and with the two Bensons side by side, it was enough to cause more than one passing female take a nice, appreciative inspection.

"So you just got back from London?" Joey asked. "Great place."

"Yes, it is," I said. "Lots of culture and history." Too much of my own history was there.

"Joey painted a car that was on a TV show last month," Charlie said.

"It was so cool." Frances patted Joey's chest and smiled. "His name was even on the credits."

"If you'd have blinked you'd have missed the car," Joey said. "No big deal."

We stood there and talked for another hour, and I watched Joey closely. He barely spoke, and when he did it was a paltry few sentences. Frances was her usual animated self—hands in motion, face showing her every feeling, and quick with a story. They seemed like such opposites. She was soon leaving to pursue her PhD, while he had skipped college to paint and repair cars. How compatible were these two? I wanted the best for my beloved friend, and this rushed wedding had me on alert.

"We should go," Joey said. "We have that huge to-do list you wanted to tackle."

I hugged Frances and made myself say something positive. "Let me know what I can do to help."

"You're the best maid of honor," Frances said. "Dress shopping next week?"

I pushed some enthusiasm into my voice. "Sounds fun."

I watched the couple walk away, arm in arm, uncertainty clanging in my head.

"Let's hear it," Charlie said.

"What?"

"Your take on my brother. You were watching him like a scientific specimen."

"He's very nice."

"And?"

I had to tread carefully. This was Charlie's flesh and blood. "He's not who I see her with."

Charlie's amiable smile slipped as he settled his hands on my shoulders. "You know what I think?"

"That it's time to get me that funnel cake?"

"My brother isn't that Ian guy."

"I know that."

"Do you? Just because Ian hurt you doesn't mean my brother will do the same to Frances. If he says he loves her, then he loves her. Stop projecting your own fears onto your friend."

"He proposed after ten weeks. It doesn't take a broken heart to think that's moving way too fast for a life-long commitment."

"Is that what you have?" Charlie asked. "A broken heart?"

"What Ian did to me has nothing to do with how I feel about Frances getting married."

"And what about us?" Charlie's eyes held me captive. "Does what Ian did have anything to do with what you feel for me?"

"What is that supposed to mean?"

"You're running scared from a lot of things right now." Charlie moved until he was but a breath away. "It would be nice if one of them wasn't me."

Chapter Eight

J UST BEING NEAR an airport made my head ache and my left eye twitch.

On Monday morning, Maxine and I drove my parents to the airport for their very long sojourn to Haiti. I knew that they were going to do some good work in an orphanage, but I was feeling a little orphaned myself. I had only been home a week, and already James and Millie were leaving.

"You're sure you're feeling okay?" Millie asked, as I pulled her carry-on behind me through the sliding doors. People milled about like ants, zipping here and there, talking on cell phones, staring blankly at iPads, hugging family members.

"I'm fine," I said. "Not a thing wrong with me."

"Actually," Maxine said, "you have panty lines."

We stopped near a self-check in kiosk, and I tried to look my fill of my parents. I wanted to remember this moment, recall their faces, the sound of their voices. They could get on that plane and never make it back. I knew very well how precarious life was once you hit the clouds. The sky was a dangerous place to travel, and I wouldn't rest until I knew James and Millie had safely landed.

"Call me when you get to your connecting flight," I said. "And right before you takeoff. And when you land in Haiti. And after you deplane."

James chuckled and pulled me into a warm hug. "Don't worry

about us."

"Are you sure you won't reconsider driving?"

"Too many toll roads." James kissed my cheek. "I've left all my notes on the property buyout in my office. Look over those. It will give you something to do."

"I'll pore over them."

"I'm sure you will," James said. "But it's just to be informed. This isn't your fight. The property owners have an attorney, and Millie and I will be back in three weeks. I'm not going to let them take the Valiant without giving it all we've got."

"This is my theater, too," I said. "My hometown."

"One way or another, it will be okay," Millie said.

But would it? I couldn't lose that theater. I had poured my very life into it, and so had James and Millie. And at the moment, it was my only job plan.

"Don't eat junk," Millie said. "I left some meals in the freezer for you."

Maxine made a little gagging sound. "Seaweed salad and bean balls. Don't invite me over."

After an incredibly long group hug in which Maxine purposely kept blowing in my ear, the family separated, said our "I love yous," and Millie and James left to get in line for security.

I blinked back tears as Maxine and I walked to the car, the Texas sun hot on my skin. I'd spent so little time with my parents this year, and now that I was home, they were gone.

"Are you gonna ignore me forever?" Maxine asked as she slid into the passenger seat.

"I'm not ignoring you." I shoved the key into the ignition and fired up the red beast. My car was ten years old and had spent the last year bunking in Millie and James's garage. It was good to drive again. On the right side of the road.

"I've told you something vitally important three times, and you've yet to so much as look my direction."

"What was this vital question?"

"Dairy Barn is having BOGO on hot fudge sundaes 'til noon."

"I can't."

She tsked and shook her head. "I've heard some people are never the same after a bad concussion."

"I have to get back to try on dresses with Frances." Lord knew I'd rather be eating two-for-one ice cream.

"Oh. Well, then I want to go."

"Not this time."

"Please don't be mad at me, Katie," Maxine said. "I'm too old to find a new best friend."

I gripped the steering wheel as I pulled onto the interstate, knowing I couldn't stay mad with words like that. She had pulled a lot of stunts in our time together, but scheduling an audition in New York might've topped them all. It was even worse than the time in high school when she got me to climb the water tower with her so she could hang a banner declaring her love for her estranged Sam. She had fallen over the railing, held on for dear life, then miraculously been saved by a truck full of hot fire fighters. The woman always landed on her feet. Or on a beefcake in uniform.

"I'm not mad," I said.

"Oh, good."

"But I'm not happy either."

"I didn't mean any harm talking to your director."

"He's not my director. We've never even met. But harm is exactly what you caused. Now I have to call him back and explain what happened."

Maxine turned the radio to her favorite pop station. "You could avoid that awkward conversation."

"By telling him you're insane?"

"By going on the audition."

"No."

"It wouldn't hurt to just—"

"I'm done with acting. Done with the stage."

"Then what are you going to do? You have too much talent to waste it here." Maxine tapped irritated fingers on the armrest.

"Maybe I'll go to Vegas and be a show girl like you were."

"Look, Sweet Pea, I'm being for real here. What's the plan?"

I turned the corner a little too sharply, sending Maxine leaning a hard right into her door. She grabbed the overhead handle and shot me a look that would scare misbehaving children and men with any sense about them.

"I said, what's the—"

"When Delores leaves, I plan to take over the Valiant." I had already informed James of my idea, and while he wasn't happy I was abandoning acting, he knew I would take care of the Valiant better than anyone else.

"And if it's not saved from the chopping block?"

"I don't know," I said. "I have no idea, okay? It's not like I knew I'd already need a career change at twenty-three."

"Then don't change. Or at least not 'til you have a good reason to."

"Do you want to know how I got the role of Beatrice?"

"A sassy, smart-mouthed heroine who shoots one-liners like arrows? Can't imagine why they'd cast you."

"I got it because the director liked me." Note to self, *never date your boss again.*

"Well, of course he did. You're a brilliant actress."

"That's not what I meant." Though Maxine's version made for a much nicer story.

"I don't know what happened in London," Maxine said, her voice gentling, "but your incredible gift got you to London in the first place. You were all but plucked from obscurity at that college. How many kids graduated from your university and were invited to work in London?"

"One."

"And how many from the entire state of Texas?"

"One."

"Remind me what her name was?"

I sighed as I switched lanes. "Katie."

"See. End of story. You need to go on that audition and show them what you've got. Your acting career isn't over. It's just taking a new direction. And maybe that direction is New York."

"I'm not going on the audition."

"Fine." Maxine cranked up the radio volume. "I'll go in your place."

DIAMOND'S BRIDAL SAT on the corner of Twelfth Street and Main in a town called Newman, one hour and five Golden Arches down the highway. Traditional red bricks made up the outside of the shop, but inside was a harem of lace and satin, ivory and white, sequins and tulle.

Frances's mother, Maxine, and I perched on pink pin-striped chairs, sipping sparkling water in wine glasses and waiting for Frances to resurface. We had already watched her model six dresses, and by now they all looked the same. If Frances had liked the dress, her mother had not. Dresses her mother adored, Frances couldn't stand. And Maxine? Well, I was pretty sure Maxine had swapped her sparkling water for the vino at least four dresses ago.

"I guess this engagement took you by surprise?" I asked Mrs. Vega. "So sudden and all." Maybe if Frances's mother and I tag-teamed, we could talk some sense into the bride-to-be.

"It was quite unexpected." Mrs. Vega didn't take her eyes off the dressing room door.

"I'm sure you'd feel better if they waited a bit. Took some time to really get to know one another."

"Mmm." Her monosyllabic sound of agreement did not provide

much information. "Frances, are you coming out any time soon?" Mrs. Vega checked the gold watch on her wrist.

"If she stays in there much longer, they're gonna charge her rent." Maxine tapped a red fingernail to her glass. "Where's that waitress?"

"This isn't Applebee's." I snatched that flute right out of her hands.

"Come on, girl," Maxine called toward the door. "I'm fossilizing out here."

"Get ready!" Frances yelled back. "I think you're going to love this one."

The dressing room door creaked open, and Frances walked to the mini runway that led to a three-way mirror so big if we aimed it at the sun, we'd light the whole town on fire. Frances wore a strapless, fitted gown of antique ivory lace. It gaped at the top and ballooned at the bottom.

Her mother pushed her glasses up her nose, much like Frances always did when needing a closer inspection. "What's that style?"

Frances turned in a circle. "It's called fit and flare."

Maxine's lip curled. "You need to burn that flare."

"I don't like it," Mrs. Vega said. "Too much cleavage, not enough bling."

"Yeah." Maxine waved her hand toward the dress. "You gotta pimp that thing out. Get some sparkle. Some razzle dazzle."

I nudged my grandmother. "You said you'd sit quietly. That was our deal."

"I want to renegotiate our terms."

I knew I should've dropped Maxine off at the Dairy Barn. "You're not helping."

"No," Frances said. "She's right. And my mother's right. This dress doesn't work. None of them have." She turned to face the mirror. "Something's missing with all these gowns."

"I bet the winter collection is worth waiting for."

"Subtle," Maxine whispered. "Really subtle."

"You could wear my dress," Mrs. Vega suggested. "We could get it altered this week."

"Your dress hasn't been in style since frosty blue eye shadow and acid-washed jeans." Frances's shoulders drooped and she stepped away from the mirrors. "I'm sorry. I'm projecting my wedding stress onto you all. When I see the right one, I'll know it. But so far, these are all very vanilla. I'm wanting—"

"Cherry chip mocha with hot fudge, butterscotch, peanut butter, toasted pecans, whipped cream, and extra sprinkles?" Maxine looked at each of our blank faces. "I guess that's just me."

Frances lifted her skirt above her heels and shuffled back into the dressing room.

"How is Mr. Vega taking this?" I asked when Frances was out of ear-shot.

Her mother shook her head. "Not well. Frances is our first born, his baby girl. It's hard. We've had to have a lot of talks about it."

"I'm sure his concerns are understandable."

Mrs. Vega smiled. "Her dad's just having a difficult time letting her go. He thinks she should still be in pig tails and Hello Kitty."

"Do you. . ." This was such a delicate matter, I wanted to tread carefully. "Do you think Frances and Joey should date a little longer?"

"Yes, but her father and I can't say a word."

"Why not?"

"Because," Mrs. Vega said dreamily, "Juan and I married on date number six."

Chapter Nine

LONELINESS WAS A funny thing.

It could flood your mind with memories, thoughts, and countless what-ifs.

It could also scatter all that away like a swift wind and leave you thinking of nothing but one person.

Tonight I was thinking of one person.

Charlie Benson.

I sat on the back deck of my parent's home, missing them and unable to stay inside that quiet house one more minute. Listening to the crickets and the tree frogs, I stared into the dancing flames of James's fire pit. It was too hot to be lighting fires, but the crackle and snap soothed my ragged nerves.

My feelings for Charlie made no sense. I had just broken up with my long-time boyfriend. Why wasn't I sitting here moping over Ian? Yet I thought of him less and less with each passing day. I didn't want to feel this Herculean tug toward Charlie, as if he held this magnet, pulling me in with a force I was helpless to stop. We had a history, so many moments as close friends and more. He had been my confidante in some of my life's darkest hours. But he'd also wounded me more than once, throwing me over for someone better, prettier, girlier. I'd despised every one of those girls. And sure, I'd done the same to him at least once, but it wasn't like I had a pattern of walking away, of seeking out blonder pastures.

Charlie Benson was a risk. Could I really believe that he had changed in the last few years? I didn't even know what I wanted to be when I grew up. The last thing I needed was to get involved and complicate my life further.

"Is this a private bonfire or can anyone join?"

I jumped at the voice, my breath seizing in my chest. "Charlie." I laid a hand over my galloping heart. "You scared me."

"Sorry." With a sheepish grin he climbed the few stairs to join me. He eased his tall body into the seat beside me, his long legs stretching before him. "I've been calling you for a few hours. I was getting a little worried you were getting into trouble with Maxine now that your folks were gone."

I leaned my head back on my chair and laughed. "She has a whole list of things for us to do now that I'm back in town. Some of them are even legal." I picked up my phone and took it off mute. "I guess I still had the volume off from wedding dress shopping."

"Find anything?"

"Frances didn't." I gave him the bare details of Frances's dress travails, knowing the long version would just make his eyes glaze over. "We did find my bridesmaid dress."

"Is it awful?"

"It's actually pretty." It was a bright coral full-length gown, Grecian-style, with a high waist, flowing skirt, and one wide strap that crossed my left shoulder. I really did like it, but Frances's assurance I could wear it again was simply laughable. Nobody wore bridesmaid dresses again. They sat in closets and gathered dust and moth holes.

"I bet you look amazing in the dress," Charlie said.

The boy did know how to turn a head. "Thank you. I guess this wedding is really happening."

"Accept it."

"I am trying."

"My brother's a good guy."

"I'm sure he is. It's just that it's happened so fast, and nobody seems to be concerned about this." My best friend was not frivolous or spontaneous. "And she's about to start her PhD program."

"And my brother works with cars."

"There's nothing wrong with that. I'm not being a snob here. I'm the first one in my family to have a degree—high school or college. But her brain is not normal; you know that. She's Mensa. She's Jeopardy champ material. She wrote a college text book her sophomore year, for crying out loud." And sixty universities used it. "I can barely keep up a conversation with her. Is your brother going to be a good conversation partner when she wants to dissect Middle Eastern religion's role on global affairs?"

"Maybe what they have goes well beyond how good they might be on paper. So what if they don't match up in education or even intellect. Have you been around them?"

Charlie knew the answer to that, so I didn't bother to reply.

"Give Joey a chance," he said. "He loves Frances. I know this."

"Marriage is hard in the best of circumstances. I just don't want to see her make a mistake."

"Love's a risk," Charlie said. "But it's theirs to take."

I had taken a risk with Ian. And lost. And now I found myself regularly thinking about this dark headed Southern boy, as if my heart didn't know I needed time to be still and dateless. Time to watch chick flicks, eat Cheetos, and disparage the male race.

Instead of spending time with the enemy.

"So what's going to happen after the wedding?" Charlie asked.

"Frances and Joey go on their honeymoon?"

"I meant you. Are you really not going back to London?"

"No." I didn't know what I would do for a career, but I was certain it wouldn't involve a return trip to the U.K.

"You're just going to walk away from acting?"

"Yes," I said. "No. I mean, I don't know." My brain was a Magic 8 ball, and all it kept coming up with was *reply hazy, try again.*

"And what are those?" Charlie gestured to the papers on the

floor.

"It's nothing."

He reached over me, his chest heavy and warm on mine, and grabbed the stack. "What is this? They're from New York."

I managed to snatch a few back. The man had no boundaries.

Charlie held up a trade paper and read. "You have some auditions circled. Are you going?"

"No. My friend Caroline from college lives in New York. She sent them to me."

"Because she knows you should go."

"Because she enjoys harassing me like someone else I know."

"You can't give up on—"

"I came out here for some peace, Charlie." I pulled the rest of the papers from his hand and tossed it on the ground. "I don't want to talk about my job plans."

"Okay." He captured my hand before I could pull it away. His fingers interlocked with mine, and his eyes dared me to do something about it. "Then let's talk about us."

Oh, even better. Because I totally had that element of my life all figured out. "Why don't we talk about something simpler. Like ending global warfare or how to solve the national debt?"

"So you're saying we're complicated?"

I merely lifted an eyebrow.

"It doesn't have to be." His voice was smooth and husky, and it skimmed over me like a caress.

It was time to change the subject. "I've been looking over James's paperwork on the Thrifty Co. takeover. They've really been low-balled."

Charlie leaned back in his chair. "This moment is totally unsexy now."

I laughed. "Were you weaving a magic spell there, Romeo?"

"I got no game when you talk business."

I patted his shoulder. "That's sweet you think you got game, period."

He ran a finger over my hand, tracing a slow line up my arm. "I seem to remember you liked me on a recent airplane ride. Need me to refresh your memory?" He leaned in, so close I could smell his cologne, see the fire brighten his eyes.

I struggled to find my voice. "We need to forget that."

"I can't." His fingers made lazy swirls on my skin. "I can't forget that kiss. And what you said right before it. And I know." His hands made a slow migration to my face, cradling my head. "I know you remember it. What I don't get is why you won't talk to me about it."

"Charlie, what are we doing?" When had my hands moved to rest on his chest? And why was my face a mere breath from his, as if I was all but begging for a kiss? "I'm not in a good place."

"I don't care." He lowered his head—

Only to be interrupted by the blast from my phone. A Katy Perry snippet sang from beneath my chair.

"James!" Relief flowed like honey at the sight of my dad's name on my screen. "Am I glad to hear from you," I said as I answered his call. He spoke briefly, assuring me he and Millie had safely landed in Port Au Prince. *Thank God.* I felt like anyone flying deserved a Purple Heart of Bravery, and I didn't know when I'd ever be able to step on a plane again.

The call was over almost as soon as it began, and a tired James told me he loved me and would ring back in a few days.

"Your parents got there okay?" Charlie asked.

I nodded.

"Are *you* okay?"

"Yes," I said. "I've just been worried about their flight. I've been tracking it on radar all afternoon, and they were going through some rain."

Charlie's hand reached out, and he massaged the back of my neck, where tension sat in knots of coiled pain. "You got issues."

"Just part of my charm. Oh, wow, that feels incredible. I don't even want to know where you learned that."

Charlie laughed, then stood. With a tug of my hand, he pulled me to my feet, only to sit down in my chair and draw me onto his lap. I started to protest, but when his hands skimmed over my back, I lost all motivation to complain. I didn't remember ever feeling this comfortable when Ian touched me. Never this dueling sense of desire and calm.

"How's that head?" Charlie asked, his fingers doing something heavenly to the base of my neck.

"It's fine. I get the stitches out later in the week."

"I guess now that you know your parents are safe, you can focus all your attention on being happy for Frances and Joey."

"While that is a worthy project"—My gosh, his hands were bliss—"What I need to focus on is saving the Valiant. A little more to the left, please. Ah, right there." Was it wrong to purr? His fingers pushed into the tight knots on my shoulders, and I took a few cleansing breaths. I could've stayed like that forever. Just me, Charlie's hands doing their thing, and the gorgeous night sky above. "I've been studying James's notes."

The massage stopped. "When you weren't tracking weather and planes?" He resumed his ministrations, his hands moving slower, gentler.

"I'm a great multi-tasker. And you're an excellent masseuse. I could fall asleep right here."

"Guys do not like to hear our presence puts a girl to sleep." He pulled my hair to the side, his fingers running down my neck, making my nerve endings hum.

I lolled my head to the left. "Don't take it personal. I haven't slept in days."

"And why is that?"

"I don't know. I have a lot on my mind, I guess."

His hands slowed. "Like me?"

"You wish." But that was definitely a good part of it. Charlie and

I had picked up right where we'd left off, as if we'd not gone two separate directions. As if we hadn't both chosen to not be together multiple times over the years. The man smelled like heaven. It was a mix of spice, outdoors, and soap, mixed with tangy notes of arrogance and charm.

"Calvin Klein ought to bottle up your scent," I said lazily.

"Maybe call it Sweaty Texan?"

I smiled. "I still have a few of your t-shirts from high school. In college when I'd get homesick, I'd pull one out and sleep in it. They used to smell like you." Like home. Like the boy I had loved.

Charlie turned me until I faced him. His hands cradled my jaw, his thumbs sweeping across. "I love it when you get too tired to filter," he whispered. His lips brushed against mine—once, twice. "Anything else I need to know? Like you have my name tattooed somewhere fun?"

"Maybe." I wrapped my arms around his neck. "But you're not checking."

"I love a good challenge." His smiling lips descended and captured mine. I soon forgot what we were talking about, and all I knew was this man. I held onto Charlie like he was a lifeline, my raft in the tossing waves. His mouth was soft and teasing, sending spiraling sensations to every limb, every cell. It was wonderful not to think, to let my brain take a few minutes of respite, while the rest of me just. . .felt.

A loud crashing had us both breaking apart.

Heart pounding, I scanned the yard until I saw the familiar intruder.

"Armadillo," Charlie said. "He was probably watching us." His hand slid down my back. "Want to give him an encore?"

"Not tonight," I said as Charlie pressed his lips to a spot behind my ear. It was difficult to form a coherent sentence when he did that. "Charlie—" His evening stubble shaded his cheeks, and I couldn't help but ran my hand over the places where tomorrow a razor would go. "I think I've found my purpose here in In Between."

Charlie leaned into my hand. "Us?"

"Not what I was talking about."

"We'll work on that." He traced my collarbone with his finger. "Your stage career?"

"No." I could barely focus. All I could think was *please don't stop whatever you're doing.* "Um. . .no, not my career. That's pretty much dead." *Focus, Katie.* "I'm talking about the Valiant. Nobody's going to take that from me." For my twenty-first birthday, James and Millie had added my name on the deed. I'd happy-cried for days. "It's horrible timing that James isn't here with all that's going on, but I'm going to fight for it. I'm going to make sure Thrifty Co. never touches it. Maybe this is what I came back for. Maybe God led me away from acting to come back and save the Valiant."

"Let me get this straight. You think God told you to quit acting? When you think of giving up your theater dream forever, that gives you the holy tingles?"

No, but Charlie sure did. I forced myself to rise from the chair and walk to the edge of the deck, needing some distance between me and the overpowering magnetic pull that kept drawing me back to him. Between that and the fact that I was completely sleep deprived, my brain was as sticky as cotton candy. "Before I came home, the attorney hired by James and the rest of the group quit. My dad said Loretta found another one last week. Ever heard of Reggie Barker?"

"Name sounds familiar."

"I guess I'll meet him at the town hall meeting tomorrow night. James wants me to size him up. You could go and help me."

Charlie stood beside me, his side pressed into mine. "I might be there. Katie, I think we should talk. I need to—"

"The stars are so beautiful tonight. And look at that full moon. There's nothing as pretty as In Between, is there?" I turned to Charlie and found him watching me with an intensity that had made weaker girls toss their t-shirts and morals.

"I could think of a few things more beautiful." His gaze not wavering from mine, Charlie reached out and captured a strand of my wayward hair, running it through his fingers. "I've always thought you were the most beautiful girl in the whole town. When I went to college, I never met anyone who turned my head like you."

"You do know how to sweet talk a girl."

"I know you're in rebound mode, and you're hurting from that Ian guy, but whether you deal with it now or later, you and I have unfinished business. If you need time, I can give that to you."

My hands slid up Charlie's chest, as he pulled me close. "I do need time." Didn't I? "It can't be right to jump out of one serious relationship right into another."

"This is me," he said gruffly. "I'm not some new guy you met at Starbucks. You know me. You know *us*. And there's always been an us."

"I have horrible judgment, especially with relationships. I don't exactly trust my heart right now."

"Then trust me with it, Katie." He hugged me to him and rested his head on top of mine. "Please. . .trust *me*."

Chapter Ten

WHEN THE ALARM went off at four Monday morning, I rolled over and thought about crying.

But the kind of energy that required wouldn't kick in 'til five.

The lazy sun hadn't even made an appearance by the time I walked into Micky's Diner and reported for my first day of work.

"You sure about this?" Loretta asked, swigging from a mug of coffee.

"I think so." I went to the carafe not labeled decaf and helped myself.

She took another sip and assessed the blousey hang of my super-sized t-shirt I had uselessly tried to shrink in the dryer. "You gonna work two weeks then get knocked up and leave like my June hire?"

"No plans to get preggo."

"You gonna be the best darn plate balancer ever, then run off with my fry cook like Miss November?"

"I can't balance anything." Though hooking up with a fry cook could have its perks.

"Or you could be like Miss February and give extra bacon and burgers to your drug dealers."

"My dealers are vegans."

Her lips quirked. "Maxine said you were sassy. You get that from her?"

Not one drop of Maxine's blood coursed through my veins. "Probably so."

"She also said you're gonna help us run Thrifty Co. out of town. Nominated you as our new leader in your dad's absence."

I choked on my classic roast. "I'm all for helping, but that sounds a little over my head."

"You got a fancy college degree."

"And if you want me to teach you all how to express your protests in mime, then you're in luck. Otherwise, I'm not really qualified to take charge."

"Either you give it a shot, or I put you on dish washing duty for the rest of your career here."

"I was secretary of our Brownie troop in second grade, so I will take your kindly given challenge." I could not catch a break if someone handed it to me.

"I'll get you a list of our group's contact info. The property owners are gonna meet before the real show gets started, and you can jump in then. Maybe you can bring some fresh ideas." She threw an apron at me. "Put that on. And be at the town hall meeting an hour early."

"Do I need a secret password?"

"Yeah." Loretta waddled off, her spikes especially pointy. "Thrifty Co. sucks."

"You ready to get started?" Kourtney with a K chewed on a pink piece of gum with lots of snap, crackle, and pop.

I banished all the thoughts of my happy days on the stage and thought about my sad, sad bank account. "Let's do this."

Before Kourtney with a K could tell me how to be a waitress, she decided to give me a fifteen minute tutorial on bleaching your own hair. "I do it all the time." She held up her fried ponytail that was colored a shade of orangey-white not usually found in a stylist's palette. "I could do yours if you want."

"Thanks," I said. "Maybe when I get paid." And when I no longer had brain matter.

She then took a whopping five minutes to explain the rigors of waitressing before the doors opened and sleepy In Betweenites trickled in like harmless zombies.

"Orders are pretty simple at breakfast," she said, shoving me toward my first table. "Just keep the coffee flowing."

It sounded so easy.

Half an hour later, I was thinking performing heart surgery or splitting isotopes might be simpler. Did everyone have to be so picky? Tea with light ice. Could I substitute hash browns for an extra egg? Semi-crisp bacon only. Was the ketchup organic? And then there was Mr. Sherman, eighty on his last birthday, trying to give me a bum-pinch every time I walked by.

I carried out three plates of biscuits and gravy, proud of myself for not spilling so much as a crumb, and delivered it to table number seven, three ladies from the In Between Garden Club.

"Hi, there, Katie." Mrs. O'Reilley settled her napkin in her lap as I placed a plate in front of her.

"Good morning, ladies." It was hard to smile at this hour on such little sleep.

"We heard you're gonna help us save our town from the evil claws of commercialism."

"Uh-huh." I watched another customer bustle in like her pants were on fire. "Did you want more coffee?"

"No." Mrs. O'Reilley patted my arm. "The Garden Club welcomes your help. We know you don't want to see the Valiant and our other fine establishments come to ruin."

Across the diner, a wide-eyed Maxine locked me in her sights and waved with her entire upper body. She clearly was trying to make her way toward my direction, but various chatty diners were not letting her pass without a howdy-do.

"Mrs. O'Reilley, I'm going to try and help," I said, "but I just got into town, and I'm not ready to roll out any big guns at tonight's meeting."

"But you must go," said Ms. Delmonaco, vice-president of the club, whose claim to fame was growing the tallest sunflowers. And luring the police chief away from his second wife.

Their tablemate Mitzy Kipper poured sugar in her coffee. "It's a done deal, girls. Katie would be wasting her breath to go tonight."

Mrs. O'Reilley huffed. "This is a town divided. Half are for this behemoth of a store, entranced by dollar signs and empty promises. And the other half are on the side of reason and protecting the integrity of our fine town."

"Yoohoo!" Maxine pushed past the mayor and finally reached my side. "Good heavens, that man is long-winded. Like I care about his denture saga." My grandmother took a cleansing breath and blessed the Garden Club with a brittle smile. "Ladies."

"Maxine," said Mrs. O'Reilley. There was bad blood between the Garden Club and my grandma, but I had no idea what it was. I had lost track of all who had dared to cross Maxine Dayberry and find themselves on her hissing list. "You look as wilted as a fern in Florida. Something the matter?"

"I need to talk to my granddaughter."

"I'm working," I said.

Maxine's grip on my arm tightened. "Surely you have five minutes for your dear grandmama."

"I have to go take table twelve's order and—"

"Here." Maxine grabbed Kourtney as she sailed by. "Kiki, go see what those folks want to eat." She gave her a healthy shove in that direction. "And pull up that shirt. Are we selling breakfast or boobies here?" With clasped hands and a face of feigned innocence, Maxine returned her attention to me. "A word, if I may?"

There was only one way to get rid of Maxine, and that was to give her what she wanted. "I'll be right back to check on you," I said to the Garden Club.

Maxine linked her arm in mine, then turned back to address my table. "Oh, and by the by, the yoga club *loves* me. They made me president."

"There's no such thing as a yoga president!" Mrs. O'Reilley called.

Maxine hauled me into a corner next to the only empty booth. "Your hair is just glorious this morning," she said. "New shampoo?"

"I haven't washed it in three days. What do you want?" Apprehension sizzled around me like a griddle of fried eggs, as Maxine didn't suck up for nothing.

"Poopsie, I might've made a little human error." She chuckled and waved a hand. "We all do, right?"

"Did you enroll me on a dating site without my permission again?"

"No!"

That fiasco had taken me weeks to straighten out.

"Dear, it's quite possible I really bungled things up this time. But I had the very best of intentions."

"Like the time you got me a wax session for my birthday?"

"Sweet Pea, you know Grammy loves you, right?"

Oh, geez. It was bad. And who was Grammy? "What did you do, Maxine?"

"I. . ." Her hands loosened their death grip on me to twist and twirl the gob of beads at her throat. "I didn't know the circumstances, or I never would've called. But I was desperate for help. At one of our committee meetings they told us to think outside the box, so that's what I did."

"Can you just spit it out please? I have tables waiting on me."

"I didn't mean to stir anything up. Well, I wanted to stir up a solution. And who better to advocate for a dying theater than a theater professional? And I just wanted advice. I didn't think he'd come here. I mean, imagine, traveling all this way and—"

"You didn't. He didn't." I shook my head, pushing her words from my rattled brain. Nope. Not possible.

"I did." Maxine's contrite face clanged the alarms in my head. "He does have experience with these sort of things. He's been involved in theater preservations before. And I didn't know you were broken up and you were on your way home or I would've never—"

"You called Ian?" At the stares of table five, I dropped my volume. "What were you thinking? How did you even have his number?"

"Please," she said. "Give me some credit. I didn't call him."

That was a small measure of relief.

"I sent him a Facebook message," Maxine amended. "I'm hip like that."

The panic had returned. "And he responded?"

She nodded miserably. "In a big, big way."

"And he said he's coming here?"

She made a strangled sound in her throat.

"To In Between?"

"Yes."

The haze dissipated like a slow-lifting fog. "Ian's in the throes of a production. In another country. He's not going to leave London, leave his cast, and fly here."

"But that's what I'm here to tell you."

"Maxine, I have work to do. It's my first day, I have no idea what I'm doing, and we're swamped. Go home and rest easy. It's not even remotely possible he'd hop on a plane and come to In Between."

"Katie." Kourtney pointed to the giant clock on the wall behind the cash register. "It's your lunch break. See you in thirty."

I untied the little apron where I kept my order notepad. "I'm meeting Frances at Vivi's Bridal Boutique. She wants to try on this dress again."

"But I'm not through talking to you," Maxine said. "What I'm trying to tell you is—" Maxine's eyes widened and she began to make little venom-spitting noises. "Sissy McKinney sitting with the Garden Club? The only gardening that woman does is watching her twenty-one year old Latin landscaper trim her shrubs. I will not have it!" Maxine stomped off to vent her wrath, and I left the diner, grateful to breathe fresh air and think on anything but Ian Attwood.

Chapter Eleven

I T WAS ONLY eleven a.m., and I was already exhausted. My ponytail hung limp, my skin had a nice oily sheen from multiple trips to the hot kitchen, and I was spending my lunch break watching Frances try on another dress. The same one she'd tried on three different times on three different occasions.

I walked the two blocks, cutting through the alley by the library, gracelessly hustling like my pants were lit by kerosene. Vivi's Bridal Boutique was an odd shop that showcased Vivi Moreau's hand-sewn designs. Vivi had immigrated from Canada forty years prior, bringing a single carry-on and her Singer sewing machine. Inside the shop you could find wedding dresses, formal dresses, Sunday dresses, sun dresses, Christening dresses, communion dresses, and a small section of lingerie made of French lace that nobody paid much attention to. The store had floundered for years, surviving on nothing but hope and the occasional wedding dress purchase until someone created that Internet. Five years after Vivi got her first website, she bought a Mercedes, opened another shop in Houston, and paid off her business loan at the Mercantile and Trust with a suitcase of crisp hundred dollar bills.

I stepped inside the shop and found Frances standing in front of a wall-sized mirror. She wore a satin number that stopped just below her knee, with short-sleeves and a fitted skirt. It reminded me of something an actress from the forties might've worn.

"What do you think?" Frances turned to face me, her black glasses sitting crooked on her face.

"I think it looks just like when we saw it the last time."

She spun back around and studied her reflection. "It would be cute with a little pill box hat, wouldn't it?"

"It would."

"I think I'm going to get it. It fits perfect. I don't even need alterations. How crazy is that?" She clapped her hands over her mouth. "I just made a dress commitment!"

"I'm so proud. Don't move." I whipped my phone out of my back pocket and snapped a quick photo. "I'll send it to your mother."

Frances smiled for the picture, then threw her arms around me in a hug. "I'm getting married, Katie. The dress makes it so real, doesn't it?"

"You have less than three weeks left as a single girl."

"And before the big move."

I didn't even want to think about that.

Five minutes later, we stepped out of Vivi's, ready to move on to Hank's Hot Dog Hangout, a food trailer that promised Chicago-style dogs of twenty-three varieties.

"Oh, no!" Frances thrust the plastic-bagged dress into my arms. "I think I forgot my dad's credit card. He'll make me elope if I lose that."

I stood in front of Vivi's, holding a wedding dress and hoping Frances would hurry. I had twelve minutes before I was due back at the diner.

"Hello, Katie."

The sky could've rained ice and the clouds thrown snow, and I wouldn't have been as chilled as I was at that voice.

"Ian."

The world moved in slow motion as my brain registered it truly was Ian walking down the sidewalk, mere feet away. I told myself to move, to say something, to just *do* something. It was much like those horror movies where the girl fell to the ground, and you knew the knife-wielding slasher was coming, but she couldn't seem to recall how to stand to her own two feet.

"You look surprised to see me."

Surprised? That was like saying the Middle East was a little tumultuous. That the ocean was big enough to swim in. That Channing Tatum was a wee bit attractive. *Surprised* was a paltry word for what I felt.

"What . . .what are you doing here, Ian?"

He smiled. He was always smiling. It was one of the things I had fallen for. Me and about a dozen other women. His thick, dark hair was a contrast to his ever-present white button down, crisply ironed and starched. He wore charcoal dress pants, as if on his way to a meeting. Instead of busting back into my life.

"I came to see you," he said. "Didn't your grandmother tell you?"

I guess she had attempted to. But why would I have believed Ian would actually come here? "I don't understand."

"I'm here for you," he said. "You and your theater."

I opened my mouth with a slicing retort when I noticed a woman walking toward us. My eyes narrowed as she came into focus. "Her?" I was going to kill this man. Right on the Mayberry streets of my hometown. "You brought *her?*" His little two-bit twit Felicity sauntered her way to Ian, her heeled feet daring to touch the sacred ground of In Between. "You two need to get out of my city. I don't know what Maxine told you, and I have no idea what you're up to, but we don't need your help."

My ex-boyfriend did a thorough study of my outfit, his nose all but wrinkling as if smelling the Queen's pantyhose. "What is that shirt?"

I crossed my arms over a top big enough to shelter an entire kindergarten class. "It's my new uniform. I have a job. Can we get back to why you're in the neighborhood?"

Felicity's tone dripped disdain like syrup on a hot cake. "Micky's

Diner? You're a . . ."

"Waitress, yes."

"Why are you waiting tables?" Ian asked.

"Isn't it what all starving actresses do?"

"You were hardly starving before you quit and deserted our production."

"Well, now I produce eggs and bacon. And you cut me from the show, if you recall."

"I gave you a break. You needed one. You should've been thanking me instead of—"

"Thanking you?" The nerve of this man! "You are the most arrogant, egocentric—"

"The fact of the matter is I'm here to help you," Ian said.

"Do I even want to know what *she's* here to help with?"

"We both quit *Much Ado*. I'll be directing a Samuel Beckett production on Broadway next month. Felicity will continue to be my assistant."

"I'm sure she'll give you a lot of. . .help."

"What happened to your forehead?" Ian asked.

"Remains of my lobotomy. Now why are you two in In Between? And more importantly, what time does your flight leave?"

The door behind us opened and out came Frances. "Got my card." She extended her perky smile to the two interlopers. "Hi." She stuck out her hand. "I'm Frances. Friends of Katie's?"

"No," I said.

"Yes." Ian slowly shook Frances's hand, and I could see his charm already reaching out like invisible tentacles. Nobody was immune.

"This is Ian." His name tasted like a bitter berry on my tongue. "My ex-boyfriend. And this is his. . .his. . ."

"This is Felicity."

Frances's mouth hung in a small oval. "I don't think I understand."

"Kind of defies logic," I said, my narrowed eyes on Ian.

"Your grandmother asked me to help your town," he said. "Theater preservation is a passion of mine."

"Are you seriously trying to tell me you flew all this way for that?"

Felicity wrapped her hand around Ian's bicep. "He didn't fly here for you, if that's what you're asking."

Ian put a halting hand on my shoulder before I could wrap my fingers around Felicity's throat. Or at least get in a good hair yank.

"You clearly have some strong feelings, Katie," Ian said. "One could only expect that. Things didn't end well, and I know I hurt you deeply."

"A mere paper cut."

He looked at me with such pity in his eyes, like I was three steps away from throwing my sad self off the nearest bridge. "No matter your anger," he said. "I have a job to do here, and that's what I'm going to do."

"What job? Seducing the skirt off every woman in town?"

He laughed, a throaty sound that had once all but made me float on air, but now made me want to claw his face with my nails. "Your grandmother needs help saving your theater, and I can be of use. I have many connections, and we can create a PR storm the likes those Thrifty folks have never seen."

"And what's in it for you?"

"You screaming across the stage as you tackled him during the intermission of your last show." Felicity put a bracing arm around her dear Ian. "Does that ring a bell?"

"Yes," I snapped. "I envision his black eye every night as I say my prayers and give thanks to the Almighty."

Ian sighed. "It's just like you to act so irrationally without any thought to anyone else."

"Were you thinking of anyone else when you had your hands all over your assistant *during* the show? You couldn't even wait 'til it was over? Until we were all gone?" The curtain had just gone down for intermission, and I had ran back to Ian's office to tell him that a major critic was in the fourth row and found him and his perky, skinny, skanky assistant entwined on his desk. Had I walked in just a few minutes later, I would've seen something straight out of a Rated R movie.

"You humiliated me," Ian said. "That critic absolutely crucified us all in her review."

"You probably dated her once too."

"If you can't keep your personal life off the stage—quite literally—then you are not cut out to be an actress."

It was a rusty scalpel to my heart, and Ian knew how to twist it until it hit a critical vein. There were lots of reasons I wasn't stage material. And we both recognized it.

"Katie is a brilliant actress," Frances said.

Ian merely smiled.

"This has been such a refreshing conversation," I said. "I love how you still spin the tale and cast me as the evil villain. And now that I've heard it—*again*—you can leave. We don't need your help. The very idea that you could save my town is just laughable. We'd have more luck shining a bat spotlight into the sky."

"I already have press lined up," Ian said. "A writer from the Huffington Post contacted me yesterday. Fox News, CNN, the *Today Show*. I've had bites from all of them. Even a few across the Pond. You need someone with connections, and that's me. And you need someone who speaks theater as a director and a businessman. Also me."

"Why would you do this?"

"Investors breathing down my neck. Your intermission show was an absolute scandal. Videos on YouTube, articles in the papers, our production made into a mockery."

"Kind of like our relationship."

"Oh, grow up, Katie. You had to know it wasn't working between us."

"No, actually I didn't. We'd been together nearly a year. You know what I expected from you? Integrity. I expected to be able to trust you."

"And all of that's in the past," Felicity said. "We're over it, so you need to move on. It's not like we appreciated being shoved on a plane to Texas."

"Arrangements could probably be made to shove you elsewhere."

"I don't want to be here anymore than you want me here," Ian snapped. "If we save your little homespun theater, then I'm taking the glory back with me. Call it humanitarianism, call it a PR stunt, but I call it a job. And I'm going to do it. The same money that's fronting *Much Ado* is also behind the New York production. I've lost all credibility with the London theater community, and they need time to forget our little intermission sideshow."

"And New York has yet to hear of it?" I could fix that.

"And they're not going to," Ian said pointedly.

"Please go back to London before you mess this up even more."

Ian took a step, his tall form leaning way too close to mine. Geez, he still smelled good.

No! Stop sniffing! That was the scent of cheating and lies.

"Don't think you won't be seeing me often while I'm here." And then Ian's tone shifted, softened, and he sounded more like the man I had fallen for. "Face it, Katie. You need me."

"You know, I've come to realize I never needed you. Today is no exception."

"Let's go home," his new girlfriend whined, her voice hitting an octave known to set off choruses of yipping dogs.

"Go to the car, Felicity," Ian commanded.

"But—"

"I'll be there shortly." His gaze locked on mine as his companion huffed then sashayed away.

"You need me to help save your theater," Ian said. "Just like you needed me to turn you from a spare cast member into a star."

There it was, that poison dart right to the throat. I wanted to deny it, to tell him he was wrong. That I was a good actress, that I did have what it took to be on the Great White Way or the West End.

But I couldn't form the words. Not any that I believed.

Ian shook his head. "I thought we were going to be so good together."

I swallowed and looked away before he could see the singular tear. "Sorry for having such unreasonable expectations."

"You're nothing without me. Your career is dead, and—"

"Nothing?" Frances bowed up like she was about to show Ian how she'd earned her black belt her senior year. "Katie's already so much better without you. Do you see that bag in her hand?"

Oh, no.

"Do you know what that is? Do you?"

Ian shrugged a careless shoulder. "I do not."

"It's a wedding dress."

"No, Frances," I warned.

"It's *her* wedding dress. That's right, Katie is getting married."

Ian slid his piercing stare to me. "To whom?"

"The love of her life, that's who," Frances said. "The boy she dated in high school and college."

"Is that so?"

I just frantically shook my head. "Frances—"

"That's right. They reunited on an airplane that nearly crashed. You're welcome to Google that. He carried her unconscious body to safety, and they realized they never wanted to be apart."

"Very touching," Ian said. "That's quite a story. And just who is this dashing hero who's asked you for your hand?"

"Everything okay here?"

I could not contain the groan as I turned around to see Charlie standing behind us.

"That's him." Frances pointed a finger at Charlie. "That's Katie's fiancé."

Chapter Twelve

I T WASN'T EVERY day your best friend announced your impending nuptials.

To a groom you weren't even dating.

There were perfectly acceptable things to fib about. How many doughnuts you'd really eaten. That you would never deign to watch that reality show about arranged marriages and obstacle courses. Your bra size.

But this? This was bad.

"What just happened?" Charlie asked as Ian walked away.

"I can explain." I sounded just like Maxine.

"Is that your ex-boyfriend?"

"Yes," I said.

"The one who lives in *London?*"

I nodded weakly.

"Funny story," Frances said, her perky smile replaced with one as plastic as her father's Visa. "The guy shows up out of nowhere, harasses Katie, and I just. . ."

"Told Ian Katie and I were getting married."

"It just came out," Frances said. "The guy's a total jerk." She gave Charlie the Cliffs Notes version of the exchange.

"I'll fix it." I checked the time on my phone. "I've got to get back to Micky's." I had five minutes before I had to clock back in. Before I had to spend the rest of my afternoon waiting on tables like my ex hadn't outrageously hopped a plane out of London, and like Frances hadn't just betrothed me to Charlie.

"Katie, I'm sorry." Frances eased the dress from my death grip. "Will you forgive me? If you want me to talk to Ian, I'll clear it up. I'll talk to him and—"

"Nobody's talking to Ian," Charlie said. "Not yet." Fists settled on his hips, he glared in Ian's direction. "Just hang on, okay? I need to think about this."

What was I going to tell Ian? How in the world did I explain this? *I'm sorry my friend lied, but she gets a little psychotic when you talk to me like I'm a worthless nobody?*

"I'll go find him," Frances said. "I'll make it right."

"I'll take care of this." Charlie put a strong arm around my shoulders. "Frances, you run back to Micky's and tell Loretta Katie will be a little late."

"I'm sorry." Frances looked as miserable as I felt. "I'm so sorry." She clutched her dress and ran down the sidewalk.

I watched the street long after Frances had rounded the corner. Seeing nothing but images of London replaying in my mind.

"You okay?" Charlie gave me a little nudge.

"I'm not really sure."

"A few minutes of being engaged, and my fiancée already regrets it."

"What am I going to do?"

"Pick out a dress?"

I turned anguished eyes to Charlie. "This stuff doesn't happen to anyone else. Just me."

"Why don't you sit down for a bit?" Charlie led me to a nearby bench, his hand at my back. "Take a few deep breaths."

"It's just that Ian showed up, and Felicity was there. And she's so skinny, Charlie. I mean, she seriously needs a burger. And she's beautiful and—"

"Tell me why Ian the Ex is here and not in England."

"I don't know! I mean I do know, but it makes no sense." Right now nothing did. I briefly filled Charlie in on Maxine's scheme to enlist my ex-boyfriend for help. "He kept saying he knew I was hurt, that I needed him. And Miss Slutty Britches was all like, 'You owe him for coming here. You couldn't hold onto him, and I'm better than you.'"

"She said all that?" The man all but cracked his knuckles and rolled up his sleeves.

"No. But she communicated it." I massaged my temples and closed my eyes. "With silent girl telepathy."

Charlie stretched his arm across the back of the wooden bench, pulling me to him. He kissed the top of my head. "Do you want me to beat Ian up?"

"No. Well, maybe just bust a kneecap."

Charlie's head rested on mine, and for a moment, he said nothing. This had always been one of my favorite spots, his chin resting on my hair, fitted so close, safe. Besides my parents, nobody made me feel as secure as Charlie. He was a protector, a defender. And not just on spastic airplanes. I tried not to analyze the status of our relationship. We were friends. Very good friends.

Very good friends who now frequently made out.

Birds sang in the trees lining the street. A young mother pushed her baby in a black running stroller down the sidewalk toward the pharmacy. Three white-headed men went inside Foster's Hardware, and I knew they weren't going in for hammer and nails, but conversation and coffee. How could a corporation want to take all that away?

"Katie, do you still love this guy?"

I let this question roll through my head like a tumbleweed in the vacant space of the desert. "We're over." How did I explain what Ian was? "I would never take him back. He said. . ." I stared at my hands in my lap. "He basically said I didn't have enough talent, and I had gotten where I was because of him. I just felt so. . ." The words gathered and formed a lump in my throat. I blinked past the tears, angry with myself, furious at Ian.

"Talk to me, Parker."

It was like opening a diary page of your most pitiful day and handing it over. I so wanted to tell Charlie how I felt, but it was embarrassing. Humiliating. "When I was fifteen the police knocked on my door."

May nineteenth at six-fifteen p.m.

I had been alone for most of the week, my bio-mom on one of her benders. I had assumed she was with one of her Boyfriends of the Week.

"They told me my mom had been arrested for the drugs, then they took me and whatever I could stuff into a plastic grocery bag to the group home." My mom hadn't wanted me. Her family couldn't have picked me out of a lineup. Even surrounded by an entire facility of girls, I'd never felt more alone. "I never wanted to feel that way again. But when Ian stood there just now saying all that stuff, it threw me right back. I was that kid again." Hot tears of shame slid down my face. I'd never told anyone this. Ever. "When you've lived that, you have this stupid need. . . to be wanted. And to never let anyone see that."

"It's not stupid."

"But it is. I have the best family in the Scotts. They've shown me what real love is. They've always taught me I could do anything I set my mind to."

"You can. Ian can't take that away from you."

"Ian didn't have to." I was seconds away from having to use my shirt to wipe my drippy nose. Some girls cried prettily. I looked like I was having an allergic reaction requiring the stab of an EpiPen. "In the last month I've had such a good dose of reality. It's one thing to be a star in a college production, but it's quite another to be anything out there with the pros."

"Are we talking about your career or your relationship with Ian?"

"Both pretty much kicked me straight to the curb."

"You can't let a breakup convince you you're not worth loving. Ian *cheated* on you. Do you really want to be with someone like that?"

"Of course not. We were falling apart way before that. It's not so much the cheating." But the old voices whispered if I'd been enough, he wouldn't have strayed. "It's mostly how he treated me after. It's the things he said today. I wanted him to know he hadn't hurt me. That I didn't need him. That I wasn't this discarded girl who could fit her meager belongings into a bag from the Piggy Wiggly. So when Frances blurted out that I was engaged to you"—Maybe this was the most terrible part—"I didn't stop her." I looked at Charlie. "I could have, and I didn't."

"Like the spirit of Lies and Matrimony just took over your body."

Amen and testify.

"I don't like that this guy is here, but in inviting him, you grand-mother was just trying to help," Charlie said. "She had no reason to think Ian would abandon his production and travel across the globe to help In Between. If that's what he's truly here for."

"I doubt Ian believed my sudden declaration. I mean who gets engaged two weeks after breaking up with your boyfriend?"

"Two people who used to love each other."

Oh, my.

When a man looked at you like Charlie looked at me now, it was hard to form complete sentences. He made me want to believe in true love and fidelity and happiness. He made me want to believe that I was worth it.

That I was somebody's first choice.

And not someone just tossed away. Again.

"Do you think he's really sticking around?" Charlie asked.

"Yes. It's a big PR stunt to appease his play backers. I kind of made a muck of things before I left. Before I got benched."

Charlie's lips curved. "Do tell."

"I might've added an extra scene in *Much Ado About Nothing*. Let's just say Beatrice went sprinting across the stage chasing her rat-fink boyfriend, screaming out every insult that came to mind."

"Shakespeare would've been proud."

"The theater community was not."

Even if I wanted to, I would never work in London again.

I stood up, pulled Charlie to his feet, and gave him a hug, letting his scent fill my senses. "I'm going to go find Ian. Tell him the truth."

"Katie?

Eyes closed, I took a cleansing breath. "Yes?"

"Stay engaged to me."

The depraved part of my brain thought that sounded incredibly hot.

The logical part thought maybe I hadn't heard correctly. "What?"

"If it's important for Ian to see the breakup didn't bother you, then we'll show him."

"Why? Why would you do this?"

"Because I don't like him."

"This makes two of us."

"And I don't trust him."

"Try finding him pretzled with Felicity."

"If you think he traveled all the way from London to do some community service, you're fooling yourself."

"He doesn't want me back."

"I'm not too sure about that. But whether he does or doesn't, he's not here with total Good Samaritan intentions."

"You can't pretend to be engaged to me."

"What happens if you tell Ian the truth?"

"I'll be humiliated, what's left of my dignity will be shredded, and he'll gloat the entire time he's here."

"Then don't do it."

"Charlie—"

"We're doing this. A little diversion from the stresses of work."

"Does your job make you smell like bacon too?"

"Something like that."

The warm breeze ruffled through his hair, mussing it, making him look boyish and young. His devilish smile had me hearing the peals of real wedding bells, and I shook my head to dislodge the sound.

"You realize this isn't going to work though, right?" I mean, pretending for a day was one thing. But longer than that? Impossible.

"We should probably get our stories straight." Charlie slipped his arm around me, folded me into his side, and we walked toward the diner. "You girls like a June wedding, don't you?"

"I think I might be sick."

"I'm more of a destination wedding guy myself. Hawaii. A beach in Florida. But your dad will expect you to have a church ceremony." His hip bumped into mine. "Help me out here. I don't know about any of this."

"You're doing a pretty good job." Frighteningly so. "The whole town will have to be in on it. We'll have to tell them what's really going on. And our parents are pretty much going to kill us." Especially mine. My dad was a pastor, for crying out loud. I could already see this for sermon material. *Please turn to the book of Matthew and let us discuss that all too common problem of when your daughter lies to a British gigolo and one small Texas town . . .*

"Ian will probably be gone in a matter of days," Charlie said. "If he truly has a play to get back to."

"We're seriously doing this?" I wanted to save face, but did we dare?

He stopped at the corner of the diner. "Seems that way."

"Thanks, Charlie." I leaned up on tiptoe and kissed his cheek, and before I could step away, Charlie caught me in his arms.

"Is that all you got for your beloved?" His gaze dipped to my mouth.

It was more than the Texas sun warming my skin. "We don't like public displays of affection. We're a very private couple."

"Must've been your last fiancé." And with that, Charlie pulled me to his chest and kissed me like I was his first pick, and not someone who'd been left behind. Like I was cherished. Loved. My insides nearly liquefied as his arm hooked behind my neck, bringing me closer before changing the angle of his kiss. It was sweet tea, sunshine, and the most indulgent chocolate all rolled into one.

I finally took a step back. If I didn't return to the diner, Loretta would fire me and make me return all my super-sized t-shirts. "You're kind of good at that."

"I'm willing to practice more."

His eyes held promises I didn't know I could accept. "Anything else I need to know about us?"

Charlie slipped his hand into mine as we walked. "We like to golf."

"I've never even held a club."

"You love to sit with me and watch SportsCenter."

"I sound amazing."

"And you adore cooking for me on a Friday night."

"I do make the best frozen pizzas."

"Anything I should know?"

"You're pretty swell, Charlie Benson."

"That's it?"

I gave his hand a squeeze. "It's enough."

Chapter Thirteen

"**Y**OU'VE REALLY STEPPED in it this time."

"I know that."

"I mean big, big doo-doo."

"Yes, Maxine."

Maxine hopped over a crack in the sidewalk as we walked to a closed Micky's Diner that night for the committee meeting. "I'm saying you need man-sized waders to walk through this level of—"

"I get it." My teeth hurt from clenching them so hard. "But who invited Ian here in the first place?"

"And your parents thought *I'd* be the problem child while they were gone, but—"

I held open the door of the restaurant. "Yes, you're a virtuous saint."

"What you did was impulsive, reckless, and just a tiny bit scandalous." Maxine winked as she walked past me. "I love it."

"No, do not even start that. This will be over before it begins." I followed her toward the back of the dining area where the others sat at a large table.

"Georgie and Michael had an arranged marriage on *General Hospital*, and it turned out just fine. Well, except for when that mob boss gunned them down. But they showed up alive again a year later, so it all worked out."

"A truly inspiring story."

"Gosh." She pulled out her chair and sat down. "Being fake-engaged makes you grumpy."

I settled into a seat beside her and said hello to the group of fifteen or so townsfolk who were there because their business was on the chopping block or they just wanted to be involved. The chatter swirled around us and hovered like a cloud, but no matter who was talking, it was the same conversation. Thrifty Co. was a bully, there were lives on the line, and they weren't going to let the corporation win.

Maxine put a thumb and finger to her lips and produced an ear-splitting whistle. "Let's get this meeting started. My granddaughter needs to go shop for honeymoon lingerie."

All heads turned toward me.

"Yes, we hear congratulations are in order!"

"When's the big day?"

"I'll do your wedding cake!"

"The Lonestar Motel has a bed that vibrates for a quarter."

"Um, thank you. For all that." I took another look to make sure it was just us in the diner then lowered my voice. "There is no wedding. It's a long story, but for reasons I don't want to get into, I'm kind of faking this whole thing."

"Honey"—Mrs. Gleason gave her husband the side-eye—"I've been faking it for forty years."

"I need everyone to just kind of go with it," I said. "And if any of you outs me to Ian, not only do I walk away from this project, but I make sure someone spits in your coffee at Micky's for the rest of your lives. Any questions?"

A gray-headed woman raised her hand.

"Yes, Mrs. Higgins?"

"Are you in some kind of legal trouble?"

"No."

"Are we going to be interrogated by some immigration agent?"

"I was born right here in Texas."

Maxine took a sip of water. "You look pretty alien to me."

"If you needed someone to marry you, I would've volunteered."

"Mr. Henry, you're fifty years older than I am."

"I have my own chicken house empire." He waggled his white brows. "You could've been my first lady."

Maxine patted his veiny hand. "If she and Charlie don't work out, you are definitely her runner-up."

"Let's get started, shall we?" Good Lord, whoever said you couldn't go home had clearly not been from In Between. Nothing had changed. "As I mentioned in my email to you all—"

"I prefer text."

"I don't do the computer."

"More of an Instagram man myself."

"As I said in my email, we need data. We need to show them the numbers. How many workers will lose their jobs? How much income will be lost? How much in taxes to the city does your business contribute?"

"Let's have everyone's information to Katie by Wednesday," Loretta said.

"We also need to collect testimonials."

"FiberLax is really effective stuff." Mr. Delmott removed his Dekalb ball cap. "Keeps things moving and grooving, if you know what I mean."

No wonder Thrify Co. had easily bought their way into town. "I meant a testimonial of how your business has affected someone in In Between."

"Oh. Still,"—He nudged the guy next to him—"good stuff."

"That lawyer we hired didn't ask for any of this. Are you sure he's worth a hill of beans, Don?" Loretta asked.

"He's my grandson from Houston. Mary's kid. Of course he's good."

"Why isn't he here?" Loretta asked.

"He'll be at the town hall," Mr. Henry said. "He told me to take notes." The man clicked the end of his pen and returned it to the napkin he'd been writing on. "Did Katie say this was a shotgun wedding or one of those arranged situations?"

Loretta's eye roll was as dramatic as it was disgusted. "I'll give you a testimonial," she said. "Last year when John Thomas's house burned down, Foster's hardware store donated all the lumber to rebuild it."

"And Miss Loretta takes leftover food to the shelter every Thursday," said Mr. Gleason.

"That's exactly the sort of thing I'm looking for. We want to appeal to logic and emotion."

"Are you sure you don't want me to make your wedding cake?"

"There is no wedding, Mrs. Holcomb."

"But we will need some samples," Maxine told the woman. "For authenticity's sake."

"Well, whatever it takes to help you, Katie dear," said Mrs. Holcomb. "You're our leader, and we want to help you like you're helping us."

"We're gonna make this fake engagement look real authentic," said Mrs. Gleason. "Just you wait and see. It's the least we can do."

"All I need you guys to do is just keep the secret, okay? That will be more than enough."

"We won't let you down, Katie." Mrs. Holcomb pretended to lock her lips and throw away the key. "You just leave it to us."

THE IN BETWEEN meeting hall was really just a big converted barn. The town used the red, rustic facility for dances, dinners, meetings, events, voting, and even the occasional wedding. Last summer Mr. And Mrs. Harris even rented it out for their Happy Divorce party. But tonight hundreds of In Betweenites sat shoulder to shoulder, occupying rows of gray metal folding chairs. These were the people I had grown up with. I knew their children, their stories. The Valiant was everything to me, but just as it held my heart, so many folks here had just as much, if not more, at stake.

I followed Maxine and the committee to the center section, front row. The group wanted to be eye to eye with the mayor and representatives from Thrifty Co. when they took the wooden stage and spoke to the town. I scanned the area, smiling at familiar faces, but searching for one face in particular—Charlie's. Since his home was now in Chicago maybe In Between losing some landmarks wasn't that important to him.

"This seat taken?"

My stomach sank as Ian slid into the chair beside me.

"Actually I'm saving it."

"For your fiancé?"

"Yes." Geez, the lies. They multiplied like weeds.

Ian crossed his arms over his chest, his body leaning a little too close to mine.

"Want to tell me how you could be engaged mere weeks after breaking up with me?"

My brain shifted and stuttered. "It's. . .it's like you said—we'd been over for a long time. Charlie and I reconnected, and it was just. . .magical." Micky's Diner didn't serve syrup any sweeter than this. "Charlie was my first love."

"I'm not really buying this."

"Your feelings on this don't matter to me either way."

"You're not impulsive." Ian gave an infuriating chuckle. "You don't jump into anything. It took you three weeks in London before you braved the Tube—armed with your spreadsheet you'd made of the stops. Six months of planning before you ventured to Paris. You waited—"

"Okay, I get it. But when it's right, it's right." Now I was quoting Frances. "If you must know, when Charlie and I had our near-death experience, it just opened my eyes to what really mattered. When that plane went down, all I could think about was. . .him. The only face I saw was his." I cleared my throat, a little uncomfortable with how right that felt to say. That kiss replayed in my mind, falling to the earth with Charlie's lips on mine. It had felt . . . right.

"Nearly dying put things into perspective for me," I said. "I realized life is short, and it's certainly not guaranteed. I got a second chance, and I don't want to waste it."

"On me."

"On people who don't appreciate me. Respect me."

"And this Charlie does that I assume?"

Ian's tone was so condescending, I wanted to leap out of this cold folding chair and bang him over the head with it. "Charlie is honest, loving, and kind. He's a man of integrity. And I can trust him to remain faithful for a long time. You know, like the fifteen minutes of an intermission."

Ian's smooth smile slowly disappeared. "People make mistakes."

He was not sucking me in with this. Ian might've been a director, but he could act with the best of them. "I don't want to talk about us anymore. We're over. It's in the past. I don't know why you're really here, but if you were hoping to find me languishing without you, you can see I'm far from it. I've never been happier."

For long, painful seconds Ian said nothing, then finally he straightened and focused on the mayor taking the podium on stage. "There are four TV news reporters in the back," Ian said grimly. "At least three newspaper outlets. I'll do what I can to help you, but I need you to help me as well."

"In Between doesn't need you."

"Do you really want to test that theory? Because if you're wrong, and you throw away my assistance, my connections, then you will have made an error that cannot be rectified—all for your pride. Because once this store gets the property, it's over."

"We have an attorney."

"Where is he?"

I had wondered the same thing.

"You can't sue Thrifty Co.," Ian said. "Their legal team is bigger than this town. They'll drain you of everything you have before you even go to trial." His voice dipped low and deep. "Good press could save both of us. You need Thrifty Co. to look like a pillaging bully, and I need to look—"

"Like the hero."

The microphone gave a screech loud enough to annoy the dead. Mayor Crowley tapped on the device, a weasel's smile lifting the lips beneath his handlebar mustache. He'd been mayor of In Between since I was in high school, and while he was a terrible leader, no one else had ever wanted the job.

"Ladies and gentlemen, good people of In Between, welcome to our town hall meeting." The chatter diminished to a low buzz as the mayor looked upon the crowd, many of them ready to fight to the last breath. While some of them were just ready to get some discounted milk and toilet paper.

The mayor took a handkerchief from his back pocket and wiped his wrinkled brow. "Tonight we're here to hear any concerns you might have on the Thrifty Co. purchase. It is a hard loss, to see familiar and beloved businesses go, but I believe what we gain will be so much more. We have two microphones set up in the middle of the left and right aisle, and you may begin lining up to present your comments. Let's remember we all have In Between's best interests at heart. We want to keep this real nice and civil, okay? No yelling and sucker punches like the first meeting."

Beside me Maxine snorted. "So my arm just accidentally flew toward his face. Big deal."

"Didn't you date him once?" I asked.

"Sometimes you gotta kiss some frogs." She leaned forward and shot a pointed look toward Ian.

Another man joined the mayor onstage. "This is Bill McKeever," the mayor said, "vice-president of public relations at Thrifty Co. He's flown in all the way from Detroit to talk to us, to reassure us, and to hear what you have to say. He is a guest in our community, and we're going to make him welcome in the way only we can."

Maxine sniffed. "Spit wads?"

"Behave tonight," I said. "James only left enough bail money for one of us."

Loretta tapped me on the shoulder and held out a notebook. "Here are our questions. I've got them in order of importance with possible rebuttals."

"Me?" I stared down at her scrawl. "But I'm barely up to speed."

"I still don't get why I can't be our spokeswoman," Maxine said. "I won't call the mayor a chicken-eating, pig-snorting nincompoop this time."

Loretta patted my back with her worn hands. "You can do it. Get on up there and show them city folks what you got."

"Be sure and give the press something to use." Ian stood up, as if to go with me. "Be quotable."

"I don't need you to join me."

"Humor me."

With no time to argue, I walked back up the aisle to the microphone, that skinny intimidator daring me to screw up, to make the committee regret putting this important moment in my hands.

Mr. Denton, owner of the town's only grocery store, stood on the opposite side of the hall and launched into his concerns of the chain store taking all his business. Mrs. June Smith spoke at my mic, telling the crowd that she was tired of paying exorbitant prices and looked forward to finally getting a break in her grocery bill.

"Uh, yeah." Randy Millhouse, barely twenty-one, tapped the microphone, then all but put his lips right on the thing. "I have an important question I think a lot of us are wanting an answer to. How much do you discount cigarettes?"

Mr. McKeever of Thrifty Co. smoothly answered that in one non-committal sentence about how all products were discounted, then transitioned into a spiel about the chain's record of service to their community.

"What about the loss of family-owned businesses?" Joe Phillips, a badge-wearing sheriff, asked. "That hardware store's been in my family for three generations. Where is your responsibility to the businesses you're taking? Why can't you purchase land that isn't occupied?"

The mayor squared his shoulders and glared at his law-enforcing employee. "The city has the right to take any property we want. The government gives us the ability to wield that power when its benefits the greater—"

Mr. McKeever nudged the good mayor out of the way. "We know this is upsetting. Thrifty Co. understands there are families, real people, behind each property. That's why we've offered generous settlements above the appraisals. When we purchase a property, those owners are often able to retire. Many of them get the chance to take it easy for the first time in their lives, travel, spend quality time with their families."

"If the offers are not accepted," the mayor said. "The property owners will meet with a special commission at the county courthouse a week from Friday. I really don't think you want to put yourselves through that legal hassle."

"Thrifty pays way above property value," Mr. McKeever said. "It's important that it's a win-win for all parties involved."

"But it's not," I barely had the words out before Ian gave me a small push forward, closer to the mic. "If we don't want to sell, we shouldn't have to. Many of us don't want your settlement deals. We want our businesses."

Mr. McKeever smiled. "And you are?"

"Katie Parker Scott. My family owns the Valiant. That theater has stood there for nearly one hundred years. It's weathered wars, a Depression, neglect, and even vandals. No amount of money can replace what it is to my family and to this community." Applause exploded in the hall, and it served to bolster me on.

Mr. McKeever looked so sincere. "I understand your frustration—"

"Frustration? This goes way beyond that," I said. "My family has
poured everything we have into making the Valiant a success. It has a
legacy, a history. It serves a purpose in this town. And so does
Micky's Diner. Loretta Parsons can't simply open up in a new
building and just pick up where she left off. Can you give her back
the character of her restaurant? The booth where Mr. and Mrs. Dylan
have sat every Friday morning for fifty years? And Foster's Hardware.
Randall Foster's father built that place by hand with the help of the
community. These aren't just buildings. They're like community
members of In Between. And when the checks are written, everyone's paid off, and your pretty new store opens its doors, all these
promises of community involvement and helpful resources will be
gone. Just like you will. But we'll be here, Mr. McKeever. This is our
town." I pointed my finger right at the man as the emotion swelled.
"And we want it back."

All around me friends and fellow inhabitants of In Between stood
to their feet, clapping wildly. They made me smile, these folks who
loved this town as much as I did. I let the sound pour into my weary
spirit. After all the plays I'd performed, this might've been the best
standing ovation I'd ever received.

"Miss Parker Scott—" Mr. McKeever held up his hands in what I
wished was absolute and total surrender. "To you and the fine people
of In Between, I want to personally assure you that Thrifty Co. has a
reputation for following through on our promises to invest in our
store's communities. We don't just build a store and leave. We believe
in the communities we become a part of. Thrifty Co. will do everything we can to help In Between thrive. Not only is that a long-term
commitment, but it's already begun." He gestured toward the back of
the building. "There's someone I'd like to introduce you all to. Come
on up here."

All heads turned as Mr. McKeever invited his co-worker to join him on the stage.

"Thrifty Co. not only believes in this town. We're one of you. Ladies and gentlemen, I'd like you to meet our newest Community Outreach associate."

A collective gasp rent the air, and the breath seized in my throat as the person in question stepped into view.

"Please welcome a man who is a friend to In Between and Thrifty Co., Mr. Charlie Benson."

The room spun around me, and I reached out a hand, gripping the chair beside me to steady myself.

"Isn't that your fiancé?" Ian asked.

I mutely nodded my head.

He smiled. "Very trustworthy indeed."

Chapter Fourteen

"KATIE, WAIT."

Charlie's voice was a mocking song in my ear as I raced to my car. I was leaving behind my dignity, my backbone, and my stranded grandmother. But I didn't care. I had to get out of there.

"Please, stop. Let me explain."

"Not listening!" My car was in sight, and I whipped my keys out of purse, mashing on the unlock button like it could beam me into another universe.

"Just wait."

"Kiss it, Charlie Benson!" A hot breeze blew my bangs right in my face, and as I swiped the hair out of my eyes, the keys slipped from my grip. "Shoot!" I dropped into a squat, reached for the keys and—

Charlie's tanned hand beat me to it.

"Give me the keys."

He held them tight. "Hear me out, okay?"

"No. That's exactly what Ian said a few weeks ago. There was no excuse for him, and there's no excuse for you. Men! I can't stand the lot of you."

"Don't lump me in with that guy."

"Why? He lied to me, and so did you."

"I didn't ever lie to you."

"Oh, I'm sorry. Withheld the truth."

"I tried to tell you about Thrifty Co."

"Really? Did you try? What's the matter, did our *kissing* get in the way?" I rubbed my hands over my face, wishing when I opened my eyes, this would all be a bad dream. "I'm so stupid! How could I fall for this again?"

"I did try to tell you. Every time I would begin to explain, something would interrupt me."

"Like your cowardice?"

He took a step back as if I'd struck him. "This is a job. And like it or not, it's *my* job. It has nothing to do with how I feel about you or this town."

"And how do you feel about me? Want to know how I feel about you?"

"Yes, let's talk about that, shall we? God knows you've been dancing around it ever since that plane touched down. In case temporary amnesia has conveniently overtaken you in the last five minutes, you said you loved me."

"I thought I was dying!"

"You said—and I quote—*I never stopped loving you.* Does that sound familiar?"

"You know what is familiar? A man getting caught in lies and changing the topic and making this about me. The issue here is that you work for the very company that's trying to take the Valiant and ruin this town. You've had every opportunity to tell me."

Charlie ignored that and returned to my crash-and-burn declaration. "*Never stopped loving* me implies that you were aware of your feelings the entire time you were dating that English loser."

"Any warm and tingly inclinations I might have had disappeared the second your boss called your name. Stay on topic!"

"You care about me."

"I care about the Valiant. And Micky's. And the other businesses that are going to be obliterated by this stupid money-hungry corporation you work for. How have you been sleeping at night? How do you look yourself in the mirror?"

"It's a good company. It employs millions of people and invests in towns."

"By pillaging them first." I held out my shaking hand. "Give me the keys."

"Listen to me and let me explain."

"I thought you were different. I thought I could trust you." I needed to get out of here before I lost it. Before the tears took over. "I even let myself begin to think we had a chance."

"We do. My job doesn't have to affect us."

Was he insane? Maybe the doctors should've checked *him* for head trauma. "I'm not sure what we were, but we're over. Forever. You laid there with me on the floor of the Valiant and let me pour my heart out. While I went on and on about how this theater was everything to me, *you* said nothing. Nothing!" I could picture us right back there, and I ached for the way I had just gone on and on that night, while he had probably been studying the theater for the best possible spot to drop the wrecking ball. "You must've thought I was pretty pitiful."

His nostrils flared, and seconds passed before he responded. "That day ripped me in two, Katie. I know the Valiant means a lot to you. I was right there with you from the beginning when you came to In Between as that angry teenager. I watched you fall in love with theater—with life—on that stage."

"Then how can you take it away from me? How can you be a part of that?"

"If I could save it, I would." His voice was a raspy whisper. "For you—I would do anything to stop the hurt. You think I wanted to be assigned to the In Between store—where I know every face? Every life story? Everything I could be taking away? But I have no choice."

"There's always a choice. And you made yours."

"Oh, Katie!" came a shrill female voice. "Katie, dear!"

Maxine buzzed toward us like a queen bee, her cluster of activists swarming right behind her. Sixty more seconds and I would've been in my car, on the road, and far away from this disaster.

"We're not done talking about this," Charlie said.

"Yes, we are." I ripped my keys from his lying hand. "You and I are totally done."

"Oh, Sweet Pea!" Maxine hugged me to her. "You did a wonderful job!" Her lips pressed near my ear. "Your ex-boyfriend is right behind us. Take off the psychopathic killer face and look like a woman in love."

"There you two are." Ian glanced between me and Charlie, that smooth smile never slipping. "The local ABC affiliate would like to talk to you both. I've already given them my statement. Unless you're busy, that is. I'm sure tonight was quite the shock."

"Not at all," Maxine said. "You think Katie didn't know her fiancé worked at Thrifty Co.? Bah! These two are so tight, he can't tinkle without her knowing. Isn't that right, Snookums?"

I could only glare at Charlie.

"That's right." Charlie's fierce gaze held mine. "Katie knows everything about me."

"You did a great job," Loretta said, then gave Charlie one of her best glares. "One of our own. Your momma raised you better than that, son."

"We're going to do right by this town." Charlie's eyes returned to me. "For everyone."

"Is now a good time to talk to you about catering your wedding?" Mrs. Tanner stepped forward. "Are you two more smoked wienies or salmon?"

"Now is not the time." I had stepped into a Monty Python script.

"The press would like to speak to you both," Ian said. "I've already made my plea for artistic and historical preservation. Now they want to hear your opposing sides." He cast a curious look between us. "What an interesting story angle you've given them. Would've been nice to have known about this." And with that, Ian marched himself back into the building, the committee following him like ducklings.

"Well." Maxine crossed her arms over her chest and fixed Charlie with a scowl once reserved for stage managers who stole her showgirl tips. "I am not very happy with you right now."

"I understand," Charlie said.

"You are not the man I thought you were," Maxine said. "You can just forget any gifts for your fake wedding from me. No toaster cozies for you!" She leaned close enough to hiss. "May you stew on that regret the rest of your days." Maxine grabbed my hand. "Come on, Katie. Let's get you away from this traitor."

"I'm sorry it happened like this." Charlie's voice was almost believable. Oh, he was good. "Please, let's talk about it."

"Katie's not speaking to you, Judas."

"She told me she loved me."

Maxine's pause was so brief, it barely registered. "Is that what she said? Katie tells strange men she loves them all the time. It's a mental condition. Yesterday we found her downtown pledging her heart to the statue of Sam Houston. Sometimes she forgets to take her medicine." She tugged on my hand. "Get to steppin'"

"You care about me," Charlie said, as I stepped past him. "I know you do."

"Maybe my feelings for you are as fickle as yours are for your hometown." I took one last look at the achingly handsome man who had become the enemy. "You and I are over."

❧

I PULLED INTO Maxine's driveway, my brain a mess of shouts and sobs. The car seemed to have driven on auto-pilot, as I had no recollection of making turns, or if I'd observed stop signs and traffic lights. I needed to go home.

But Maxine made no move to open her door.

"So," she said. "You told Charlie you loved him?"

"It doesn't matter."

"Doesn't it? Finding out he works for Thrifty doesn't really negate the words if you said them."

I let my head drop to the steering wheel. "I have the worst picker."

"Nose picker?"

"Man picker! I'm absolutely terrible at it. I'm my mother." I'd done everything I could not to become her, and yet, here I was. Just because I was dating men a little more upper class than Bobbie Ann Parker's average drug dealer didn't mean I was choosing stellar winners.

"Sweet Pea, you are not your birth mother. I mean, like her, your chest is flat as the hood of this car, but other than that, you don't have a thing in common."

"I thought I could trust Ian. And then. . .Charlie. This whole time he was here on business for Thrifty Co., and I couldn't even see that. I should've figured it out."

"Well, it's hard to think when you're lip-locked and making declarations of love. You want to tell me about that?"

Not really. I wanted that moment on the airplane to go away forever. "The plane dropped altitude. I thought we were dying, and I was having my last moments alive." I lifted my head and stared at the dark sky beyond Maxine's passenger window. "I told Charlie I loved him." I gave her the rest of the details, and Maxine responded by fanning herself and cranking up the air.

"Maybe you should talk to Charlie," she finally said. "Hear what he has to say for himself."

"When the Valiant gets bulldozed, Charlie will be part of that. When that stupid store goes up in its place, Charlie will be right there for the ribbon cutting. His Thrifty Co. will stand on the graveyard of

In Between businesses, and he helped it happen."

"Babe, despite my perfectly flawless skin and impeccable neckline, I've lived a lot of years. Buildings are things. It's the people that matter." She rested her hand on mine. "I know the Valiant means a lot to you. Nobody wants to see it go down. But you need to examine that heart. Because if you truly do love Charlie Benson, will you be able to just toss it away?"

"I could never be with someone who's doing what he's doing."

"It's terrible, for sure. But like he said, it's a job."

"Are you hearing yourself? This is our theater we're about to lose."

"I get that. But, hon, I've been married to two wonderful men. Dear Mr. Simmons loved me something fierce. And now my own spicy love machine Sam—"

"Get to your point."

"My Sam worships the ground I walk on. And I wouldn't trade that feeling for anything. And I've seen the way your Charlie looks at you—the way he always has. And the way you look at him."

"No matter what I feel for him, if he had any care for me, he wouldn't go through with this. Charlie knew what that theater meant to me, how it had transformed my life."

"Life's full of tough choices," Maxine said. "Sometimes we just have to stumble through some together. Don't give up on him yet." She opened the door, flooding the car with light. "Say, what did Charlie say when you told him you loved him?"

"Nothing." I reached for the controls on the air conditioning, cold to the bone. "He said nothing."

Chapter Fifteen

I ROSE THE next morning before the sun and got to the diner just as a sleepy Loretta unlocked the door.

"It's four-thirty. What are you doing here?" She walked inside and flipped on the lights.

"Couldn't sleep."

"That Benson boy threw you for a loop, didn't he?"

The industrial-sized coffee pot beckoned, and I flipped some switches to bring the thing to life. "Did you know?"

"His uncle is a big wig for Thrifty Co. That was all I knew. I had suspected your friend might be involved, but I wasn't for sure."

"You could've shared your suspicions with me."

"You seemed to have enough on your plate."

I grabbed two white ceramic mugs and waited for the coffee maker to spit out its heavenly elixir. "Is his uncle from around here?"

"Naw." Loretta climbed onto a swiveling stool. "The uncle and Charlie's dad are both from back East. So you won't get any hometown sympathy from either one of them."

"Charlie's dad's involved in this?"

"The bank president? Hon, you think he doesn't see dollar signs every time he drives down Maple? Of course he's in on it."

I snagged the pot and filled our mugs, grabbing two creamers and a white packet of sugar for Loretta.

She blew on the cup, grimacing as she took a sip. "Pretty stout."

"The day seems to call for it."

"It's your tips at stake." Loretta gave a half smile. "Not mine."

I joined her at the counter and took my first drink, hot and black.

"The committee met after the town hall last night." Loretta stirred in more sugar.

"Why didn't you call me?"

"With you getting engaged, your ex-boyfriend showing up in town, and discovering your beloved is a corporate Grinch, we thought you might need some alone time."

"I spent the entire evening watching infomercials and eating Chunky Monkey. I could've penciled you in."

"We decided you need to stay engaged to Charlie Benson."

"We're not really engaged."

Loretta wrapped her wrinkled hands around her mug. "Whatever you're doing, keep it up. You said you don't want that Englishman to be sniffing around, and the more you're with Charlie, the more likely you can glean information."

"I don't really think there's any secret ammo. His company wants the property. The city is letting them have it. The end."

"Is it? Is it the end? Where's your sense of sleuthing?"

"There's no mystery here, Loretta. What we need is a miracle."

"We got one. It's you. If there's any loophole, any kink in their armor, you're gonna find it." Loretta stood up and handed me her mug. "Sure hope you can do that better than you can make coffee."

The closed sign got flipped at one minute 'til five, and customers trickled in, eager for their breakfast and any gossip that might've bloomed overnight like evening primrose.

Kourtney with a K and I hustled it, both of us running back and forth from the dining room to the kitchen and back. It got so busy, Loretta had to leave her register to refresh empty coffee cups and bus some tables.

The Garden Club ladies were at their usual table, and after losing three rounds of rock-paper-scissors with Kourtney, I hustled over to get their order.

"Good morning." I flipped open my order pad. "I see Loretta's already got your drinks. What can I get you to eat?"

Mrs. O'Reilley lifted her menu to cover her mouth, as if secrets were about to be shared. "We get what you're doing."

"I'm taking your order." I had five other tables waiting on me, and I did not have time for their nettlesome conversation. "Mrs. O'Reilley, did you want bacon or sausage?"

"Marrying the enemy to get insider secrets," Ms. Delmonaco said with a dreamy air. "Just like a war spy."

Mitzy Kipper nodded. "You're so brave."

"I'm not marrying anyone, and Charlie and I are not speaking, so unless he can give up some info through smoke signals, charades, or homing pigeons, I won't be sussing out anything useful for our case. Now what would you like to eat?"

"I once dated a judge to get some assistance in a little public disturbance case," Mrs. O'Reilley said. "Cleavage and cobbler, my dear. That is all you need."

"Bacon it is." I scribbled a few words on my order pad. "How do you want your eggs?"

"And then there was the time I got frisky with a police officer who—"

"Over-easy. Coming right up." I scurried away from the table of flower-loving floozies, only to shoulder swipe Kourtney. Her bleached hair had a hint of green in it today. Apparently her latest root touchup had gone south.

"Can you get table twelve please?"

"Sure. I—" Table twelve sat in a corner by the window. It was one of the best seats in the house. It was also inhabited by Charlie Benson and his little sister. "No. You get it."

"Isn't that your fiancé?"

I wasn't going to bother explaining the charade. "Absence makes the heart grow fonder and all that crap. I'll give you twenty bucks if you get his order."

"Loretta just gave me a ten top. Sorry." She scurried away, leaving me with no choice but to wait on Charlie's table. I took my sweet time getting there, taking the orders of folks who arrived after him, topping off coffees that had barely been touched, and sitting down a spell with Mr. and Mrs. Dylan to talk weather and politics, two of my least favorite topics. Fifteen minutes of stalling, I finally made my way to table number twelve.

While some of the townsfolk were shooting Charlie the hairy eyeball, most just left him alone. A few people had stopped to say hello, which clearly identified them as Team Thrifty. Charlie had been smart to bring his little sister. Tensions were high, and many people were fighting mad. And to not only have a target for that anger, but to find out it was your own native son, was just too much. But the good people of In Between would not stoop so low as to show their ire in front of the little girl in braids drinking orange juice to Charlie's left.

"What can I get you?" I addressed this question to Sadie.

"Hello, Katie."

Charlie had the good graces not to look polished and well-rested. In the place of his usual button-down, he wore a t-shirt from his college alma mater, his hair was still slightly damp from a shower, and he clearly hadn't shaved. He still looked handsome as ever; meanwhile, I had puffy bags beneath my eyes, my ponytail and headband combo barely contained my bed-head, and my makeup could only be described as minimalist spackle.

"Do you know what you want to eat yet?" I asked Sadie.

Sadie was no slouch in the brains department, and from the way she hesitantly looked to her brother, I knew she was picking up on the tension pinging like a divining rod.

Charlie nodded at his sister. "Go ahead. Tell her what you want."

"I'll have the happy face pancakes and sausage."

"Happy face pancakes it is." I jotted it down then spoke to the space near Charlie. "And you?"

"I'd like to apologize."

"Not one of our menu options today. How about angry face pancakes? Loser face pancakes? Back-stabbing jerk who withheld information face pancakes?"

Charlie leaned near his sister's ear. "Sadie, I see our neighbor Mrs. Tanner over there. Why don't you go say hello?"

"She doesn't like me."

"Now's a perfect time to win her over."

Sadie plunked both elbows on the table, rested her chin into her hands, and leaned in. "This is more interesting. Keep talking."

With an aggravated growl, Charlie dug into his wallet, pulled out a ten spot, and slapped it into his sister's waiting palm. "That buys me ten minutes."

Sadie gave her brother a smacking kiss on his stubbly cheek. "See ya in five."

She toodled off, leaving me standing awkwardly beside Charlie's table, torn between wanting to update him on every angry and well-composed comeback that had come to me in the middle of the night, and wanting to freeze him out with silence, not giving him one single word.

"Will you sit down?" he asked. "Just for a minute."

"I'm working. Either order or I'm walking away."

"Excuse me," interrupted a male voice.

I turned to find Dr. Kapoor.

"Can I get you something?" I asked.

"I hear congratulations are in order for you two," he said much too loudly. "I'd like to offer you a year's worth of free pregnancy tests."

My cheeks flamed red as his words echoed in my ears. "Dr. Kapoor, what are you doing?" I whispered.

He smiled at the nearby tables as his voice dropped conspiratorially. "I'm Team In Between. Your grandma told us to do what we could to support your fake engagement." He handed me a business card and patted my back. "Congrats!"

"My ex-boyfriend isn't here."

"Oh." He snatched his card back. "In that case, they're only half off."

I watched him walk away, completely horrified. "How is this my life?" When the committee had told me they'd help with the engagement sham, I should've known it would not end well. I now lived in fear of one of them popping out of the shrubbery with champagne, CrockPots, and poorly delivered lines.

I counted backwards from ten before turning back to Charlie. "This is your last chance to order."

"Katie, I know I've hurt you," he said.

"You knew you would, so don't act like you have a problem with it."

"In my head, I'd planned it differently."

"In my head, I sell you and your boss to a tribe of aboriginal cannibals who want to roast you over the spit like stuffed pigs." I pushed a chunk of hair from my face. "Do you want the special?"

"If I didn't work on this deal, I was out at the company."

"That's too bad. I'd hate for you to have to find a different job. I'm so glad you chose to shut down half a street of our city so nobody would be inconvenienced."

Charlie's jaw was locked so tight, I wondered if those perfectly straight pearly whites might turn to dust. "I can't explain this right now, but I need to talk to you." He glanced at the prying eyes of the tables around him that weren't even pretending not to stare. "Somewhere alone."

"That doesn't work for me. I think we said all we needed to last night. I'll bring you the three egg special and have Loretta refill your coffee."

"Katie, wait—"

I sprinted toward the kitchen, nearly barreling over a three-year old playing in the floor, and completely ignoring Mr. Pickens rude call for more coffee by raising his mug to the sky like Thor's hammer when I sped by.

The kitchen door swished as I pushed through. I clipped Charlie's order to a clothespin suspended on a wire contraption, then slid it toward the cooks.

"You okay?" Loretta asked, balancing six plates as if they were glued to her arms. The cook's twangy country music drifted from a radio nearby.

"Charlie Benson's table needs refills."

She opened her mouth, probably to tell me how much she appreciated being told what to do by an underling, but then changed her mind with a slow nod. "Okay." This was a woman who had seen a handful of husbands and heartaches. She knew pain when she saw it. "I'll take care of that. You step out back and get some air. I'll handle your tables."

I didn't argue.

Outside the clouds gathered in gray clusters, threatening to sprinkle more gloom into my world. I sat on an old plastic milk crate, right next to an oversized coffee can filled with cigarette butts. I currently had a little insight into why people gave into the urge to light up. Life was hard. And it seemed to be this snowball of mishaps, as if God thought one singular bad event deserved some company.

I had barely rested my feet one full minute, when the door swung open, and out walked Charlie.

I made to leave, but he only blocked my path.

"Please, Katie." He wasn't going to let me ignore him, and resolve flashed in those eyes. "You've got to hear me out."

A wave of weariness rose over me like an ocean billow, and I let it take me under. I was too tired to argue anymore. I had used up all my fighting words.

I crossed my legs and leaned my back against the building. "Go ahead."

Charlie studied me for a few moments, like he was not quite certain I wouldn't bolt. He began to pace, his long legs making quick work of the limited walk space in the alley.

Finally he stopped. He lifted his eyes toward the dreary sky, as if scanning it for help, then finding none there, turned his attention to me. "My uncle is vice-president of Thrifty Co."

"I'm aware."

"Back in high school, my dad made some bad investments. We lost. . .everything. Or we would've. Things were bad. If he had gone under, he would've lost his bank job, our home, and maybe even lost my mom. My parents separated for the better part of my senior year."

He'd never told me.

But, no, I didn't care!

At least that's what I reminded myself.

I knew poverty. Before living with James and Millie, I'd had nothing. Charlie didn't know anything but wealth. Even if they'd have lost everything—which they didn't—his family certainly wouldn't have been reduced to living in their Cadillacs.

"My uncle gave my dad a huge loan. One he's yet to fully repay. He saved our family, and. . .I owe him."

"You could work anywhere," I said. "With your school credentials, you could've gone to any company."

"There was never really a choice," Charlie said.

"That's an unfortunate perspective."

"My family is in Uncle Steve's debt."

"Until when?"

Charlie paused, as if he hadn't ever asked himself this same question. "I don't know."

"It's your father's debt," I said as a raindrop hit my arm. "Sounds like it has nothing to do with you."

"My father and uncle would disagree."

"Why didn't you tell me what was going on our senior year?"

"I couldn't."

"I told you everything."

"This was. . ." Charlie rubbed the back of his neck in frustration. "This was different. I had to keep it confidential." His expression darkened. "Do you get what I'm saying?"

"Some legal issues?"

"If my dad didn't make the money reappear quickly, he would've gone to prison."

I didn't pry further. I didn't know if it was shady stock trading or bank embezzlement. All I knew was that nothing had really changed. "I'm sorry that happened to you. And I'm sorry most of all that you feel the need to do all the sacrificial dirty work for your father, while he's sitting pretty in a nice office with no complaints. You're pulling the plug on our town, on my theater—"

"You think I want to?"

"No. I don't. But I also don't think you get what it's like to watch something taken from you that has your whole heart and means everything. And no matter how much you love it and want it, there's nothing you can do to stop it. You have *no* idea what it's like to lose something that important."

"I'm pretty sure I do." Thunder rumbled in the distance as Charlie lifted those gray eyes to mine.

And when the sky opened up and poured out rain like tears, I was still standing in the alley.

Completely alone.

Chapter Sixteen

ON SUNDAY MORNING, I decided to go to church. My hope was that while I sat there in a stiff-backed pew, and Maxine belted her off-key renditions of praise songs, God would beam down some wisdom and show me what to do like Moses and the Ten Commandments.

If nothing else, I would sneak downstairs to the children's area and get myself a handful of cookies.

The In Between Community Church was where my father preached the gospel every Sunday except the few he took off for family vacations, and as in today, mission trips. The church was where I had met some of the best friends of my life, like Frances. Charlie's family attended there as well, so it should've been no surprise when I saw him walk into the lobby.

And yet it was. I guess I thought when you robbed and cheated innocent people out of their property for a living, you probably weren't keeping up with your church membership.

Charlie joined his mother, his little sister holding his hand. Their father was noticeably absent, but he'd always been on the Easter-Christmas visitation plan. The youth pastor's wife chatted with Charlie's mother while he scanned the room. Before I could look away, our eyes met, and he inclined his head in greeting.

I turned and gave him my back, tuning into the conversation between Frances, Maxine, and a quieter-than-usual Joey.

"No, I truly had no idea." Frances sent her fiancé a sour look. "*Someone* didn't tell me."

Joey shrugged. "It just never came up."

"I knew Charlie worked for his uncle's company," Frances said, "but I didn't know what that was. Joey and I had more than a few cross words about this."

"One or two." He kissed Frances's cheek.

I imagined most of the words had come from Frances.

"Well, my dear Katie was absolutely bamboozled," Maxine said. "And she's been a complete mess every since."

"No, I haven't," I said.

Maxine inspected my hair and makeup. "You keep telling yourself that. But somebody needs a little hair trim and waxy-poo."

"Katie, truly, I didn't know," Frances said. "And I know you're angry at Charlie right now, but he is Joey's best man. You'll be together quite a bit during the wedding and—" Frances's words died as she caught sight of something behind me. "Don't turn around, but Ian's here."

"My Ian?"

"Your *ex*-Ian," Maxine corrected.

What kind of loose government was I living in, that some foreigner could just come and go without any thought to the lives of American ex-girlfriends? Ian was *everywhere*. How could I text immigration? Why were we letting cheaters within our borders? "What in the world could he be doing here?"

"To hear the word of the Lord and get spiritual nourishment as a child of Jesus?" Maxine proposed.

Frances and I answered in duplicate. "Nah."

"Ladies, hello."

I turned at that perfectly enunciated accent, dread filling my every cell. "What do you think you're doing, Ian?"

He stood there looking GQ in a dark suit, without Felicity the simmering twit on his arm. "I came to hear your father preach."

"He's in Haiti," I said. "Why don't you go find him?"

Ian ignored that. "Hello, Mrs. Dayberry, Frances."

"You didn't answer my question, Ian."

"I'm here because it makes me look good." He straightened his tie and smiled. "Do me a favor and take some photos of me later, okay? I'm going to send those to the paper. And back to some strategic folks in London."

"Oh, Katie, dear!" Mrs. Livvy Hightower waddled her way to us, her flower-covered hat bobbing precariously on her white head.

"Good morning, Mrs. Hightower." I tried not to stare at the frayed silk rose that dangled near her ear, as if contemplating jumping off.

"I've been working on the music for your wedding?"

"The music?" I widened my eyes in a silent plea for her to stop.

"Yes. I do a mean Adele." The octogenarian then proceeded to sing a song I had previously liked somewhere between the key of G and awful.

"Thank you," I said when she finally finished.

Maxine removed her fingers from her ears. "Lovely."

"I'll keep working on it." Mrs. Hightower winked with her good eye. "For your wedding. The one that's coming up. Because Charlie really asked you to marry him. Because you're truly engaged and—"

"*Thank you*, Mrs. Hightower." This town was going to do me in. Instead of helping me, it was like they were conspiring to see who could make this engagement the biggest farce.

With an assurance that the well-meaning woman could have the wedding solo, Mrs. Hightower happily walked away, and I returned my attention to Ian. "So you're using my dad's church for PR?"

"Using is a very harsh verb." Laughter lurked in Ian's eyes, and I knew he wasn't buying the engagement story. "I prefer mutually helping us both. By the by, you have a phone interview with the Dallas Gazette, and the NBC affiliate in Houston is wanting us to do an interview for their morning show."

"There's no *us* here. And where is Felicity?"

"Since my stay here is going to go longer than I'd anticipated, I sent her back to Manhattan." There was nothing sweet about that smile he still wore. "We do work really well together. Maybe when you get your head straightened out, you can come out to New York, and I'll see if I can get you a part."

Maxine shoved herself in front of me like a human shield. "My Katie can get herself a part all on her own."

"Sure she can," Ian said. "Maybe with some acting lessons, she'll be ready in a few years."

"A big time director's been calling her nonstop, and Katie happens to have an audition."

Frances gasped. "You do?"

"She does!" Maxine clapped her hands.

"Is that so?" Ian chuckled. "Do you really think you're ready?"

I wanted to shove this Bible right down his throat then pull it back out his nose. "I don't need you to—"

"There you are, Katie"

I startled as Charlie suddenly joined us. As I stood there swallowing my zinger for Ian, Charlie wrapped his arm around me, tucked me in close, and planted a careful kiss on my bandage. "Had to take Sadie to children's church." He pulled a napkin-covered package from the pocket of his pin-striped shirt. "They're serving the good kind today. Oreos. For my girl."

Cookies. For me.

I would not be charmed by this. Faking it or not, Charlie was not going to lure me in with crunchy, cookie goodness.

Oh. They were double stuffed.

Get thee behind me, Nabisco.

"We were just talking about Katie's audition in New York," Maxine said. "The one that director has been begging her to go on."

"The audition. Right." Charlie's fingers massaged my shoulder. "She's been fielding lots of calls. We can't even make it through ten minutes of dinner without her cell ringing."

Ian cocked his head and smiled indulgently. "Is that a fact?"

"Yes, it is. We're into facts around here," Maxine said. "And that's. . .definitely one of them."

Holy offering plates, she was a terrible liar. How could someone so devious be that awful at lies? "We were just going into the sanctuary," I said. "We'll see you later."

"Is this the church where you'll be getting married?" Ian asked.

My pause was as obvious as the orange spray tan on the worship pastor's wife. "Yes. My dad will marry us here." I looked up at Charlie with an expression I hoped was full of love.

"And when did you say that was?" Ian asked.

"We haven't set a date," Charlie said. "It all depends on Katie's busy schedule."

"At the diner?"

Charlie smiled. "On Broadway."

I wanted to disappear into the laminate flooring that was trying so hard to be a nice bamboo. But it wasn't. And I wasn't a Broadway caliber actress. I was community theater, and Ian and I both knew it.

"And your honeymoon plans?" Ian asked.

"Probably not London." Charlie's hand made a lazy S down my back.

Ian looked like he was actually enjoying this. "I couldn't help notice you're not wearing an engagement ring."

"I only want a simple band."

"It's being sized."

Charlie laughed amiably as he lifted my left hand and gave my fingers a sweet kiss. "Katie has a ring, but so far I can't talk her into wearing it."

"It's a doozie." Maxine made a giant circle with her arms. "Gigantically, epically, monstrously mega big."

"Well, we should get going." I took a step toward the sanctuary. "Maxine gets twitchy if she doesn't get her pew."

Frances gave my grandma the side-eye. "I know that's right."

"I'll see you at the committee meeting after church," Ian said. "At the diner, right?"

How had he known about that? I had specifically left him out of the communication loop.

"I'm sure you forgot to let me know," Ian said. "Being busy with all your phone calls and impromptu wedding plans. But Loretta gave me a ring on my mobile."

"Don't feel like you have to go," I said. "We've got it under control."

Ian held up his phone, showing a text. "Actually your lawyer just quit ten minutes ago. But I'm sure you knew that."

I made a move to step out of Charlie's embrace, but the man tightened his grip and just smiled. "Katie and I don't discuss the Thrifty Co. buyout together," Charlie said. "You and Katie can talk business later. When we're not at church."

"A sound idea," Ian said. "She can ride with me."

"She's not going anywhere with you." I felt the muscles beneath Charlie's shirt flex. "I'll take her."

"What is this, *Downton Abbey*?" Maxine snapped. "This little filly is fully capable of driving herself."

"Thank you," I said. "Ian, if you insist on going, I will see you there. And now, I'd like to go sit down before we miss the entire sermon."

Charlie reached for my hand then led me inside.

"I'm ready to tell Ian we're not engaged," I mumbled as we walked down the aisle and slipped into a row.

"Wait 'til he's gone." Charlie sat down and rested his arm on the pew behind my back.

I scooted over an inch, but Charlie merely followed. "I'm still very angry at you." I tried to turn off my girlie-senses that were attuned to his every move—his heavenly scent and those heart-stopping good looks.

"Duly noted."

"I would prefer it if you didn't touch me."

"Too bad."

I snapped open the church bulletin and read over the prayer requests. "I'd also rather you keep some distance."

"That would look real authentic."

"All couples go through rough patches."

"Not us," he ground out. "We're *blissfully* happy."

"You must have me confused with Thrifty Co."

Frances and Joey soon joined us, and I turned down some of my rancor. Ian sat somewhere behind us, and this was not lost on my fake fiancé. Throughout the service, Charlie leisurely played with my hair, clasped my hand in his, or ran the tips of his fingers along my back.

All the while the assistant pastor spoke heartily from the podium.

On the challenges of marriage.

Chapter Seventeen

"ND THAT'S WHY we want Thrifty Co. to build somewhere else. To save our heritage and to save the livelihoods of many families."

I sat in a cushy, blue chair across from Kiley LeBeaux, the co-anchor of the Channel 5 morning show. The perky bobbed-blonde nodded at my response and directed her final question to Ian.

"And you came all the way from London just to help out this town?"

"I care about theaters, and the Valiant is too much of a historical gem to let it be bulldozed just to provide a parking lot for the new store. Directing is my career, but I have a passion for theater preservation."

"And you came all the way from London?"

The poor woman couldn't let that one go. I had to admit, nobody really understood it.

"I've traveled further for the cause, believe it or not."

I was going with not.

"The theater community takes care of our own, Ms. LeBeaux," Ian said. "Katie and I worked together on a large production on the West End, and when she told me what was going on, I knew I couldn't stand idly by. I was en route to New York to begin a new show, and it was the perfect time to offer my assistance."

Kiley consulted the notes in her lap. "And Ian, you've had hundreds of your theater friends sign an online petition, gotten an official letter of support from the president of the Actors Equity Association, started a Twitter hashtag campaign that is generating some buzz on Broadway, and even gotten the attention of some famous actors. Do you feel this is making a difference? Is it enough to stand against the fifth largest American retailer?"

"As Katie said, these aren't just buildings Thrifty Co. would be taking. These are family businesses, only sources of income, and in the case of the Valiant, a beautiful theater with a rich history that would be lost if Thrifty took over that part of town. The Valiant, like many theaters, is a work of art in itself, and it's been an anchor in In Between for decades. It must be saved."

"Thank you both." The woman looked directly into camera two. "Thrifty Co. could not be reached for comment at this time."

Ten minutes later, Ian and I walked to the parking lot of the Houston news station. After last night's committee meeting, Ian had worn me down until I'd finally agreed to make the long drive with him this morning. The way there had passed uneventfully, with Ian making polite small talk, and me pretending to be engrossed in a texting conversation with Charlie. When in fact, it was Frances who had obsessively texted me, giving me updates on her wedding dress drama. She had returned the gown to Vivi's and was now back to being a bride without a dress.

He unlocked his car, then hurried to open and hold the passenger door. Something he'd never done in nearly a year of dating.

"So that went well," Ian said as he merged the car onto the highway, doing remarkably well for usually driving on the other side of the road. "You did a wonderful job."

"Thanks." The next compliment hurt to even say. "You were great as well."

"Tomorrow I'll be chatting with three radio stations. It's a shame you're working and can't join me." He sent me a chummy smile. "We make a pretty great team."

"When did you say you were going to New York?"

"Ouch." Ian's brow furrowed as he fiddled with the radio volume. "Very subtle. So you want me gone?"

"I just want an idea of when I can quit expecting to see your face in my hometown. It's weird."

"Like a suddenly getting engaged kind of weird?"

"Why do you care if I'm engaged? It's not like you wanted me."

He drove for the better part of a pop song before responding. "That's not true. That's just not true."

"Ian, get real. You were having an affair with Felicity. If that didn't reveal the status I had in your life, then I don't know what would."

He took his eyes off the road and looked at me. "Do you ever think about me?"

"Yes," I admitted. "It usually involves hot tar and chicken feathers."

"Kinky." He laughed. "I can hang with that."

I couldn't hold back the smile. Ian would never be my Mr. Right, and losing him had thrown my life into a tailspin, but he still possessed a certain level of charm. He made people feel as if they were his favorite person, like you were the one he wanted to sit and talk with. When you were with Ian, you felt like you were the most fascinating individual, and he was in awe just to be in your presence.

At one time, it had been a heady drug.

And I had fallen under its power.

But I was now clean and sober of Ian Attwood.

"Are you going to tell me the truth about this Charlie guy? You can't possibly be engaged to a Thrifty Co. employee, especially one assigned to tearing down your theater."

"It's an obstacle," I said. "But our love will see us through."

Ian chuckled again. "Right."

"I've known Charlie a very long time. He and I have had lots of stops and starts. But we always seem to come back to one another."

And that, I thought, was true.

"If Felicity hadn't been in the picture," Ian said, "you still would've left me."

At this I said nothing. I didn't like where this was headed.

"You were never all in," Ian said. "Like you knew I wasn't the one. But I wonder." His knowing eyes found mine before returning his attention back to the road. "Does Charlie really have it either?"

I SPENT THE rest of the day trying not to think about my conversation with Ian. It helped that I had gone to the doctor to get my stitches finally removed. While there was a nasty pucker that would scar me and forever ruin any chances of my becoming a super model, I felt lighter without the lovely bandage and Frankenstein needlework.

As it began to rain outside, I celebrated my separation from the stitches by going home and poring over articles on the internet of businesses and homeowners who had also found themselves the victims of eminent domain. There were few success stories, and it only served to depress me even more. James and Millie had called, updating me on their experiences in Haiti. Their group had roofed a few houses, painted the church, and provided toys to a local orphanage. My parents were difference makers. And I wanted to be one too. Right here at home.

On hour five at my computer, I rubbed my dry eyes and leaned my aching head down to utter a quick prayer.

God, please save the Valiant and the other businesses. Save us from that monster known as Thrifty Co. And help me get my mind off Charlie Benson and back on figuring out my career. Do I go to New York and audition? Or are my acting days truly over?

Oh, and forgive me for my lies.

All 2,980 of them.

Okay, 2,981.

Amen.

I rolled my shoulders and heard my back pop. I had been sitting there way too long. I was starving, it was somehow dark outside, and my bladder told me I was seconds away from a tragic incident.

Minutes later, I hobbled downstairs on stiff, creaky legs, more excited over the leftover pizza in the fridge than Millie would approve. Her organic weirdo meals were still sitting in the freezer, untouched and dying a slow, cryogenic death. But Hawaiian pizza? My beloved ham, bacon, and pineapple trio had never done me wrong.

I stepped off the last stair.

Into a puddle of water.

What was this?

Oh, no. Oh, no, no, no.

Water was everywhere. On bare feet, I padded my way through the shallow pond that had overtaken Millie's shiny hardwood floors and followed the mess into the kitchen.

Where water poured from the pantry door.

I flung it open and found the water heater gushing and hissing and doing its best imitation of Niagara Falls.

Crap! What did I do?

Didn't it have a place to shut off the water? A knobby thing? A switch? A magic button that said *IN CASE OF MONSOON, PRESS HERE?*

I slammed the door, then ran to the kitchen phone. Picking it up, my fingers hovered over the numbers.

I couldn't recall one phone number.

Cell phone! Where was my phone?

I sloshed across the kitchen and back up the stairs to my room. At this rate, I was going to need my life jacket and nose plugs to go back down there.

With a punch of a few buttons, I dialed Maxine. Sam could fix this. He knew how to repair anything.

No answer!

I dialed Sam.

Voicemail.

With visions of the dining room table floating down the hall, I called Frances, who answered from a bridal shopping trip in Dallas. Totally useless! Next I tried two of the neighbors, one of the deacons, Loretta, and my gynecologist.

Not one person answered.

Where was everyone?

Phone in hand, I ran back downstairs, knowing there was one number I hadn't tried.

Charlie.

It was either let the house flood to the rafters or call.

"Hello?"

"I have an emergency," I said. "I'm at the house, and the water heater seems to be flooding."

"Did you turn the water off?"

"I don't know how to do that."

"I'll be right there."

"I'm still mad at you."

I could hear his smile. "I'm guessing you called ten other people first."

"Eleven. Please hurry."

He made it in four minutes and sixteen seconds.

"Where's the water line?" he asked as he filled my doorway, all handsome, strong, and tool belt carrying.

"I don't know."

He nodded and palmed a flashlight big enough to light the football field. "I'll be back."

"I'll get my umbrella."

"Just stay inside."

"I'll hold it over you."

"Stay in the house."

"But what do I do?"

His eyes took a slow perusal of my shorts and tank. "Think of some creative way to repay me."

"It won't involve anything dirty!" I called as he walked away.

He cast a look over his shoulder and sent me a wink. "A man can try."

Five minutes later, Charlie came back inside, his hair drenched, smelling like earth, rain, and savior. "Water's off."

I had a fluffy towel ready, but he ignored it and marched right into the battle zone, the pool-like kitchen.

He went into the pantry, rattled around in there, then stepped back out. "The PopTarts on the bottom shelf are totally ruined."

A devastating loss. "They died a noble death. I will think of them fondly and write dark poetry of their sacrifice."

"Let's get some of this furniture to the living room."

"Water's in there."

"To the garage."

We spent the next three hours transferring furniture and odds and ends to the garage, then cleaning as best we could. Charlie got a wet vac from one of the neighbors and got rid of some of the water. It seemed to be everywhere I looked. Millie was going to pass out when she saw her house.

At the stroke of midnight, we were still working, so I decided to make dinner.

When the doorbell rang, I took the food from the delivery guy, looking like I had just popped up from a sewage drain. My hair hung in a wet, stringy mess, and frizz had staged a war and won. My clothes were soaked, and I knew I probably smelled.

And yet here Charlie sat in James's very dry office, settled into a leather recliner, and looking at me like I had just placed in Miss

America.

Or maybe he was just ogling the pizza.

Armed with more dry towels and paper plates, I sat on the floor and opened the pizza box, the scent nearly bringing me to revival.

I slid two slices onto Charlie's plate, then filled my own. "It was nice of you to come over." I took a bite, savoring the gooey cheese on my tongue. "You saved me. Again."

Charlie eased onto the floor beside me. "Got a little marinara there." He reached out and used his thumb to swipe a drop of sauce from the corner of my mouth. "You know, I'm not the bad guy you've decided I am."

"I don't think you're. . .a bad guy."

"That's something I guess."

I leaned back on my hands and closed my eyes for a moment, letting the tension ease from my neck. "This is a nightmare."

"It'll be okay."

"Is that what you told yourself when you got assigned to In Between?"

The mood in the room shifted so hard, it was a wonder the floor didn't quake. Despite the awful circumstances, we had been getting along so well in the last few hours. Laughing even.

"Can't we pretend like we're not on opposite sides for tonight?"

"Are we on opposite sides?" I studied his face, wanting so badly to know what was truly going on in that brain of his. "Do you really want a Thrifty Co. here more than you want to save our businesses?"

"It's complicated."

"Try and explain. I'll Google the big words."

"Nothing I can say is going to make this go away." Charlie reached out his hand and pushed a damp strand of hair from my face. "I wish I could fix this. But if I wasn't here in this job, someone else would be. I'm not the person shutting down your theater. I'm just the low guy on the totem pole who has to stay and put on a good face when it's over."

"Lots of people in town don't like you very much right now."

His expression darkened as he slowly nodded. "I guess that's a work hazard."

"I just. . .I'm just so disappointed this is your job. That it's okay with you."

"It's not okay with me. I lie awake every night, seeing the faces of those angry business owners, people who were a part of my teenage years. Good people who know me." He rested his hand on my dirt stained knee. "Mostly I see your face. Hear your angry voice and see that disappointment in your eyes."

The crickets sang their lonely night song outside the windows, filling our silence. Charlie's gaze held me in place, but I didn't know what he wanted me to say. I was too tired to fight. Too sad to keep repeating what I'd said time and again.

Charlie picked the discarded crust from my plate and bit into it. We'd shared many a pizza like this. This was a man who had never feared carbs.

"Where were we headed before you knew the truth about my job?" He gave my knee a light squeeze. "You and me."

"I don't know."

He rested his hand on the floor behind me, his body slanted toward mine. "I think you would've bailed on me at some point anyway."

"Why?" I licked my lips, suddenly uncomfortable with this new direction of conversation. "Why would you say that?"

"Because that's what you do. When things get too close, you jump ship. Maybe that's what you did with Ian."

"I'd like to remind you that Ian was getting it on with his assistant. Pretty sure my *bailing* had nothing to do with my emotional inadequacies."

"How was it going before you found him cheating?"

It was hard to chew when he kept bringing up Ian. "I guess if it had been going well, he wouldn't have strayed."

"At some point, you're going to have to dig in and stay. Fight for the relationship. Love that man enough to do it afraid."

"I'm not afraid."

Charlie was so close, his lips were a breath from mine. "Aren't you?"

I said nothing, just shook my head.

"I think you are. I think you're afraid for someone to love you. For someone to honest-to-God love you."

"I've been in love," I said.

"I'm talking about the kind where you stay. Where you have to. Even when it's tough, even when it's ugly, and nothing makes sense except for one thing. That one thing you know is that that man loves you, and you love him. And you stay, Katie."

"Are you telling me I should've stuck it out with Ian?"

"No." Fire lit the dark flecks in Charlie's eyes. "You should be as far from that jerk as possible."

"So we're talking about you."

"What if we were?"

"I can't even trust you," I said. "And given my last relationship, I'm not going to toss my heart over to someone who—"

"You know me," Charlie said. "No matter what I do for a living, no matter who I work for, you know who I am."

"Do I?"

"I'm still that guy you sat next to on Flight 247."

"No. That man who threw himself over me to protect me from an imminent crash, who carried my unconscious body off the plane—that guy does the right thing. He doesn't follow money or try to walk in anyone's footsteps to prove—"

"I am *not* my father."

"Really? You can't tell me when you're losing all that sleep, that that thought doesn't cross your mind."

"And who are you becoming?" Charlie stood up, dusting the grime from his jeans. "You've got a string of auditions you could go on, and you're here."

"My family's here. And in case you hadn't noticed, I'm kind of needed. This corporate giant is trying to ruin my town. And if you manage to leave the Valiant alone, I'll be managing that soon."

"You're running. Again."

I wasn't going to have this man tower over me. I stood to my feet and marched out of the office. In case Charlie had forgotten where the front door was, I would lead him there. It was past time for him to go. "I'll return to acting when I darn well feel like it."

Charlie followed me into the hall. "No, you won't. You'll stay here, settle in, and become something that was second or third on your list. Like teach or social work."

My pulse beat a hot tempo at my temples. "There is *nothing* wrong with either of those jobs."

"Of course not. Unless it's something you settle for because you were too scared to pursue your dream."

I flung open the door, letting it crash on its frame. "I think it's time you left. I'm grateful for your help, but—"

"Anything worth having doesn't come easy, Katie. Whether that's us or your stage career. You're all about it as long as it's easy, then as soon as you meet any resistance, you quit."

"You call finding out you're not who I thought you were *resistance?*"

Charlie loomed over me as he brushed past. "Yes. And I also say you're too chicken to go out to New York and go on a stupid audition. Or two. Or three. Heck, it might take twenty or thirty to get a part. But you'll never know."

Hot tears pressed against the back of my eyes. "I'm glad you've got my life all figured out." I shoved a towel into his chest. "But maybe you should take a good, hard look at your own. Because if I'm settling, I can assure you I'm not the only one."

My attempt to slam the door was halted by his arm. "One more thing."

"What?" I yelled.

Charlie's chest rose and fell in heavy breaths, and he briefly looked away, as if searching for patience in the umbrella holder by the door. Finally he lifted his head, focusing those tired eyes on me. "I called Maxine. She and Sam are expecting you tonight."

I lifted my chin. "I can take care of myself."

"That may be, but you'll be doing it without a bathroom. Your water's turned off."

Oh.

I guess he could be right about something.

"Fine." I could attempt to be civil too. "Thank you. Thank you very much for your help." Though the advice was totally crappy.

"You'll need to call your insurance."

"Okay."

"Tonight."

"Just as soon as you leave."

"I'm gone." And he shut the door behind him.

But he was still in the driveway when I pulled out of the garage fifteen minutes later. And his familiar rental car followed me all the way to Maxine and Sam's, not leaving until I was safely inside.

"So," Maxine said as she led me to the guest room. "Were you and Charlie able to get any of it cleaned up?"

"Maxine"—I put my bag down and threw my arms around my grandma—"I think we just made an even bigger mess."

Chapter Eighteen

"**D**ID YOU CALL the repairman?" Maxine asked as we pulled into my driveway bright and early the next morning.

"No." A Patterson's Home Repair van sat in the street, and at the sight of my car, a uniformed man climbed out.

"You Katie Parker?" he asked when I stepped out of the car.

"Who wants to know?" Maxine popped her gum. "What are you, some ambulance chaser of a fix-it guy? You hear talk of my grand-daughter flooding her home, and you all come running with your wrenches, water suckers, and thingie-mabobbers?"

"It's already paid for." He pushed up the brim of his black company cap, his gray hair springing out the sides. "All I know is I've been dispatched to this here house to replace a water heater."

"Who paid you?"

"That fellow right there." The man pointed behind us, where Charlie Benson was pulling in.

"He bought you a water heater." Maxine sigh was a slow drawl. "That is so romantic." She linked her arm with the repairman's. "Follow me. I'll lead you to the culprit. You know, I do so admire a man in uniform."

She guided the repairman inside, while I stood on the front step watching Charlie slowly walk my way. He had a way of carrying himself that spoke of confidence and strength. I could see him one day being president of Thrifty Co. He would get there sooner than later, and while family connections may have opened that first door, it was his own abilities that would push him to the top. I wondered how long it would be before he was the one making the decisions to tear down businesses and brush hog the small man.

"Do you know something about this repair guy?"

Charlie pushed his hands into the pockets of his khaki shorts, and his black Aviators hid whatever might've been brewing in those eyes. "Fred's one of the best in the county. He'll get you taken care of."

"I don't need you to pay for it."

"Too late."

"Insurance would cover it."

"Yeah, and it would take them days. Did you want cold showers in the meantime?"

I didn't know what to say. I had zero experience in pricing hot water heaters, but it couldn't have been cheap.

"You're kind of dressed down for the day, aren't you?" I took in his flip-flops and a t-shirt that advertised some beach town in Florida. "Did the man-eating boss give you the day off?"

Charlie's full lips curved, and he propped his hand on the porch beam right over my head. "I took the day off so I could help you. Now are you going to invite me in, or do I have to wait for an invitation from my friend Fred."

"Fred is pretty handsome. You could do worse."

Charlie's grin deepened.

I would not smile at him. I wouldn't. All he had to do was breathe, and charm and charisma surrounded him like the wings of an angel. I had to keep my wits about me. My mother would've fallen for those brooding eyes, chiseled jaw, and body of a Hollywood action star, but I wouldn't.

I couldn't. But I did have business with the boy. There were words I needed to give him that had sat heavy on my heart all night.

"You gonna let me in, Parker?"

"No."

Charlie merely lifted a brow, stared down at me. . .and waited. "Is there a problem?"

"Yes." My word, he looked incredibly dashing today. And he smelled like that cologne he'd always worn, the one I had gotten him that one memorable Christmas. "I mean, no. I. . ." So hard. The words lodged in my throat like Millie's bean balls. "I wanted to . . . apologize."

One single brow lifted. "Is that so?"

"You came over last night and were an incredible help. I have no idea what I would've done if you hadn't answered your phone."

He shifted closer. "I will always answer your calls."

The heat index under this porch had to be climbing. "And I'm sorry I turned it into an argument. You didn't deserve that. I mean, you do deserve what I said, because I was right, and I can't stand what you're a part of, and I think you're making a huge mistake." I took a breath. "But last night wasn't the time."

Charlie took off his sunglasses and focused those grays right on me. "I kind of got lost in some of that. Was that an apology?"

"Yes." I returned his smile. "Somewhere in there, there definitely was one." I leaned on tip-toe and before reason prevailed, I gave him a kiss on the cheek. "I'm sorry."

I didn't know if I robbed the man speechless, but he didn't move. Charlie simply stood there, so close I could move right into his arms if I wanted.

And glory, how I did want.

Charlie studied the ground, head bent, as if his thoughts weighed him down. "Katie, nothing in this buyout deal is simple," he finally said. "It's more complicated than you could ever imagine."

His tone sounded defeated and heavy, yet laced with something I couldn't define. "Enlighten me."

"I can't."

"Because of family obligations or Thrifty Co.?"

"Both," he said. "But I care about you. I care about this town. And I want to do the right thing by everyone."

"Including your company."

"My *uncle's* company." He looked around, like he expected someone to be lurking in the landscaping. "You guys need a new lawywer," he advised quietly. "The longer you let that go, the worse your case is."

"James said he's in contact with someone." It was killing my dad to be so far away, with such limited communication while the case completely unraveled.

"It can't wait. And you can't pick just any attorney. You need someone with experience in this sort of thing."

"Why are you telling me this?"

"Nobody likes to see a total shutout. They want a fair fight."

"You mean it's bad press for you guys if it's a total shutout. Thrifty Co. ends up looking like the giant who squashed the little man."

"Not quite what I meant."

"This morning three major cable news networks picked up the story. They went live with it on air and their websites"

"I'm aware."

Of course he was. It was his job. "Sorry if that's making trouble for your career pursuits."

"Your first apology was half way believable. That one was just pure sass."

"Ian always said my acting skills were weak."

"I guess your ex-boyfriend is good for something—he's garnered more attention for In Between than your attorney ever did. When did you say your British chap was leaving town?"

"Is Thrifty Co. feeling our choke hold yet? I guess you didn't expect us to come up swinging. Is our little portion of the street really worth your company's reputation being dragged through the mud?"

"How much more you got?"

"Remember that time we went four wheeling after the storm on old man Holt's farm?" We'd ridden for hours, mud flying, brown from scalp to shoes, laughing 'til I ached. "That day won't even compare to what we're going to bring." I was bluffing really. I knew Ian was at the point where he had exhausted all his contacts. It was simply a waiting game to see if the small media fire he lit would catch and grow into an inferno.

"I remember that day." The look in Charlie's eyes told me he recalled more than just the mud slinging. It had been our senior year. I'd just been put in the friend zone by my boyfriend Tate weeks before, and Charlie and I had gravitated back toward one another like fate had tugged us in with this invisible string. It was that day that I'd sat behind him on the four wheeler, my hands tight around his waist, and knew I was where I belonged.

"And then college came, and you forgot me," I said.

"Is that what you think?" Charlie leaned down, his face near enough to tempt. "I seem to recall it was the other way around."

"And now?" I asked. "You're leaving me behind again."

"I'm not." Charlie's hands slid up my arms and rested on my shoulders. "This is my job. And I can't walk away from it. I don't expect you to understand that, and that might make me the enemy to you. But we both know that's not what I want you to see when you look at me."

"I don't know how I can see anything else. What are you going to do when they bulldoze the Valiant—hold my hand. . . or hand me a check? You work for them, Charlie."

"If you can't trust in what I'm doing, then trust in the man you know I am."

"I can't do that." I wished I could. "I'm losing too much."

"What if *we're* more than those buildings?"

"You're asking me to choose you over the Valiant?"

Before Charlie could answer, the repairman opened the door. "Hey, Mr. Benson, I got something I need you to take a look at."

Charlie's eyes never left mine. "I'll be right there." He exhaled slowly and took a step back. "Katie, you tell me to leave, and I'll leave. I'd like to stay and help. But I will not talk business or buyouts with you, and I'm not going to fight. Maybe I can't be who you want me to be tomorrow, but today. . .I can at least be who you need."

I stood there on the front porch, right next to the very door Charlie had come through so many times when we were younger. Dates. Prom. Church.

We certainly weren't those kids anymore.

"Stay," I said. "I'd like you to stay."

We walked in together, and Maxine met us in the soppy living room. Her arms crossed over her chest, she stared Charlie Benson down like a firing squad.

He inclined his head. "Mrs. Dayberry."

"I hear you worked your tail off last night with this disaster."

"I helped a bit."

"Well." Maxine moved a hand to her hip. "I would've answered Katie's call of distress, but it was my bingo night. I'm a ten card player, and I take no prisoners or outside communication when I'm in the zone, you get me?"

"We wouldn't want to interrupt your sacred time," I said.

Maxine straightened the row of gold bangles decorating her wrist. "It's not like *I* get crazy like some of those bingo nut jobs."

"You take a whole bag of troll dolls."

"Moral support."

"And don't forget your statue of the Virgin Mary."

She turned to Charlie. "I'm very spiritual."

"We're not Catholic."

"At least I don't blow up water heaters."

"Nope, just chicken trucks."

"That was a long time ago and I—"

"Ladies." Charlie stepped between my grandmother and me, his hand grabbing mine, as if to restrain. "How about we get some work done?"

"Excellent idea," Maxine said. "Dibs on role of supervisor."

"Katie and I can handle it. You take it easy, Mrs. Dayberry."

Oh, he was putty in her manicured hands.

"Thank you, dear boy. I lost to Peg Pickering last night more than once, and I am just not feeling full of vigor. Plus that tramp stole my lucky dauber."

"What a tough night you had," I said. "Really puts mine into perspective."

Maxine's grin seemed to hold plenty of vigor. With her poison apple red nails, she gripped Charlie's chin in her hand. "You're a good boy, Charlie Benson. And if I were thirty years younger and Sam didn't worship my every breath, I'd snatch you up myself."

He looked to me for assistance.

But I just smiled.

She roughly patted his cheek. "We'll take that help. We'll take any help you got." Her cobalt eyes narrowed. "You know what I'm saying?"

"I believe I do." His easy smile dimmed, and the face of the Chicago businessman appeared. "Today I'm just here to clean a house."

Maxine scrutinized him for a moment. "Good enough. Oh, and keep your paws off my sister here."

"I'm your granddaughter," I corrected.

She rolled her eyes and sashayed away. "Details."

We worked all day, stopping only when a restoration company came and ripped up the hardwood and tile in spots where the damage had been too great. They set up fans loud enough to be airplane propellers. Sometimes I would work side by side with Charlie. Our arms would touch, my leg would brush against his, a hand would be at my back. Other times he'd be working across the room, and I'd look up to find him watching me, a small smile playing at his lips.

It was nice to drop the battle lines.

He could just be Charlie.

And I could just be me.

But was there any hope for the two of us together?

Chapter Nineteen

I DREAMED OF death and Charlie.

On Wednesday morning, I slowly roused, stretching arms sore from cleaning and furniture lifting. The industrial fans downstairs might as well have been sitting outside my bedroom for how loud they were. I rolled over, fluffing the pillow beneath my head, and recalled I had dreamt that I had slept on a runway and was just about to be mowed down by a low-flying jet. But right before the airliner charged over me like a giant bird of doom, Charlie appeared, sprinting toward me and pulling me to safety in the nick of time. I had shown my appreciation by raining kisses all over his face.

Then a gorilla drove by in a VW bug, Snickers candy bars fell from the sky, and a marching band serenaded us with the greatest hits of Justin Bieber.

When I awoke, I knew I needed to deal with my feelings for Charlie Benson.

And I was never eating those frozen burritos again.

My anger over Charlie's role in the buyout seemed to spring from a bottomless well, but I had to admit, like an addiction, this was a boy I had never gotten out of my system. And much like that addiction, reason did not prevail. Good sense said to steer clear, but my heart said. . .*what if he's the one?*

After spending a scant fifteen minutes on my appearance, I slipped on my Micky's Diner t-shirt and cinched it in a knot at the waist. It billowed over the waistband of my jeans, and I knew I wouldn't be starting any fashion trends with this look. Today I had a full schedule. I had a full to-do list for the Valiant, a morning shift at the diner, then I had to stop by Vivi's for a final fitting of my bridesmaid's dress.

My bed bounced as I plopped in the middle and opened my laptop. I had an hour before I was to report to work, so I typed up some content on the buyout for some blogs that had contacted me, responded to some emails for interviews, and ignored Ian's tenth text about calling in for a podcast out of Manhattan. Last week I had put in nearly forty hours on research, phone interviews, calls to strategic persons of interest, three interviews with area news stations, and one meeting with a state Congressman.

We had two more days until the meeting with the special commission, and I both feared it and welcomed the finale. But if the Valiant was destroyed, what would become of me? My only plan was to manage the facility. I had been lucky to immediately find work at Micky's, but I couldn't do that indefinitely. The cobwebs and dust were accumulating on my college degree.

My fabulous shirt and I rolled into Micky's at six o'clock.

"You're almost late," Loretta said, breezing past me with a steaming coffee pot.

"Sorry. I got behind Mr. Philpot's tractor."

"Clock in then meet me at table ten."

I obeyed her snippy orders, but not before grabbing myself a cup of coffee and one of Loretta's famous cinnamon rolls. They were big as a dessert plate, and the trick was to eat the center first while it was still warm and gooey. Hot icing was an underused little bit of nirvana.

I said hello to some friendly faces and made my way to the table in the corner where Loretta sat with a man in a navy blue suit, crisp white shirt, and a tie decorated with the initials of a Texas university.

"Katie, this is Daniel Stephens," Loretta said as I sat down. "He's taken over the case in Reggie Barker's sudden departure." She had a laptop in front of her, and a folder of papers thick as a dictionary.

I shook hands with the gentlemen who looked to be about ten years younger than James. "Nice to meet you."

"I've been doing nothing but catching up on this case," Mr. Stephens said. "A little unusual that each of the property owners doesn't have their own attorneys."

"We're in this together," Loretta said. "We decided that from the beginning."

"It looks like your previous lawyer did you more harm than good. He knew nothing about eminent domain."

"None of us do," Loretta said. "But I guess we're learning the hard way."

"I'm going to be honest with you." Mr. Stephens took a quick drink of coffee. "It doesn't look good. And time is not on our side. But you've been creating a thunderstorm of bad press for Thrifty Co., and that's made an impact."

"That's all Katie and her English fellow," Loretta said.

Mr. Stephens smiled with approval. "One of their attorneys contacted me last night with a new offer. I'm meeting with the rest of our property owners today, but here are yours. Hot off my printer." He slid Loretta her piece of paper first, then mine.

Loretta's eyebrows rose to the middle of her forehead. "Whoa."

I studied my offer. "Twenty thousand dollars more than the initial offering."

She whistled low. "Mine too. That could be a nice chunk down on a new RV for my retirement."

"But we're not interested, right?" My bite of cinnamon roll turned to glue in my mouth.

Loretta pushed her paper back to Mr. Stephens. "No, we're not interested. You'll get the same answer from all of us."

"I thought that might be your answer," he said. "I just wanted to pass on the information. I'll call them right away. Tell them we'll be there Friday to hear the verdict of the special commission."

"And you let them know I have more media spots lined up so I can continue telling the world what they're doing to us," I said. "Our slightly aggressive, but mostly tasteful mud-slinging is only getting started."

"Ladies, you need to prepare yourselves for Thrifty Co. to come back with an even bigger dollar amount. I've seen settlement offers double and even triple over the initial numbers thrown out. And if that happens, I need to know how you want me to proceed. Legally, your town has every right to your property. You may have won the favor of your city, your county—"

"We've been mentioned on CNN and FOX half a dozen times," I said.

"Okay, and even on a national level, but the three special commission members will be looking at it from the perspective of what's best for In Between."

"But they're landowners," I said. "How could they not side with us? All they have to do is imagine if they were in our position."

"I hope that's exactly what they do." Mr. Stephens slipped our offers back into his leather attaché case. "But the reality is landowners don't often win. Think about their offers, okay? I promise I'm going to do everything I can, but I need you to be realistic with your every decision."

"And if we don't like what this commission says?" I asked.

"You can take it to a court of your peers." He didn't even try to sound optimistic about that option.

"You just dig a little deeper," Loretta said. "Look up more statutes, more cases like ours. Dredge up some dirt on this company. If we go down, I want it said we went down with our fists a flying."

"Yes, ma'am." Mr. Stephens took one last drink of coffee then stood. "I'll communicate your refusal of the new offer. If I hear anything else, I'll let you know. I guess in the meantime, keep doing what you're doing and. . . think about what I said."

The lawyer left our table, and when he walked out the door, I knew we wouldn't see him again until the meeting at the courthouse.

"You trust that guy?" I asked Loretta.

"Much as I trust any man." She plucked the pen she always kept perched behind her ear and used it to jot some notes inside her folder. "He seems pretty knowledgeable. Pretty together. Your dad found him."

I leaned my elbows on the table and let my head fall into my hands. I was tired of not sleeping, tired of being upset. "I'm not buyable." I looked up at my boss. "Are you?"

She let out a ragged breath that sounded as if she'd been holding it for years. "I'm not young, Katie. None of us involved are—except you. I don't want to lose my diner, but we all have a price. They just haven't named it yet. We all reach the point where the fight isn't worth what we could gain if we'd just lay our anger and expectations down and surrender." The eyes beneath her wrinkled lids watched me close. "Do you understand that?"

I swallowed against the lump in my throat and picked up my fork, slicing my cinnamon roll into bites. But I had no stomach for it.

"Speaking of waving a white flag, I have something I'm supposed to give you." Loretta dug into her folder of papers until she found the ones she wanted. "My sister said to hand this to you. Said you'd know what it was."

I took the offering and knew what I was holding upon reading the first word. It was pages of auditions Mrs. Hall had printed from sites with theater job postings. Three pages of Broadway roles. Two for Chicago. Two for touring companies. With a red pen, my former drama teacher had circled some she thought were especially note-worthy. A few entries even got smiley faces.

The instructions were all the same. Show up for the audition. Have an audition piece prepared. Bring picture and resume stapled together. And how far would I get without my London history on my own resume? Or worse yet, *with* it?

"Well?"

I looked up from the listings. "Well what?"

"Are you gonna go on those auditions or not?"

"Are you trying to get rid of me?"

"You still can't balance three plates on each arm."

"No man will ever marry me now."

Loretta's cracked lips quirked. "You need to go live your life, Katie. What's for you here in In Between?"

"The Valiant. My family. A sweet-tempered boss."

"And what if the Valiant gets razed to the ground? Then what?"

The very thought sent hot needles of panic through my system. "I'll figure it out then. Right now I want to focus on saving the—"

"You heard what the lawyer said. Our odds are terrible. You need to face that and get a plan. I'd give anything to have my whole life in front of me like you do." She tapped her pen to Mrs. Hall's list. "What's really stopping you from going after this?"

"A lack of talent?"

"I've seen plenty of your high school productions. You've got something."

"I think they call it mediocrity."

"Well, if f fear is what's stopping you, it's a dumb excuse. When you get old like me, you realize how many chances you let pass you by because you were afraid—of looking stupid, of rejection, of failing. Take it from me, you've got more to lose by not giving this acting thing a shot than by going out there and falling on your face."

"I thought Mrs. Hall loved her teaching job."

"But she'll always wonder. What if she had tried to make it on Broadway? Where would she be now?"

"I've had my taste of it."

Loretta folded her arms on the table and leaned toward me. "And how was it?" She let that question soak in for a while. "How did you feel up there on that big stage in front of all those people? How did that applause sound?"

I could picture myself there. Standing in the spotlight. Delivering that first line.

Listening to the crowd laugh at my character's witty barbs.

"It's a high." I couldn't afford to recall every blessed nuance. "There's no feeling like it."

"You know what that sensation is?" Loretta asked. "It's what it feels like when you're doing exactly what you were put on this earth to do. Katie, if a dream grabbed you fiercely with its mighty teeth, then don't let it drop you. Don't let this go. Because nothing else will satisfy you. And if you think you're bitter now, you just wait until twenty years pass by. Because that bitterness only grows by the day. There's no greater waste than a life unfulfilled."

"I'm truly not good enough."

"Says who?"

"People who know what they're talking about."

"I want names."

I chuckled lightly. "I can give you names, newspaper reviews."

"You can't be a total genius right out of the chute. You got a lucky break getting that big role right out of school, but maybe it was too much too soon. Maybe what you need is practice. Experience. You think I could flip those omelets in the pan on the first try?"

"Yes."

"Okay, I could, but I'm just freakishly gifted." She chortled and swatted my arm with her big hand.

"I should get back to work." I stood and pushed in my chair.

"Katie?"

"Yes?"

"Your drama teacher?" Loretta pushed her pen back into her hair, and her gaze held no more teasing. "She bought a bus ticket to New York when she was seventeen. Our daddy found out and called her three kinds of a fool. Told her she was wasting her time, that few people would ever make it, and she wouldn't be one of them."

"Did she go?"

"No," Loretta said. "No, she didn't. She went to college and got married to the first boy who told her yes. But what if she'd gone?" The questions rang with a reverb in my ears. "What if she'd made it? What if she had followed her passion . . . instead of her fear?"

I didn't have the answers.

And I didn't know if I ever would.

Chapter Twenty

"HOW CAN I get married without a dress?" Frances asked when I met her at Vivi's after my shift for my very last fitting. "What kind of bride am I if I can't even make this simple decision?"

"Don't panic yet." There was no need. I was panicking enough for both of us.

"I've still got the one from that shop in Dallas, but it's not the one. Remind me never to get married again. I'm terrible at this."

"I'm sure it's the nerves. You have a lot going on all at once." I pulled open the heavy glass door and walked inside. "How's Joey holding up?" Let the record show I was trying. I wanted to like my best friend's future husband.

"He's great." Her forehead wrinkled in a rare-sighted frown. "But he still hasn't found a job in Cambridge. He's pretty worried about it."

"And you?"

"I'm a little concerned too. But it'll work out, right?"

"I'm sure it will." Even I could hear the doubt in my voice.

"Ladies, welcome back!" Vivi held out her arms like wings. "Your bridesmaid is here for her last fitting, correct?"

"Yes," I said.

"Excellent. Right this way." In a cloud of perfume, Vivi led me to the back where she retrieved the dress then guided me to a dressing room.

"I'm excited to see the gown again," Frances said.

Vivi pulled my door shut. "It's a lovely choice."

I shucked off my clothes, wishing I had thought to bring another shirt to change into. My Micky's Diner tee didn't seem quite worthy to be in the same store as thousand dollar dresses.

I had managed to remember to bring my special strapless bra that was a cruel form of torture no female should have to endure. I slipped it on, then zipped myself into the dress as far as I could.

I stepped out of the dressing room and onto the stage area in front of the three-way mirrors.

"Gorgeous!" Vivi exclaimed. She had pins stuck in a tomato-like cushion banded to her wrist like a watch. She pulled the zipper the rest of the way up, then walked a full circle around me and back again. "I think the length is just right, don't you?"

"It's perfect," Frances said, all traces of gloom gone.

I took a good look at myself in the mirror. The coral provided a nice contrast with my pale skin, but didn't clash too badly with my red hair. The bra, though about as comfortable as a corset, was padded enough to make my chest look almost impressive. The empire waist accented the hourglass shape I had yet to lose on Loretta's cooking, and the skirt fell in even, flowing pleats to the floor. I felt like a princess.

"What do you think, Katie?" Frances asked.

"I think it's just right." Nothing else in my life was—my relationship with Charlie, my career outlook, the fate of my Valiant. But this dress? "It's exactly how it should be."

Minutes later, Frances and I walked toward the register, Frances with her smile back in place, and me with the coral dress in a garment bag over my arm. We passed a wall of wedding dresses, one more beautiful than the other.

"Oh, look at this one." Frances stopped at a lace strapless gown. "She must've just gotten this one in. Do you like it?"

"It's very pretty." But an ivory A-line next to it caught my eye. My traitorous hands had a mind of their own and reached out to touch. It was total vintage chic. Sleeveless, but not strapless. Lace covering the satin bodice, with a tucked waist and a circular skirt that flared and stopped inches above the ankle. It wasn't a dress for a long veil; no, this one needed a pert little fascinator with netting that peeked out to cover the face. This dress wouldn't want to go to a formal church wedding, but rather a rustic setting, like a renovated barn or farm. Or my Valiant.

"Try it on." Frances lifted the dress from the rack. "Do it."

"No. Don't be silly."

"Come on. It'll be fun. It'll give you something to do while I'm trying this one." She handed me the gown. "You know you want to."

I did want to.

One more costume change later, I again stepped in front of the mirrors, only this time looking like a bride.

The dress was a size too large, but it was still a show stopper.

"My gosh, you're beautiful."

I looked up at the sound of the male voice, and the mirror showed Charlie standing behind me.

I turned around, slightly horrified. Who wore wedding dresses if they weren't a bride? Crazy people. The type who stalked men from the shrubbery and had a collection of restraining orders in their name. "I'm just killing time waiting for Frances."

But Charlie didn't look frightened. No, he looked. . .enchanted.

He came my way, his gaze taking in my every lacy part. He lifted my hand, then spun me in a slow turn, causing my heart to thud like a kick drum. "You should get that."

Every girl should be looked at like this once in their lives. Adoration. Admiration. Heat. Want. And something so much more.

"I should get this for my Friday night trips to the library?"

He kept my hand held lightly in his. "You're stunning, Katie."

My breath caught at the reverence in his voice. The warmth in his eyes. "This old thing?"

"Go out with me."

I blinked at the topic jump.

"Go out with me tonight. Just you and me. Forget everything that's going on. Forget how you want my head on a stake." Charlie drew his hand along the edge of the neckline. "I want to see you."

"I'm. . .I'm busy."

"Doing what?"

He had me so rattled, I couldn't even think of a good excuse.

"Well, hey, Charlie." Frances saved me from sputtering and joined us at the mirror. "That dress did not work at all. Way too poufy." She gave Charlie an enthusiastic hug. "What's my future brother-in-law doing here?"

Charlie seemed reluctant to take his focus off me, but he gave Frances an easy smile. "Picking up our ties. Joey got the wrong shade of pink, so Vivi had to order them for us."

"It's very sweet of you to do that for him." Frances grinned as she looked from me to Charlie, as if she had just happened upon a lovers' tryst. "All rightie then, I'm going to go up front and settle up. See you outside. Take your time. Talk as long as you want. I'm in *no* rush."

Frances all but frolicked away, leaving me standing before Charlie in a wedding dress that would belong to someone else. Someone who had her life figured out.

I took a small step back, my lips lifting in an embarrassed smile. "I probably smell like bacon and maple syrup."

There was that dimple in his left cheek. "Which makes you a man's walking fantasy."

Well, then.

He took a step closer, and the air around us seemed to still, like the electric pause before a warm summer storm. "You were saying we should go out tonight."

I strangely couldn't recall anything I'd uttered since waking. "I believe that was your idea."

He considered this as he reached for my hand again. "It was a good one."

"So wedding dresses do it for Charlie Benson."

"Just when Katie Parker's in them."

Reasons for not going anywhere with Charlie slowly began tapping on my conscience, whispering in my ear. "I should probably stay at home tonight. Get my plans finalized for Frances's bachelorette party." Work on my Thrifty Co. defense.

"You gotta eat. And I have it on good authority a number of your provisions got waterlogged."

"I can go to the grocery store. Eat the stuff Millie left for me in the freezer."

"Spinach casserole?"

"Don't forget her famous beet loaf."

"You hate that stuff."

"True. But—"

"I'll pick you up at eight."

"I didn't say I'd go."

He dared a quick kiss to my cheek, his lips lingering near my ear. "There will be pie."

"Make it seven-thirty."

Chapter Twenty-One

YOU'D HAVE THOUGHT it was my first date.

I spent the rest of the afternoon cleaning Millie's house until finally retreating upstairs to get away from the roar of the fans. Surely everything was dry now. And anything that wasn't had been ripped up to be replaced. The kitchen, dining, and living room looked like a battle zone. All because of one little water heater. James and Millie wouldn't be home for well over a week, and I couldn't wait. I was tired of our sporadic talks via their iffy internet connection, and if I ever needed their wise counsel, it was now.

The head-banging band of butterflies in my stomach seemed to have forgotten we'd been out with Charlie many times before.

Charlie.

The man who made me weak in the knees and inspired unbidden thoughts of my own walk down the aisle, a white picket fence, and children who had his dimples and skin that turned a nice tan in the sun.

Then there was the rising business executive. Who believed in a slash and burn approach to corporate expansion, with little care or thought to the lives left in the smoking ash. But what if he left the company? Was this thought dancing dangerously close to the *but I could change him* mentality that had ruined my bio-mom many times? I knew from her experience, the men never did change. You didn't bring them up; they could only drag *you* down. If Charlie stayed with

Thrifty Co., could I stand that? If we got together, how long before my resentment became a virus, a disease that took over, infecting every part of our lives?

My doorbell rang at seven-forty-five. I checked my appearance one more time in the mirror and was mildly satisfied. My hair piled on top of my head in a messy bun, with stray tendrils falling near my cheek. I wore dark jeans and flats, with a floral tank top that showed off the bit of muscle I had developed from heaving trays at Micky's. My lips shimmered with a shell pink gloss.

The bell rang again.

"Coming!" I scrambled down the stairs and opened the door. "I hope you brought the—"

"Hello to you too." Ian stood on my front porch, leaning one arm against the doorframe. "I love an enthusiastic welcome from a woman."

My face fell. "I thought you were Charlie."

"Ah, yes, your beloved. Your duplicitous, money-hungry beloved."

"I've shortened that endearment to sweetheart. Feel free to use it."

"Mind if I come in?"

"Yes."

"Invite me inside anyway."

"Pretty sure that's what Dracula said before sticking his fangs into his victims." I held open the door and gestured inside. "Be quick," I said as I led him past the first set of fans into James's office.

"I love what you've done with the place." Ian sat in James's overstuffed, comfy leather chair, his lean form not quite filling it the way Charlie had.

"Was there something you needed?" I made a point of glancing at my watch. "Charlie will be here soon."

"I've called and texted you a dozen times."

"I'm sorry." I settled into the chair opposite of Ian and ran my fingers over the faint scratches left like old love notes from the faithful dog our family had once loved and lost.

"If you had bothered to check your messages, you'd know that we have quite the opportunity. Paul Schmidt, a board member of the National Endowment of the Arts, wants us to join him on a podcast called *The Great White Way* out of New York."

"I've heard of it."

"It reaches over one-hundred thousand people world-wide. It's simply a matter of both of us calling in. It will air live, then be posted online for free download."

"The new attorney said your PR blitz was making an impact. Thrifty Co. offered everyone a new settlement."

"Are you taking it? Old theaters are a dying species. They should be used for their original intent, not to house local bands and antique stores. The Valiant is a work of art, and I've seen far too many theaters fall to—"

"We're not taking the offer. But the lawyer said our chances were not good."

"Then we'll keep fighting. Though I will be continuing the battle from my flat in Manhattan."

"You're leaving?"

He nodded. "Soon. The producers want me to wait until after your court appointment."

"To get the ending to their story."

"Yes. But I find myself wanting to see this through as well."

"And Felicity? What does she want?"

"She wants me in New York. Obviously she doesn't understand what I'm doing here."

"Yeah, but none of us do." Though I was through trying to make sense of it. I stood, and Ian followed suit. "I am grateful for the work you've done. Truly, it's made a difference."

He seemed pleased with this and was still smiling when he reached for my hand, halting me just before we left the room.

"You're really over me, aren't you?"

"You expected to find me regretting my hasty break-up and miserable without you?"

"I had hoped."

"You were right—we weren't in a good place even before you cheated."

"So this Charlie fellow has really won your heart, has he?"

Wasn't that the million-dollar question.

"I love him." I hadn't said it since the horrible flight out of Houston. But there it was, the truth that wouldn't leave me alone, wouldn't go away.

"You love him despite the fact that he works for the enemy? Even though he's a part of tearing down your Valiant and the businesses owned by your friends? Your town will never be the same when that store moves in. This idyllic community will just be another grave marker on the way to industrial spread."

A noise in the hall had us both turning.

There stood Charlie, flowers in hand, his face wiped of expression. How long had he been standing there?

"I knocked and nobody answered. So I let myself in." Like Charlie had done a hundred times before.

"I was just leaving," Ian said.

Charlie studied the two of us, close enough that suspicions could fit through the thin space between Ian and me. "Everything okay here?"

"Yes," I said. "Ian was giving me a progress report."

"On the Valiant." I had seen that look on Ian before. It was his director's face, the withering gaze he gave an actor when he'd committed a stupid, thoughtless mistake. "Your fiancée's family business. A precious treasure she's fighting to save. But I guess what she wants isn't your priority."

"Everything about Katie is my priority." Charlie straightened, drawing himself to his full height.

"Right." Ian did not back down, and doubt soured his features. "Because you're *engaged*."

"Yes." Charlie's eyes were fierce on mine, and his next sentence sliced clean through me. "She's the woman I'm going to marry."

The words were for Ian, but Charlie was sending the message straight to me.

"She may be the woman you're marrying, but at this time, she's the woman you're hurting. And I'm trying to help."

"I'm not going to explain my job to you, Attwood. I'm doing everything within my power to help."

"By lighting the match that burns her theater?"

"All right, gentlemen." There was so much truth to Ian's accusations. And yet here I was with Charlie. "Back to your corners, please. Ian, send me the details, and I promise to call in for that podcast. Charlie—" The man looked like he was ready to introduce his fists to Ian's face—"I heard dripping in the pantry. Would you please go check it out?"

Charlie hesitated, his jaw set, but with one final scorching look at Ian, he walked away.

"I'm sorry," Ian said as he made his way back to the front door. "I just see you with him and. . .I go a little nuts I guess. I can accept that you're done with me, but to see you with someone who hurts you—it's too much. You deserve better than that. You should be with someone who respects the things you're passionate about, who truly knows you."

Sticky humidity greeted me as I opened the door. "Goodnight, Ian. We'll talk tomorrow."

I watched him get into his rental car, then pull out of my drive. With a tired sigh, I walked back into the kitchen where I found Charlie leaned back against the granite countertop, his arms crossed across his chest, the discarded bouquet lying next to the microwave. "What are these?" He held up the printout of auditions from Mrs. Hall.

"Exactly what it looks like." I had come in from the garage this afternoon and thrown my purse and paperwork on the counter. "Why are you prowling through my stuff?"

"So these are theater jobs? They're dated. Do these come out every day?"

I simultaneously wished for this conversation to end and that the water hadn't ruined my hidden stash of Chips Ahoy. "Yes, there are websites you can check where shows post their jobs. It gives audition information. Mrs. Hall is apparently watching them for me. She thought I might be interested in a few."

"Are you?"

I wanted to. Part of me wanted to throw clothes in a bag and fly to New York right now. I missed the stage. My heart ached to perform, to step into the life of someone else. To be part of an ensemble that worked and surfed the ups and downs of show business together. "No. I'm not going to any of those auditions."

"I'll buy your plane ticket."

"I'm not going to New York."

"Chicago then."

"No." Anger swelled like a wave ready to crest. "Just drop it."

"Is it because you're afraid to fly? Because I'll drive you."

"Let's talk about that scene with Ian."

"I'd like to wipe the floor with his face. Is that what you'd like to discuss?"

"He's been a great source of help." Surprisingly so.

Charlie tossed the audition listings down. "Is there something going on between you two?"

"Of course not."

"It looked pretty intense when I walked in."

Because we had been talking about how I loved you, you idiot. "He's worried about me."

I expected that to relight his ire, but Charlie grew quiet. "I probably would be too," he finally said. "But hurting you is the last thing I want. I need you to believe that."

"I'm trying. The evidence is kind of stacked against you."

He snaked out a hand and pulled me to him. "I know things look bad."

"Things *are* bad."

"If you remember, on your second day back in In Between I asked you to trust me. I'm asking again. Thrifty Co. is an enormous company. And there are lots of players in this buyout game."

My hands pressed against his chest for balance. "What does that mean?"

"It means the business side you see is only part of it. There are lots of people involved, lots of stakeholders. I'm studying every angle. If I ever got confirmation of anything that could help you, I would."

"Does that mean you suspect you might be privy to some helpful intel?"

"It just means I'm not the heartless monster who wants to watch you and the others lose. I care about this town. I care about the girl who declared her love on a swan-diving plane then took it right back. I'll turn over every stone, but it's not that easy." He rested his head on mine. "It's just not that easy."

"Charlie—"

He silenced me with a kiss.

Charlie pressed me to him, and my hands slid to his back. There was no urgency. The kiss slowly unfurled, with feather-light touches meant to soothe and comfort, but they did so much more. My head filled with his scent, the heat of his skin radiating from beneath his shirt, the undeniable strength that was so much a part of him. When Charlie held me like this, the world slipped away, and all I knew was *right*. He felt like heaven.

He felt like home.

Charlie rained kisses along my cheek, then pressed his mouth to my temple. "I do have something to tell you."

"Something helpful?"

"Yes." He cocooned my body in a tight hug. "We're meeting Joey and Frances."

That was his news? "I thought it was just the two of us. I thought. . ." Anything that might've come out of my mouth at that point would just sound petty and pathetic.

"You thought we'd be alone?" I could feel his breathy laugh on my neck. "Why Miss Parker, I believe despite trying not to, you have the hots for me."

My mom had her addictions. Apparently Charlie was mine. "So we're going out with Frances and Joey."

"He drove in from Dallas this afternoon. He'll be here 'til the wedding."

"Great." I tried to sound enthused, but Charlie did not look impressed. "You might take this opportunity to talk to him about slowing things down."

"We Benson men don't do slow." Charlie tilted my chin with his finger and brushed his lips against mine. "We know what we want and don't stop until it's ours."

For a girl with too many scars from being left behind, his words were a balm on the old wounds that still festered and ached.

"Would it surprise you to know there's nothing dripping in your pantry?" His voice was dry as sandpaper.

My face was the vision of innocence. "I must've been hearing things."

"You sent me in here to cool off, didn't you?"

"Did it work?" Because my own temperature was definitely not dropping.

Charlie laughed as the tips of his fingers made looping figure eights on my back. "Babe, my brother knows what he's doing."

I closed my eyes at the endearment and held it like a keepsake "And you?"

Charlie's smiling mouth lowered. "I've got all I want right here."

Chapter Twenty-Two

BY THE NEXT evening, I had my entire life figured out.

Or at least the part concerning Charlie.

After working the morning shift at Micky's, I spent the rest of the day doing online, phone, and print interviews. With Ian's help, we had created a media hurricane, and the whole country was getting the message that Thrifty Co. was not the small town friend they pretended to be. Business owners from other communities who had fallen to Thrifty's powerful and persuasive bulldozing had jumped into the fray, adding more voices to our cry for justice.

I texted Charlie to tell him to put on something nice, that I was picking him up for dinner. And at six o'clock, wearing a midnight blue dress I had purchased on a whim in a little boutique in London, I pulled into his parents' driveway. My heels clicked on the pavement as I walked to the front door. I ran my tongue over my teeth to swipe away any stray lipstick and was about to ring the bell when I heard it. Loud shouts coming from within. I leaned closer to get a better listen.

"But I'm not you!" I recognized Charlie's deep voice.

"That much is clear! You do the job you were hired to do."

"And what about your job, Dad?"

"You stay out of mine. You're lucky to be where you are. In a matter of years, you'll be a vice-president. Don't screw that up!"

"You can't even be honest with me. Or yourself."

"I didn't get where I am by being soft and coddling." Mr. Benson accented his words with a pound to a wall or something hard. "The business world requires a steel backbone. You better find yours soon, or you're never gonna make it."

"Maybe I don't—"

Whatever Charlie said next drifted away as the two moved to a different part of the house.

Did I call Charlie? Text him to see if he still wanted to go out? Maybe just come back in an hour?

The door flew open, making my decision.

"You gonna stand out there all night?" Sadie Benson held an American Girl doll beneath her arm and aggressively chewed a piece of gum.

"Um. . ." I cleared my throat and put on a kindergarten teacher smile. "I was just about to ring your doorbell. Is Charlie home?"

She squinted one eye and tilted her head to the side. "Are you gonna marry my brother?"

This kid should never grow up to write romance novels. The couple would be swapping I Do's by page seven. "No, I don't think we're getting married any time soon."

"Mia Penbridge says when boys and girls kiss it means they're getting married."

"Mia should remember that and not kiss any boys until she's twenty-five. Did you say you'd get your brother?"

"Charlie says he's kissed you."

And why did he feel the need to share that information with a pint-sized psychotherapist? "And what else did Charlie say?"

"He said you were his—"

"Sadie." Charlie scooped up his sister and threw her over his shoulder like a sack of giggling potatoes. "Were you bothering Miss Katie?"

"She was about to tell me about some of your interesting conversations." I watched him kiss his little sister, and my heart doubled in size. "So far it's been very revealing."

"I seem to remember a pinkie swear not to repeat what we said." Charlie tickled his sister until she laughed even harder. "Need a reminder?"

"No!" she cried. "I remember. Mum's the word on our talks of Katie, things you buy me, and cookie stealing."

"That's right." He set her on her feet and gave her backside a pat, sending her running out of the room. "Well." Charlie's eyes lit on me. "Look at you."

I wore my hair down in relaxed waves tonight, though it was probably only a matter of time before I used the elastic on my wrist to bind my tresses into submission. My dress was a strapless number that had me back in that torture device of a bra. The full skirt made for spinning stopped just above my knee, with a layer of tulle to give it some bounce, while a thick ribbon wrapped around my waist and tied in a fat bow.

"You look devilishly handsome yourself," I said. Charlie wore a dark three-piece suit, complete with a very British looking vest, a pale pink shirt, and a maroon tie. Tortoise shell glasses poised on his straight nose, making him the model of intellectual chic. He looked dashing and sexy, and like he might jump into a phone booth and fly out a super hero. "New specs? I've never seen them before."

"Contacts are messed up. Besides I thought it would make me a little incognito when we went out on the town. That way no one's throwing tomatoes at our table."

With the way he looked, they'd probably be throwing their knickers at our table.

"Everything okay?" I looked past Charlie into the foyer.

"Yes, of course."

"Shall I go in and say hello to the family?"

Charlie patted his chest pocket to locate his phone then hastily closed the door behind him. "You can see them at the rehearsal dinner." When I lifted a questioning brow, he pulled me to him and kissed me. "I don't want to waste a minute of tonight."

Good answer.

Though things were clearly wrong between him and his father.

"I'll drive." I pulled him away from his car and toward mine.

Charlie opened my door before getting into the passenger side.

"I'm intrigued," he said as we drove down the street. "Where are we going in our finest?"

"A wonderful place. Very fancy."

"Do I know this spot?" He reached for my right hand sitting on the armrest and clasped it in his.

"I don't think you do." I turned onto Smith Street. "But it's got quite the reputation. Pretty elite."

A few minutes later, I pulled the car right in front of the entrance of the Valiant Theater.

Charlie had gone quiet in the last minute, figuring out exactly where we were bound.

"Katie—"

"No, hear me out." I put the car in park and let the air conditioning cool my flushed skin. A lot was riding on tonight, and my nerves were as frazzled as Kourtney with a K's dead ends. "I know this is considered enemy territory for you right now." I stared up at the impressive building, loving the welcoming hello of the old marquis. "But I'm asking you to come inside. It's just you and me and the supper I made in the basket sitting on my backseat."

He reached around and lifted the basket. "You made this?"

"That's what Loretta told me to say." I slapped his hand away from the lid. "She fixed it herself."

"I thought she hated me."

"She doesn't hate you, Charlie. She may not like the decisions you're making or your current job, but you're still one of our own." Plus I'd made her swear on her Miss Clairol that she hadn't spit in his fried chicken.

"I'm still an employee of Thrifty Co."

"Not tonight." I opened my door and stepped outside. "Tonight you're just Charlie Benson, hometown boy, and the sexiest date I've ever had." I held out my hand.

And waited.

Charlie looked at the building before him. He'd been to the Valiant so many times, but this evening I wanted him to see it with new eyes.

He took my hand and kissed my fingers, his heavy-lidded gaze on me. "What are you up to, Parker?"

My skin tingled at his touch. "I'm hurt you would even feel the need to ask."

"You're related to Maxine. Sam's already warned me of my fate."

I wondered at the permanence of that statement, but led Charlie into the theater, locking the doors behind us. The lights glowed inside, and we ventured past the lobby.

"This is our lobby."

He laughed. "I know that."

"F.D.R. stopped here on his campaign trail for his first presidency. His slogan was 'Happy days are here again,' and he thought the Valiant captured that spirit." We took a few steps. "In 1954 the Valiant underwent a little renovation, but forgot to tell one small act they'd booked. That man showed up to sing, and when he couldn't get to the stage, he put on a show right here in this very lobby. Nobody in town had ever seen moves like his before."

"And who was it?" Charlie smiled indulgently.

"A virtually unknown talent out of Mississippi named Elvis Presley."

Charlie was wary, but that little tidbit should've impressed anyone with a pulse.

With Charlie's fingers linked through mine, I pulled him to the corner by the concession area. "Did you know that Millie makes James buy a special organic blend of kernels for the popcorn machine? She's never told anyone about it, but she says you can taste the difference over that GMO stuff. People stop in here on event nights just to purchase the buttery popcorn."

"They get it to go?"

"And right where you're standing is an important spot in the Valiant history."

"Some famous actor stood here?"

"No." I took his other hand. "You did. Christmas our senior year, the Valiant's annual community Christmas party. Do you remember?"

His smile spread. "I kissed you here."

"And blamed it on the mistletoe."

"Want to relive the moment?" Charlie ran his thumb over my bottom lip. "Maybe this time your crazy neighbor won't interrupt and threaten to make a citizen's arrest."

"Would've been worth it." I gave him a quick kiss, then escorted him through the double doors. "And here we have the main theater. Those box seats over there are good for more than just making out during a slow third act. They had totally gone to rot over the years before James and Millie bought the place. My parents searched for an expert to restore what was left of the plaster facade, but couldn't find anyone in the state. Then one day John Carter knocked on James's office door. He'd lived in In Between all his life. His wife had died in the last year. He'd lost his job, and he wanted the work. James gave it to him." The suspended seating areas were now a crowning jewel in the theater. "Mr. Carter told Millie just this year that the job had been his last hope. He'd lost everything until the Valiant. Now he's so in demand, he's had to hire help."

"This way, please." I crooked my finger and Charlie followed me to the first row, center stage. "We have four hundred seats of very cushy padding, and while the upholstery is about seven years old, the color is authentically matched to the original fabric. When the theater was vandalized after I came here, many of the seats were ripped to shreds, and Sam Dayberry taught me how to wield a staple gun and upholster. I love how every row has a supporting family's name on it."

"I'm not new to the place, Katie." He seemed to be losing his enthusiasm for my tour.

"But this one means the world to me. This one is for my family. When James and Millie showed me my name was on it, I burst into tears. Even though I had been with the group who tore this facility apart, James and Millie still claimed me. I was their new foster kid, but this was their way of saying I would always have their support. And their name."

"They were crazy about you from the beginning." Charlie slid his hand up the side of neck. "I think we all were."

I could've stood there and drowned in his gray eyes, or I could've kept moving and gotten to the main event.

I chose to move.

Climbing the steps to the stage still set up for the summer production, I located the spot on the black wooden floor where it was slightly faded, where the spotlights converged on center stage. "This is where I found. . ." I breathed in the scent of the memory, the powerful hold on my heart still so strong. "Where I found my life. My first role as Juliet, and I stood right here. Got my first standing ovation."

"I remember," he said.

It felt right to share this space with him now. "After that first show, I knew this was what I wanted to do." My eyes misted with tears. "This was church to me. Where God spoke and moved. Where I was the best version of me."

"It's also where I first kissed you."

"The night before I had gone back to my bio-mom's house." I hadn't known if I'd ever return to In Between. "And you told me you were sorry you'd let me go."

"Then I righted the wrong." Charlie reached for me and tucked me into his arms. My own arms around his waist, I rested my head on his vested chest and listened to the cadence of his heart.

"I'd waited forever for you to kiss me." And he finally had, at my going away party the Scotts had thrown. I'd been blown away by the huge turnout—friends, teachers, church family, and community members. But after a few hours, I'd stolen away behind the curtains of the stage, needing a quiet moment alone. "And you found me." And once again it was the stage, Charlie, and me. "Charlie?"

He looked down into my shimmering eyes and gently wiped a tear away. "Yes?"

"I love you."

Chapter Twenty-Three

I HAD JUST declared my love—again.

And Charlie was still as the statue of Apollo in the Louvre.

It was not the response I was going for.

Maybe he didn't believe me. "Charlie, when I thought we were dying on that plane, and I said those words, I meant them. It wasn't just adrenaline or our impending demise. I have never stopped loving you. Even Ian saw that." I watched Charlie's eyes soften, and I took heart. "I love your strength, your kindness, your faith, and even your weird addiction to all things sports."

I pressed my hand to Charlie's cheek, and he covered it with his.

"I adore watching you with your little sister, the way you treat your mother, and how hard you work. You've seen me at my best and my worst, but you've always been behind me like a protector. I feel safe with you. I don't want that to be so important, but it is." I was rambling. Babbling like a drunk sorority girl at a rush party. "Say something. Please." I had just reached into my own chest cavity, dug out my bleeding, beating heart, and asked him to take it. Why was he just standing there?

"You know how I feel about you." The words tore from his lips like they pained him to say.

"No, I really don't think I do." I had been so certain I did. But everything about this was so off-script. I had rehearsed this evening a dozen times in my mind, and now every page, every line was so dreadfully wrong.

"I would give you the world if I could." Charlie's hand dropped to his side. "But you didn't just ask me here tonight to tell me how you felt. Did you?"

"I don't understand." I was suddenly cold, as if I were standing there naked in front of him. Stripped and vulnerable.

"Was there anything else you wanted to ask me, Katie?"

That bleeding heart shuttered to a stop. "Yes," I whispered. "I wanted you to see my theater. Really see it."

"I do."

"Do you?" My volume escalated to the lights above us.

Charlie took a step away from me, and that bloom of hope within me wilted. "I see you in every brick and board in this whole building. I see this place in my dreams every night—with a vision of you *crying* because I can't do anything to save it."

"If I have to lose the Valiant, I don't want to lose you as well."

"Say it, Katie. Let's just get it out there."

I sniffled and wished he had offered the words himself. "Quit working for Thrifty Co. Walk away from them, Charlie."

He muttered a curse and began to pace a path around the stage. Loretta's picnic basket of chicken and all the fixings grew cold on their spot by the first row. Dinner would not be happening.

Not while Charlie walked the length of the stage, his face taut with frustration.

Charlie's temper had always had a long fuse, but tonight it was sizzling to the quick. "You've lived your whole life playing it safe," he said. "Your mom was the wild child. *She* was the one you couldn't depend on. But not you. And now you want every thing to be a sure bet before you even consider attempting it. Me. Your career."

"There is no career."

"Because you won't even try! You go out of your way to not be like Bobbie Parker, but you're living half a life in the process. You're going to die here in In Between if you stay."

"*I* love this town!"

"God gave you this incredible talent to entertain, to act, to bring stories alive, and what are you doing with it?"

"At least I'm not hurting people with my career choice."

"What are you doing with it?" he demanded.

"I'm not good enough, Charlie."

"Because Ian said so?"

"College is over. I'm no longer the star of campus, and I have to face that reality."

"You dumped Ian. He would've said anything to hurt you. He *knew* that was your Achilles heel. You have zero faith in yourself or your ability." *Or me.*

He didn't say it, but it was there.

"My stage career is over."

"Because you're scared. What happens when you wake up twenty years from now, and you're still here in Texas, going through the motions of some job just to pay the bills?"

"You have no inkling what it's like to stand on that stage every night at the mercy of your audience's judgment. What it's like to step into a part so big, it's survived centuries, and you're some kid from small town, Texas. You can't begin to imagine what it's like to hear all the voices in your head, louder than my own voice delivering my lines. Those voices that say I can't do it. That I'm on borrowed time, and soon they're all gonna know I can't act. And that the only reason I'm there is because I caught the director's eye. Or what it's like to finish your scene, high on adrenaline, only for your director to cut you down, tell you every single thing you did wrong. Constantly telling you it's not good enough." My mascara had to be black rivulets streaking my face by now, but it felt good to open that festering sore and let it bleed out. "You want to know the truth? I knew from the beginning why I had the part. Maybe I even led Ian on."

"You wouldn't have."

"Yes, Charlie. I would have. Because I was desperate to get that role. . . desperate to be somebody."

"You are somebody."

"I flirted with him 'til I got his attention, until he was intrigued enough to give me a shot. I just wanted one chance to show him I had what it takes. One try to be the understudy." Then the lead.

"He wouldn't have given you the part if you hadn't earned it."

"But I didn't have enough talent to keep it. And I still don't."

"How do you know?"

"Broadway is for the Julliard graduates. Not for the daughter of Bobbie Ann Parker. I tried, I failed. I'm done. You can only fall on your face so many times before you have to be honest with yourself. I don't want to go to Manhattan and wait tables until I'm sixty because I'm still trying to get my foot in the door at the Gershwin."

"So you're gonna wait tables here instead."

I lifted my chin and dared him to contradict me. "I'm going to run the Valiant."

"And if it's not here?"

"Can you tell me for certain it won't be?"

"I can't tell you anything. I want to," he quietly admitted. "But I can't."

"You won't."

He slammed his hands into his pockets and studied the floor for long, agonizing moments before slowly lifting his head. "I'm not quitting my job right now."

"Then when?" But I knew the answer now. It was never. It was job first, like his father.

It felt silly to stand on the stage in the midst of this life-altering conversation with the *Sound of Music* set behind us. How do you solve a problem like. . .me?

"I asked you to trust me." Charlie yanked on the knot of his tie, loosening it with a few harsh tugs.

"How can I do that when you're a part of this company? This theater is part of my family. For a time in my life, it was all I had. It *saved* me. Do you get that? I probably wouldn't be here today if I hadn't met the Valiant. I'd be in prison or dead. But I sure wouldn't be where I am now."

"And where you are is asking me to just quit my job and go do something else. Like it's that easy."

"I didn't say it would be easy. I think I know a little bit about job transitions."

"Really? Because I don't see you transitioning to one."

That icy dagger stabbed right through me. "Not all of us are born with family connections or this genius talent. Some of us have to work our butts off to get even one rung up the ladder."

"I work very hard. I work day and night, trying to keep my head above water, while dodging hate mail from the neighbors, and attempting not to break your heart."

"Is that what you're doing right now? Trying not to break my heart?"

Charlie scrubbed his hands over his face. "I can't give you what you want."

"I'm not talking about business." The pitiful words gathered in my throat and danced on my tongue. I hated them. I hated every one of them, but I spit them out anyway. "I told you I loved you. . .and you said nothing."

"I can't be the man you want right now."

"The one who can leave a job that makes him miserable and do the right thing? You're not willing to take that risk for us? You, who keeps telling me to get on a plane to New York?"

"Loving you has always been a risk," Charlie said. "But you don't trust me right now, and I don't trust tonight's declaration. Twice you've told me you've loved me, and both times in a moment of desperation. What about on the average day when you have nothing to gain? Let's say I was able to stop the Valiant from going down. Would you still be there when it was over? Because anytime someone gets too close, you take off."

"That's not true. I was with Ian for nearly a year."

"He's got temporary written all over him. I have no doubt you knew that from the first date. You knew he wasn't the type to put a ring on your finger, so less risk for you. What about our freshman year of college? I told you I loved you, and you disappeared. I didn't hear from you again until . . . when was it? When was it, Katie?"

On a plane ride from Chicago to Houston.

"It took you four years to say you loved me back, and only then under the threat of death. So you wonder why I haven't said the words to you? Because you can't take them." His booming voice echoed throughout the theater. "And because I don't want you to leave again."

Tears fell unchecked down my cheeks. "I didn't run from you."

"Why don't we finally talk about that last night I saw you."

"Just stop." It was old history. Dark ghosts of memories that haunted me when I was too worn down to lock those doors.

"Freshman year. February."

"I don't need to hear this story again."

"You didn't even bother calling me with the news. Frances did."

My mother had died.

She was gone.

And I had spent two days throwing up until there was nothing left but bile.

Bobbie Ann Parker had always made a game of leaving me, but that time, she'd really outdone herself. She wasn't coming back. I'd known her life was one big walk on the ice pond, and it was only a matter of time before it would crack and she'd fall in. But when the police had come to our door and given me the news, I'd dropped to the floor, tearless. Numb. Emptied of all words. My mom had chosen heroin over me.

"You were in Chicago," I said. "It wasn't like you were a few hours away."

"I would've traveled across the globe to get to you."

I swallowed back tears. "I didn't want to bother you."

"You didn't need me."

"No." I shook my head, my vision blurring. "I needed you more than I could stand. It was all just too much. My mom, the funeral. . .you."

"Two a.m., and I'm driving through town, and whose car do I see at the Valiant?" Charlie's voice tendered. "When I walked inside, I found you sitting in that front row seat, holding your head in your hands."

I was right back there. Loss. Unbearable loss that I hadn't expected to feel.

"I could hear you praying."

I squeezed my eyes shut, desperate to shut off this memory. I never wanted to think about those days again. I tried not to think about her.

I hadn't shed one tear for my mom. Hadn't seen her in years, but the guilt had eaten at me all the same. What if I could've helped her? And what if I grew up to be her?

I'd sat in the Valiant for hours that night. Alone.

And then Charlie appeared like an angel of mercy.

He'd hugged me, wrapped his arms around me just like he'd done on the plane, covering my body as if to keep away any more harm.

Then I'd lost it.

My heart exploded and I convulsed in sobs, sinking to the floor of the Valiant, taking Charlie with me. Sitting there, he'd held me, murmuring soft words, praying, and giving me moments of silence with my own terrible thoughts.

And saying the one thing I hadn't been prepared to hear.

"Do you remember what I told you?" Charlie now asked.

"Yes." He'd said he loved me.

"And what did you do?"

It had been a stupid mistake. I had been young, shattered.

"You pulled away from me," Charlie said. "Ran out of the theater like I had struck you. And you never looked back. So you want to know why I haven't said the words, Katie?" His question was a land mine, and I was about to step right on it. "Because I'm afraid you'll run again. That's what you do."

"I'm not running this time."

"And what if I don't quit Thrifty Co.? Will you still love me then? Because tonight it seems like it has to be a package deal."

I wanted both—Charlie *and* my theater. Was that asking too much? "You're going to choose this job over us?"

"You don't know what you're asking right now."

"Then tell me!"

"I can't."

"If you truly cared for me, you'd do something. Anything to save my Valiant." I clamped my hands over my mouth, appalled those words had just taken on a life of their own. "I didn't—"

"There it is. That condition." I hated that acidic laugh that came from Charlie's lips. "Well, that's not how love works. It's not something you earn or work for to keep. It doesn't come with conditions and hoops to jump through. I'm not my dad, and you're sure not you're mother. And I'm not playing this game. But you want the words, Parker? Because I wouldn't want to leave you hanging."

Suddenly I didn't think I did. I couldn't bear to hear his disappointment.

His regret.

"I'm done with conversation," I said.

But Charlie wasn't.

"I've always loved you." He said it like the admission was a crime that would lead him to the gallows. "When I held you the night of your mom's funeral, I knew that as long as I lived, I would never feel for anyone else what I felt for you. Whether you'd ever admit it, you needed me. I wanted to protect you from every hurt, every tear. And when I saw you in the Houston airport, last month, I think I stopped breathing."

His leather dress shoes clicked on the hardwood floor as he walked to the edge of the stage and looked out into rows of empty seats. "The plane was going down, and I had you beneath me. Safe. Then we hit another air pocket, and I lost my hold. That's when you were hit. . .and for a few blinding seconds, I thought you were gone. You were completely out, and there was all this . . . blood." It was an anguished man who turned back to face me. "We were dropping fast, and it was just chaos. But I grabbed you, pulled you to me. And when I felt your chest rise and fall . . . I started breathing again. Because I didn't care if we were both going down on that plane, Katie." Charlie pressed his hand to his breast pocket, as if the heart beating beneath it ached. "I just didn't want to go without you."

For every tear I dashed away, five more took its place.

I wanted out of here now. I had to get out of this building. The urge to run—that black, hissing presence in my head—screamed for me to bolt.

Get out of here.

Leave him.

You will never have what you want.

You're unsafe here. I'll keep you sheltered.

But run!

"I know I'm asking for the impossible," Charlie said. "I'm asking you to trust me through this buyout. But I need to know you're going to be there when the dust settles, no matter what's left in the end. I'm asking you to take that risk. Whether it makes sense, whether it looks like you will get your happy ending or not—take that risk. Love *me*, Katie Parker."

There weren't a thousand uncertainties.

Only two.

Either Charlie was enough. . .or he wasn't.

I could put my hand in his forever and step over that precipice, not knowing where we'd land.

Or I could walk away.

From a man who couldn't give me any guarantees. Couldn't even give me all the answers.

And spend the rest of my life searching for someone who could.

On weak, shaking legs, I walked to Charlie, stopping mere inches before him. I took one good hard look at my theater, the place that had been my life support. God's mercy breathed into every nail and surface.

"I'm sorry." Reaching out my hand, I caressed his stubbled cheek one final time. "It's just not enough."

Chapter Twenty-Four

"**I**'M AS NERVOUS as the day I first took the stage at Circus Circus."

Maxine sat in the backseat of Loretta's minivan and powdered her nose for the third time. "What do you think that judge will say?"

A light mist peppered our vehicle as we drove to Mills Creek, the county seat and home of the dreaded courthouse. I traced a finger across the window, chasing the path of a raindrop caught in the wind. Conversation had been flying around me for a good half hour, but I hadn't caught a word. My eyes stung from crying in sporadic fits all night, and all I wanted to do was curl up in a ball and sleep for a thousand days.

Maxine nudged me with her bony elbow. "I said, what do you think the judge will have to say?"

"I'm not sure."

"Would you like to borrow some lipstick?" Maxine dug into her trendy leather bag and offered one of her favorites.

"No." I hadn't bothered with makeup this morning, and my eyelids were as swollen and fluffy as one of Loretta's omelets. Eyeliner would've been impossible to apply, eye shadow had been more effort than I could expend, and mascara would've just been something smeared on my pillow when I returned to my bed.

Maxine patted my knee and rested her head on my shoulder. I sat to her right, squeezed in between her and Dana Lou Tanner, who was taking up more than her fair share of seat space, while Betty McAnally of Betty's Hair Salon, rode shotgun. Behind our van, Mr. and Mrs. Foster drove in the pink Cadillac Seville she'd won thirty years ago selling makeup. Mr. Gleason and three other townsfolk rode in his dusty Ford pickup, with Mr. Henry and Mrs. Virgie Higgins bringing up the rear. We were a caravan of misfits, each of our vehicles stocked with an abundant supply of Loretta's coffee, fear, and anger.

Unable to face an empty, lonely house last night after dropping Charlie off at his home, I'd gone to Maxine's. She'd taken one look at me standing beneath her porch light and hugged me 'til my body warmed and the jagged sobs had abated.

She'd put on a pot of coffee, and we sat at her kitchen bar talking until I was all wrung out. Then we'd adjourned to her living room, huddled together on the couch beneath one blanket and binge watched some *Golden Girls*. Maxine had fallen asleep four episodes in, but I had stayed awake, alternately crying and trying in vain to get some rest.

Because I knew I needed it for this day. I needed to be sharp, on my guard, with a fully functional brain.

I was definitely on my guard, but the other things weren't even in the realm of possibility.

"You're going to be okay," Maxine whispered. "It's not over 'til it's over."

How wrong she was. Charlie and I were beyond done.

And I wasn't too sure about the fate of the Valiant as well. And if there was no Valiant, what in the world was I going to do about a job?

"Sure you don't want my lipstick? It's called *Revenge Red*."

"No, thank you." But if she had any *Boys Are Stupid* or *Not Enough Ice Cream To Fix This*, then I'd paint it all over my face.

With a shrug of defeat, Maxine retrieved her mirror and applied another coat herself. "Well." She shut her compact with a snap. "I

191

didn't want to put this out there, but these are desperate times. If things go south, I am not above seducing that judge with my feminine wiles." She pushed up her girls and sniffed. "Let's be honest, I just have a way with men. I don't question it; it just is."

Loretta caught my eye in the rearview. "Aren't we lucky to have you and your hooters in our arsenal."

"If I had a dollar for every time I heard that." Maxine straightened the scarf around her neck.

"Ladies, if we don't get good news today, I don't know how much longer I can hold out," Loretta said. "A year's worth of attorney fees is really hurting us. My Milton retired last year, and he's begging me to take the deal and enjoy our golden years together. Buy that RV and travel. See the grandkids whenever we want instead of being tied to the diner."

"This is crazy talk," Maxine said. "We must keep plodding on. My Millie will be crushed if she loses her theater. Not to mention Katie here." Maxine patted my hand. "Of course she'll be going to New York soon to make a name for herself and getting so famous she becomes snooty and uppity and too good to talk to us and gets one of those passies like Beyonce."

"Posse," I said.

Maxine snorted. "Well, I can see the uppity's already hit. Dana Lou, what about you? You're hanging in there, right?"

Dana Lou considered her answer for the duration of the country song quietly seeping from Loretta's speakers. "I don't know," she finally said. "The legal fees are starting to scare me. I lay awake so many nights." Loretta nodded her black head in agreement. "I just worry about winning the case, but losing everything I have over the cost of the fight. And like you said, Loretta, maybe it's time to retire."

"You're fifty-five," Maxine said. "You're young, like me. That's too soon to hit the rocking chair."

"I don't want a rocking chair," Dana Lou said. "But do you know because of my bakery, Max and I have only had two vacations our whole married life? And one of those was to go pick up new cash registers in Dallas. I could sleep in on a Saturday morning."

"Not get coiled as a rattle snake every quarter when it's time to pay taxes," Loretta added.

"Oh, yeah," Betty said dreamily. "Not worry about how we're gonna pay for health insurance for employees or who's gonna cover when someone doesn't show up."

"Now, stop it," Maxine said. "There are wonderful reasons to fight this and keep your businesses. In Between needs you."

"There are reasons," Loretta said. "But they're getting dimmer by the day."

"But if you guys sell out, then that will just leave us," I said. I was on a derailing roller coaster, my stomach turning over and over with nothing to hold on to and control slipping away. We couldn't do battle Thrifty Co. alone.

"No matter what happens, we've fought the good fight." Loretta flicked on her blinker then turned to the street leading to the county courthouse. "It's in God's hands. We just have to trust that we've done all we can do." She whipped the van into a parking spot, and everyone unbuckled like we were reporting to the front lines of combat.

"Why don't we say a little prayer?" Dana Lou suggested.

So right there in Loretta's Chevy minivan, with the air conditioning blasting full speed and George Strait crooning about Amarillo, Loretta prayed.

" . . . and give us the grace to know when to let go and the wisdom to accept the right choice. Amen."

I nodded. "Amen."

"Amen," said Betty.

"Ladies"—Maxine undid the top two buttons on her blouse, revealing cleavage and a cross—"Lock and load."

LIKE A DEER looking up seconds before the trigger was pulled, I felt Charlie's gaze on me before I spotted him in the room. Surely one day that sensory awareness of his presence would fade.

We filed into the courthouse, only to be directed to a room three doors down from the courtroom. The building had been erected sometime in the early 1900s, and it appeared as if this room had seen few renovations since. Faded wood paneling lined the walls, and the little circle tiles beneath our feet were in sad need of grout.

Our new attorney David Stephens greeted us, and our group surrounded him like a football team in need of the coach's pep talk.

"Good day to you all," Stephens said. He wasn't already sweating, cursing, or consulting some college textbook, so he was already better than the previous lawyer. He again walked us through what to expect, his voice kind and reassuring. I hoped we were more than just dollar signs and free burgers at the diner.

"Please come in." Judge Hollister, foregoing the robe for khakis and a polo, gestured to three mahogany tables forming a u-shape. "Do sit down."

Charlie intercepted me as I walked toward our table. "Katie." He seemed to struggle with what to say. I kind of struggled not to bloody his nose.

Seeing him and getting that fresh reminder that he worked for Thrifty Co. was like holding a can of AquaNet to the flames of my ire. The enemy employed Charlie. And Charlie had chosen his company over me.

"No matter what happens today, I want you to know I'm sorry. For whatever the rest of this process brings. . .I'm sorry."

I didn't trust myself to speak.

So I simply looked away.

"Let's all take a seat, shall we?" The judge gestured to the metal chairs that looked like they'd just been dragged off the lawn of the county fair—the silver, fold-up variety used for events when you weren't really trying to impress. Like now. "I'd like to introduce the three gentlemen on the special commission." He fired off their names, and two of the men gave polite smiles, while the third couldn't seem to make eye contact. "Now per the state law, these three have no dog in this fight, but do own land in the county. They've reviewed the case, reviewed the offers, and they are ready to present their decision. Their decision is legal and binding, but of course, you can appeal." He spoke to our table of In Betweenites. "If you do appeal, this goes to a jury trial."

Beside me Betty groaned and Loretta just shook her head. While the judge continued to talk, Charlie and his boss consulted with their legal team. Our lawyer seemed to have his wits and then some, but he wasn't a team. Thrifty Co. came with a group of attorneys in dark suits that reminded me of the mafia. Everything about them was fancy, from their tailored attire to their polished leather shoes. They spoke in hushed tones and occasionally stole glances our way. If they were trying to intimidate, they were doing a fabulous job.

"I'll just get out of the way and let the special commissioners get to the business at hand." The judge threw up his hand in a kind wave, then walked out the door.

Maxine stared toward the door, her face scrunched into a frown. "He didn't even look my way."

"You're thirty years older than him," I whispered.

She looked at her chest. "Not all of me is."

The man introduced as Mr. Spellman stood up. "Thank you for coming. We know this is a difficult situation, and we don't want to drag this out any more than it already has been. We have spent many hours studying the documentation, and we feel confident we have made the best decision for your town."

Maxine reached beneath the table and slipped her hand into mine.

"We believe the town of In Between has proven the addition of Thrifty Co. on the requested property will benefit your community economically and progressively and find in their favor."

Our table exploded into gasps and protests, and the man paused to let the shock settle in. We were going to court. It was the last thing I wanted. And I didn't even know if the other businesses would continue in the lawsuit.

"We understand the first offers for buyouts were declined," said Mr. Spellman. "Citizens of In Between, do you still stand by that decision?"

"Yes," I said. "We do not accept their offer."

"Thrifty Co., do you have anything to add?"

Charlie's boss Mr. McKeever stood and addressed our table. He wore a fitted pin-stripe suit, a smile meant to calm, and teeth too white and straight to be real. "We'd like to submit a final offer to you folks."

"We're not interested," I said.

Loretta planted her elbows on the table and leaned in. "What kind of offer?"

McKeever lifted his chin in a curt nod, and Charlie stood.

"I'd be glad to explain that." Charlie smoothed his tie and approached our table. It hurt to look at him. "We have a settlement we think will be much more to your liking." Charlie handed each member a manila folder, and when he got to me, our eyes met . . . locked . . . held.

How could you do this? I wanted to ask. My heart was somewhere on the floor, and he and his cronies were walking all over it.

"Oh, my," said Mrs. Gleason.

Beside her Mr. Henry gave a low whistle.

With a shaking hand, I opened the folder. And saw enough zeroes to know it was over.

"Your property and businesses mean a lot to you," Charlie said. "And we realized our initial two offerings didn't honor that. We consider this our first investment in the community we're excited to be a part of."

I knew Charlie had somehow gotten us more money. He'd said he was trying to help, and this was obviously the end-product of all those late hours he'd put in.

It was the last thing I wanted.

"My clients will need to discuss this," our attorney said. "And I'll need time to thoroughly study the new proposal."

"You have ten days," Charlie said. "Then we'll need to know an answer."

"But please keep in mind your alternative," Mr. McKeever said. "A trial is a lengthy and costly experience. We employ over a hundred people on our legal team. They're some of the best minds in the nation."

"You need to ask yourselves if you're prepared to pay for legal counsel another six months," Charlie said. "Or even two or three years."

McKeever put his easy going grin back on. "But spend some time with those numbers. Could it change your life? Could it make all your money worries disappear? Please give it some thought." And then he went in for the kill. "We truly want you to be happy. In Between will be our home. And we want you to be a part of our success. We hope you find our check generous. Because we care about this town. And we care about you."

"You care about your bottom line. We're just a check to you. A drop in the bucket compared to what you'll make over the lifetime of your store." I stood to my feet, my heart thudding so loud, I could hardly hear my own voice. "You care about us? What about my theater? It's an Art Deco architectural work of art that's irreplaceable. Can you bring plays to this town? A beautiful location for entertainers or guest speakers?" My words caught in my throat. "Can you change lives like that place changed me?"

"Katie—"

"No, Charlie." I held out my hand to hold off his advance. "How can you take that from me? You can't find any other property in this entire town to build on? It's that important to you? Years ago my parents restored that building from the shell that it was as a beacon to their lost daughter Amy. Then it found me instead. And saved me." Tears slid down my cheeks like rivulets of rain. "Don't take it. I'm begging you, don't take my theater."

"I'm sorry, Miss Parker Scott," said Mr. McKeever. "I think you'll find our offer to be incredibly generous. Your parents will have enough money to rebuild, most likely even retire."

"You don't get it." I hated them. I hated this company and everything they stood for, every treacly word coming from their truth-spinning lips. "I hope one day someone puts a price on something you love." I locked my cold eyes on Charlie. "And I hope you watch it ripped from your hands, your life. Then you tell me how much that precious check really means." I picked up the financial offer, lifted it high.

And ripped it to shreds.

I watched it fall to the floor like confetti from the devil's hands.

As I charged out the room and out into the sunlight, I knew there would be no chance at an appeal. There would be no trial.

My Valiant was gone.

Chapter Twenty-Five

"**I** HAVE MY dress," Frances announced the next Friday night at her rehearsal.

We gathered in the sanctuary, waiting for all the family and wedding party to show up. So far we were still lacking a groom and his brother.

I tried to keep my eyes off the door. "The one from Dallas?"

"No, I'm wearing my mother's dress."

"The giant, eighties poufy thing you hated?"

"No, my mom's cheongsam. It's a traditional Chinese dress she wore right after her ceremony. Her grandmother bought it for her and had it shipped to the United States."

"I think that's perfect."

"It's red. It's going to clash horribly with your dress."

I smiled at my friend. "Nobody's going to be looking at me."

"My mom broke out her old sewing machine, and we let out a few seams and secured some buttons. I'd fought it, but when I tried it on, it was just . . . right. It was that feeling I'd been looking for. None of the others made me feel like a bride."

"Sounds like everything is in place."

She took a few deep breaths, as if the air around her bridal head was too thin. "We're going to try and wrap up tonight early. I still have so much to do, and you really look like you could use the sleep."

Translation: You look terrible enough to scare small children, and I only want happy tears at this wedding.

The doors to the sanctuary opened, and in walked a smiling Joey and Charlie, who looked like someone had just run over his dog.

Good. I hoped he felt as miserable as I did. I hoped it haunted him for the rest of his excessively handsome life. I hadn't seen or talked to Charlie in a week. One long week of anger and what-ifs.

Joey made quick work of greeting his future in-laws, high-fiving and fist-bumping with each of Frances's siblings and hugging her mom. He stuck out his arm to shake hands with Mr. Vega, but Frances's dad was having none of that. Joey was pulled into a bear hug so intense, his eyes went round.

"Hello, Katie." Charlie stood near enough that his arm brushed my shoulder.

A hundred things I wanted to say flashed through my mind like a slideshow on high speed. But I settled for one snippy word. "Hi."

"I'm sorry about the settlement."

The words were like a stinging slap to my face. "Right." I left him standing there, deciding I'd rather talk to Frances's brother.

The rehearsal lasted an hour, one agonizing hour in which I had to stand ten feet away from Charlie, as his brother and my best friend pretended to exchange their vows. Finally the associate-pastor said, "It is good," and set us free to move onto the final phase of the evening, the rehearsal dinner.

My twisted, knotted stomach said I couldn't eat a thing, but I would go and put on a good face for an hour, then excuse myself and return to Maxine's. My grandmother and I had graduated from *Golden Girls* and progressed to a series about a gang of Harley riders who liked to beat people up. Maxine said I could learn a few things from that show.

Giuseppie's was an old post office converted into an Italian bistro five miles out of town. They served homemade pasta, butter-dripping bread, and the waiters occasionally crooned at your table. Frances's father had wanted Mexican food, her mother Chinese, so of course,

Frances chose another country entirely.

Frances's father wouldn't hear of my driving to the restaurant alone and wasn't satisfied until I was buckled into the back of Joey's SUV, Frances beside me and Charlie riding up front. It was a painful sojourn in which Frances and Charlie did all the talking, and I sat there as quietly as Joey.

We arrived at the restaurant, and Charlie opened my door.

"Thank you," I muttered.

"Katie, wait." He latched onto my elbow and gave a pointed look to the happy couple. "A moment, please." Between the resolve on his face and the pressure on my arm, I knew saying no was not an option.

Frances and Joey walked into the restaurant hand-in-hand, lost in blissful, kissy wedding talk. Oblivious to my plight.

I jerked my arm from his grip. "What?"

"I get that you hate me, but do not bring it in to that restaurant. This is their night, and we're not going to be a distraction."

"Distraction." The man needed a dictionary. "Is that what you call your company devouring part of my town? Is that what this has been for you?"

"You know that's not how I—"

"Spare me."

His hand slid down shoulder, like it had a million times before. "No matter what's between us, I do not want to see you lose your theater."

The nerve! "You want me to calmly get through tonight? Then don't speak to me, don't touch me, don't—"

"Well, hello there."

Dread soured my stomach as I placed that voice.

It could only be Ian—standing behind me.

God, give me the strength to get through this day without maiming another human being.

I turned around to face my ex-boyfriend. "Hi." My voice was as welcoming as a swarm of yellow jackets.

Ian studied the scene, that analytical brain no doubt in overdrive. The hostility between Charlie and me had to be as heavy as Loretta's cast-iron skillet.

"So. . .tough few weeks, huh?" Ian's smile was surprisingly melancholy. "Sweetheart, I really fell for your little theater. I wanted it to make it. Really."

"Do *not* call her sweetheart." Charlie curled an arm around me, ever the attentive fake fiancé.

"I know you wanted it to work out, Ian." Unlike Charlie, who apparently couldn't care less if the Valiant fell to ruin. "Thank you for helping us. It was. . .strange to have you here. But we couldn't have gotten as far as we did without you." I slipped from Charlie's embrace and leaned into Ian, pressing a kiss to his cheek. "Thank you."

"When are you leaving?"

At Charlie's rude question, I blasted him with one of Maxine's evil eyes, using way more eyebrow than necessary.

Ian just smiled. "I'm headed out early tomorrow. Thought I'd have one last dinner with the locals, and someone said this was the place to be. And you're here celebrating. . . or drowning your sorrows?"

"Rehearsal dinner."

His forehead wrinkled in a frown. "Yours?"

"No," I said. "Frances and Joey's."

"I guess you'll be celebrating your own wedding soon. The engagement is still on, right? It survived the Thrifty decision?"

"It did." Testosterone dripped from Charlie's every word.

I could all but feel him bowing up beside me, regarding Ian like a dog that had stepped into his yard.

"Katie?" Ian left the question hanging.

I was running out of energy to lie about this anymore. Who cared? "Yes." I stiffened as Charlie pulled me in closer. "Still so . . .

so . . ." I sniffled and tried to think of the word.

"Happy," Charlie finished. "Very happy."

That wasn't the word I'd been going for. "Right."

Ian's eyes searched mine. "I do hope you are happy. If you ever need anything—"

"She won't."

I mashed the spike of my heel onto Charlie's toe. "Thank you, Ian. For all you did. And tried to do. For caring about the Valiant. For understanding what it's worth and how much it meant to me." Unlike some jerk I knew.

"We should go," said the jerk. "Frances and Joey are probably ready to order."

Ian looked so lonely standing there by himself. "You're welcome to join—"

"The *family* is waiting for us," Charlie interrupted. "Ian, good luck to you."

"Thank you."

I grabbed Ian's hand and squeezed. "Goodbye."

"You take care, Katie," he said. "Oh, and Charlie"—Ian could sure do smug—"Might want to keep those steak knives from your *happy* fiancée."

With Charlie's palm pressed to the small of my back, we walked to our table.

"He's charming," Charlie muttered.

"At least he has a heart."

"Which he freely shares. You should probably request a blood test before you touch it again."

"He cheated on me with one girl."

"One more than I ever did."

I stopped right beside a table of an elderly couple. "Do you want to talk about what you *did* do? Because as long as we're maligning Ian, we might as well discuss your grievances as well."

His jaw tight, Charlie smiled at the couple now thoroughly absorbed in our conversation. "Sorry to interrupt your dinner." Grabbing my hand, he pulled me toward a dark alcove away from the listening ears of any In Betweenites.

Between the isolated spot and his hands getting a little too free with my person, I had had enough. "Don't *even* think of putting any moves on me, buster."

"Would you just quit squirming and listen?" He waited 'til I stilled and managed to meet his angry stare. "This is Joey and Frances's rehearsal dinner. It's not going to be the Katie and Charlie show. I know you're mad—"

"Furious."

"I know you're furious—"

"Like the fire-breathing, head spinning, hell summoning—"

"But no matter what you feel, we cannot ruin this for Frances and Joey. Or my mom."

"Your mother?"

He raked his fingers through his hair, releasing a gusty sigh. "Joey and I live in different parts of the country. I don't know when my family will be together again after this wedding, and I want it to go perfect for everyone involved. We're not going to bring our differences into this weekend. We get through this wedding, and then we talk. Are we clear?"

"We have nothing left to say."

"Katie, if we have anything in common right now, it's that we both love at least one member of the wedding party. This is about them." A pleading note entered his tone. "Save your anger for later. When we're done, when Frances and Joey drive away tomorrow, you can yell and curse me all you want. But until then, we're going to make sure that those two have a great wedding, and everyone's happy."

If he was trying to shame me into compliance, it was working.

Charlie stood there and waited for my response, the dim lights casting shadows on his chiseled face. A face I used to love tracing with my hands. Which usually led to my hands traveling to his hair. Which usually led to—"

"Katie," said Charlie, jarring me from my thoughts, "your word on this."

How could I be so angry at him and still find my skin tingling at his nearness, my eyes not missing a single detail of how handsome he was?

Because I was my mother's daughter.

And a woman with a pulse.

"Fine." I pushed off the wall and shoved past him. "But you're giving me your dessert."

Dinner was a loud, boisterous affair, as was any meal or gathering with the Vega family. While Frances's mother's family mostly lived in China, her father's relatives never missed an event, no matter how far they had to travel. I sat next to Frances, pushing my Alfredo around on my plate and trying to pretend that Charlie Benson was somewhere in a Speedo on a glacier in Antarctica, instead of seated right across the table.

Joey hadn't had much to say during dinner, and I worried that Frances's chatty, vibrant personality was no match for his silent, introverted demeanor. What would they talk about at dinner? On road trips? When there was nothing left to binge watch on Netflix?

"So, Joey," I began, taking a sip of tea. "Are you excited to move to Cambridge?"

"I am." He smiled and glanced at Frances. "It will be very different from Texas, but I think the new venture will be fun."

"Probably expensive too, right?" I flinched as Charlie delivered a light kick under the table.

"We'll get by." Joey winked at his soon-to-be bride. "I just got a job lined up at a body shop. Hopefully I can eventually get into paint detailing. It's more my specialty."

"I'll probably work part-time at a coffee shop or something with late hours," Frances said.

"You're going to work and be in the PhD program? That's quite a load." I took a sip of iced tea. "And you guys have an apartment already?"

Frances dipped her bread in olive oil. "We just found a really cute studio near campus."

"Cute?" Joey's laugh was boyish and bashful. "It's a pit. But we'll make it our own. We can't have a house like my parent's right away."

"It'll be great," Frances said.

Charlie smiled at his brother. "I'm sure it will."

"You must come see me soon, Katie," Frances said. "We'll show you around Cambridge."

"Maybe at Christmas?" Warm memories filled my mind. "Joey, Frances and I have these silly traditions. We drive around and look at the lights."

"While singing carols at the top of our lungs," Frances added.

"Frances hadn't told me." Joey rested his hand on Frances's. "Sounds just like her."

"I guess you'll be taking her cat Mango," I said. "How do you feel about temperamental cats?"

Joey frowned. "I'm allergic to them."

"Mango's staying with my parents." Frances said.

"But he's your baby. You bottle fed him since he was—"

"It's okay," Frances said. "He'll be happy here."

That cat was Frances's pride and joy. I knew she had to be crushed.

"We are taking my dog Bruno," Joey said. "He's a Rottweiler. Huge guy."

I assumed from Charlie's narrow-eyed glare that he didn't want me to comment on that.

"I can't believe we're going to be married tomorrow," Frances said, pulling us away from my quicksand of conversational topics. "I can't wait to walk down that aisle."

"Do you have something borrowed?" I asked.

"My mom's pearl earrings."

"Something blue?" Charlie inquired.

Before Frances could answer, the waitress stopped by with dessert menus. The restaurant was known for their homemade pies.

"I'll take peach cobbler," Joey said.

"Would you like ice cream on that?"

"Nah, can't have the stuff."

The waitress scribbled down the rest of our orders and scurried away.

"You can't have ice cream?" Frances asked. "I eat it almost daily."

"Joey's lactose intolerant," Charlie said.

Frances picked up her water glass and drank deeply. She tossed her napkin on the table and rose to her feet. "I'm going to go to the ladies room. Katie, would you like to join me?"

"I don't really have to go—"

"Yes, you do." Frances excused us both without her usual graceful charm, then walked toward the bathrooms like her underwear had just caught fire.

She flew through the ladies' room door, only to stop in front of a row of mirrors. She began to wash her hands, repeatedly soaping and rinsing as if she had something to scrub away.

"Are you all right?"

"Yes, I'm fine." She worked a puffy lather onto her hands. "Perfectly fine. I mean, never mind that my fiancé doesn't know some basic details about my life, and I had no idea he was lactose intolerant. I mean, I could've killed him. With dairy."

"A little milk probably wouldn't do that much damage."

"He can't live his entire married life with diarrhea!"

I bit my lip on a grin. "He probably has stuff he can take for it."

"Does he have stuff to take when I starve him with my lack of cooking? Did you see how he was going to town on those potatoes? I've never even bought a potato."

"He can learn to love rice."

"Can he?"

Doubts.

They were running through Frances's head so loud, I could almost hear them myself.

"Are you okay, Frances?"

"No." She shut off the water and ran her hand over the sensor to get a paper towel. Then another. And five more. "I do love him."

"Would you feel better if you moved the wedding date out a few months? Maybe next spring?"

"My whole family is out there. Even my stupid cousin Esther who just married a plastic surgeon. And my grandma who loves Esther best. You know, all my beloved kinsman."

"They'd understand." I pulled the wad of towels from Frances's hands. "You need to do what's best for you. And Joey."

"He would never understand."

"If Joey loves you he would."

Frances turned back to the mirrors, leaned against the damp granite counter and looked at the girl staring back at her. My friend was exquisitely beautiful, brilliant, neurotic, and stressed out of her mind.

"It's just nerves," she finally said. "My mother said this could happen. I'm being silly." She inhaled a cleansing breath once, twice. Then squared her shoulders and nodded to my reflection. "I can do this." She watched herself in a mirror. "Tomorrow I marry Joey Benson."

Chapter Twenty-Six

"**S**O YOU TWO get married next, sí?" Grandma Vega took a bite of her tiramisu and leveled that eagle-eye gaze on Charlie and me.

"No. No, definitely not." The woman had never liked me enough to speak to me, and *now* she wanted to chat? I needed to get out of this restaurant.

"Why not?" she demanded.

"Grandma Vega, Charlie and I are not a couple. We're not . . ." Charlie of course was ignoring my glare and offering no assistance. He almost seemed to be enjoying this. "He and I . . ."

"Katie's not speaking to me." Charlie's arm found its way to the back of my chair.

Grandma Vega shoved her dessert away and cackled. "You sound like a wife already."

"I'm probably a long way from that," I said. "I'm not very good at choosing the right guys." Take *that*, Charlie.

Grandma Vega patted her lips with her napkin. "How you feel about arranged marriage?"

I reached for Charlie's cheesecake and speared my fork into a large bite. "Not interested." The cream cheese melted on my tongue, and I was grateful for the loose fit of tomorrow's dress. "But Charlie's very open to the idea. I'll give you his address."

Fifteen minutes later, as everyone sat finishing their dessert and drinking coffee, the focus and conversation was completely on Frances and Joey.

It was the perfect time to make my getaway.

"Excuse me." I tossed my napkin on the table, grabbed my purse, and escaped to the lobby. I reached for my phone and pulled up my favorite numbers. Maxine and Sam could pick me up.

No signal.

I wound my way through the hungry, waiting crowd in the lobby and walked outside. "Come on." I held my phone to the left. "Come on!" I extended it to the right. "Too many freaking trees!"

"I can't do anything about the freaking trees," said Ian standing by his car. "But I'd be glad to assist in any other capacity."

I clutched the phone to my chest and stared at my salvation. "I need a ride to my grandma's."

He jangled his keys. "Now that I can fix."

Minutes down the road, I let myself relax, my bones melting into his leather seat.

"I'm sorry how things turned out." Ian turned down the nagging voice of his GPS. "You put up a good fight."

"Thank you."

"It has to be hard, with you being on one side and your fiancé being on the other."

"He's not my fiancé." There. I'd said it, and relief poured over me like a waterfall. I had nothing to gain by pretending anymore, and I just didn't care. "It was a stupid ruse. I had told Frances all about you, so when you showed up in town, she wanted to stick it to you."

"And thus the engagement?"

"Yes."

"Yesterday I was sitting downtown on a bench, and the Garden Club spent forty-five minutes showing me the flowers they had selected for your wedding."

I couldn't help but smile. "This is my hometown. They love me."

"So this Charlie is a . . .?"

"Fool," I supplied. "You're a fool, he's a fool, you're all fools."

"And what if *this* fool said he was sorry?" In the dark of the car, Ian watched me closely. "Truly sorry."

"You all say that."

"Fair point. But I truly am. I don't expect you to understand this, but something happens for a man when you hit thirty. You panic. You realize it's time to settle down, and your playing days are numbered."

"Pretty sure you have the extended warranty on the playing days."

"Then you came along. And you were different. I loved you."

Empty words, especially after my row with Charlie, but for a girl who had been abandoned by her birth parents, it would never fail to send a momentary jolt of happiness. "Don't fool yourself, Ian."

"Would I have asked you to marry me if I hadn't loved you?"

I closed my eyes and wished to be anywhere else. How had my life gotten so complicated in the last few months?

"Does your Charlie know that part of the story?" he quietly asked.

"No." I hadn't even told Frances or Maxine. I'd shared it with no one.

Ian turned in the seat and watched me in the dark of the car. "I might've been the player, but you were the one who strayed first."

"I did not. I never so much as looked at another man the entire time we—"

"Your heart belonged to someone you'd met years before. And when I came to In Between it all made sense."

"I told you the engagement was a total fabrication."

"You never loved me. Not really."

My lips opened to deny it. But I couldn't.

He was right. Had I been crazy about Ian at one time? Yes. Wildly so. I'd delighted in the time spent with him, soaked up all I could learn about the theater from him, enjoyed the envious gazes of the girls wishing to be me. And I'd luxuriated in those moments when he showered me with attention.

"All this time I didn't know who I was jealous of," Ian said. "But I knew this guy was out there, someone who held your heart in a way I couldn't. Then I came to your little town, and there he was."

"My relationship with Charlie is as dead as the Valiant."

"You're a hard person to love. Did you ever think about that? I don't like your Charlie, but I can't help but feel sorry for him."

"He doesn't love me." I pushed a button and the window slid down. I needed air.

"I suppose it's safer for you to tell yourself that," Ian said. "You were always holding back, always ready to bolt, like I was someone to be afraid of. Or that love was."

Did these men all read the same self-help books? "And what good would that have done? If I had totally fallen for you, you still would've cheated on me."

"Would I?"

"Yes. Or you would've found some way to leave."

He chuckled to himself. "So you went into our relationship expecting loneliness, and I was the one who got it."

"And that's why you messed around with Felicity. Because you were lonely." He would have to have been deaf to miss the irony in my voice.

"I made a mistake. But maybe I just lived up to that low bar you always held over me."

He was using me to excuse his gigolo behavior, and I wasn't having it. No matter how low my self-esteem could drag lately, I knew I deserved better than some cheating rake.

"I miss you, Katie. I miss us."

"You're probably just saying that because Felicity broke up with you."

"No," he said. "She's eagerly waiting for me back in New York. But she's not you. I miss your smile, your laugh, your curiosity. How you adored London and made me see it with new eyes. Watching you try to find your way on stage."

"You said I stunk."

"You have a lot to learn," Ian said. "But you don't stink."

"Did you give me the part because we were dating?"

"Yes."

I expected the pain to barrel through me and sever me in two.

But it didn't. More like a mallet to the kidney. It wasn't anything I hadn't known, yet hearing Ian confess it was hard.

"You're not ready for the big time yet. Come back with me. Work with me. We'll get you there." His hand rested on top of mine. "Together."

"You really did a number on my head, Ian." And he was still working it.

He pulled the car into Maxine's driveway. "You did a number on my heart."

"Seriously, where do you get this stuff?" My grip on lucidity was slipping by the second, and I couldn't hold back the laughter. "Do you expect me to buy this crap now? I bought it for a year, and you know what? I'm not that girl anymore." Indignation swelled within my chest. I was grateful for all the work Ian had done, but that didn't erase the fact that he'd cheated on me. Made a mockery of me. And was waiting for me to fail. "I was that puppy Felicity is, following you around wherever you went, reacting to your every command. You know what? I don't need you to make my career."

"Is that a fact?"

"Yes. It is. There are hundreds of parts available on Broadway, and one of them could have my name on it."

"You'll never make it without me."

"Maybe dating you did get me those roles, but I was good, Ian."

"Good doesn't cut it in professional theater. Because for every audition you go on in which you're *good*, a hundred girls will be there who are *amazing*." Gone was the husky, come-away-with-me voice. "You want to go to Broadway? You'll be starting at the bottom. As some walk on part with no lines, just like you began in London."

213

"But I *did* get to London."

"It's a rough life. You've seen that. It will chew you up and spit you out, and only the strong can endure." Ian propped his hand on my headrest. "And I don't think that's you."

"You don't know that."

"Want to hear some truth? When I replaced you with Tiffany Meltzer, the *London Times* gave us a starred review. Our ticket sales went up twenty percent in five days. My other lead actors shined like never before. *That's* what a real actress can do. She makes the show a hit. She makes those around her better. She romances her audience. What did you do? You ran across the stage shrieking at your ex-boyfriend. With a sold-out crowd."

I wanted to hurt him back, to deflate some of that egotistical air. But any sarcastic retort I might've had sputtered and failed at liftoff. His words were a guided missile, zeroing in on my every insecurity, following my confidence until it achieved total destruction.

"Why did you really come to In Between?"

"Because if I didn't do some PR and humanitarian deed, I was fired. As in never working in the theater again." His smile was a little crooked, a little sad. "And because I wanted to see you again. Might as well see you and get a tax write off in the same trip."

"Do catch me if I swoon."

"And because no matter how heartless you think I am, I felt badly for hurting you. Cheating on you with Felicity was a horrible thing to do. When I found out I was New York bound, I wanted to see you. I wanted to help, even if in some small way. It was my apology."

I'd had worse.

"I didn't expect to fall for your town. Your theater. Even your crazy grandmother."

"She infects everyone." Much like influenza.

Ian inclined his body toward mine. "I did see something in you, Katie. I saw a diamond in the rough, and I thought with the right opportunity, you could have star quality. Perhaps with the right tutelage and with time, you could still get to the top. Come to New York. I'll work with you. We'll get you a great coach, enroll you in acting lessons, and I can put in a good word for you with directors."

"Your faith in me is so bolstering."

"You're a state university drama major. Your resume includes six months as an understudy and a few in a lead. If I had to guess, I'm betting you won't even list your last few London roles. No, I don't think you'll make it without some connections. We all know how the theater works. It can be just as much about who you know as it is talent. Your talent might not be Broadway quality, but you've got me. I know people. Let me be the one who helps you."

I opened the car door, the dome light a glaring mimic of a spotlight. "Goodbye, Ian."

"Katie, wait—"

"Maybe you're right." I set my feet on the pavement, wondering that I had the strength to stand. "Maybe I'm a made-for-cable movie actress in a sea of Oscars. But I don't need you. If I can't earn a role on my talent, then I don't want it. I don't want to be an actress so badly that I let someone use me—again. I won't be your protégé, and I won't have people whispering about me when I walk by."

"You're making a mistake. My offer won't last forever."

"Give it to some other poor, desperate girl. I was stupid to ever listen to you. Go home, Ian."

"You'll never make it without me."

"Then I'm all the better for it." I slammed the door, my heels hitting the driveway with an angry staccato. His headlights arced across the front porch as I heard his car back up, then finally drive away.

I stopped at the front door and kicked off my shoes, then bent to scoop them into my hands.

And that's when I saw a scrap of yellow in the shrubs.

"Maxine?"

Nothing. Just the chirps and croaks of night and the distant hum of cars.

I sighed loud enough to raise my bangs and tried again. "I have ice cream and hot fudge inside."

The bushes rattled, leaves shifted. And my grandmother stepped out like a Chanel-wearing Chupacabra.

She dusted off her black slacks and picked a spiny piece of flora from her shoulder. "Just out on my neighborhood watch." She spit out a bit of mulch. "Don't worry. The place looks secure."

"I assume you heard all that."

"Just the parts where you were yelling."

I stared up at the moon with watery eyes. "Ian said I was a mediocre actress."

"Frank Sinatra once said I'd never master the high kick, but who's laughing now." She proceeded to demonstrate just how wrong Blue Eyes had been. "Yep, still got it."

Standing on my grandmother's front porch, I laughed for the first time in days.

"Hon, you just gotta decide."

"On?"

Maxine slipped her arm around me and hugged. "If your fear's gonna be bigger than your faith. You can either dream it. . .or fear it. But either way, Sweet Pea—it's never going to let you go."

Chapter Twenty-Seven

"**Y**OU LOOK BEAUTIFUL."

Frances took her ivory wedding bouquet from my hands, her smile wobbly.

We had dressed in a side room down the hall from the sanctuary at the In Between Community Church. I wished James could've have been there to marry Frances and Joey. I wished James could've been there just to talk to. I had spoken to him via the computer days ago, updating him on the Thrifty Co. buyout, but he'd had little to say other than, "I'm sorry." When I'd pushed about an appeal, he'd gone silent, the answer in his apologetic face. "We'll talk about it when I get home," he'd said. But I knew there was no hope in our family taking on the company by ourselves. I had to push that out of my mind. Because today one of my best friends was getting married.

"The dress is perfect," I said, earning a beaming smile from Frances's mother.

Frances turned to a large mirror we'd brought in and looked at the bride staring back at her. "My parents pushed their cultures on me so hard all my life, and I wanted to be like the other kids in In Between—all American. But I'm not. I'm a blend of two amazing families and histories. It feels right to wear my mother's dress." The fitted red dress showed off Frances's willowy curves, and the bold colored threadwork complemented the regal peacock pattern.

"I'm proud of where we come from," Frances said.

I had no idea why, but tears sprang to my eyes. I had been a weepy mess in the last few days, and today was only going to offer more tearful opportunities.

"I'm my Chinese mother's daughter." Looking like a member of royalty, Frances held her chin high. "My Mexican father's first born." She gave a watery grin. "And Katie Parker's best friend." Not caring about wrinkles, Frances hugged me fiercely. "Thank you. Thank you for always loving me for me."

I choked back a sob. "Oh, Frances. You were my first friend here. The one who didn't care that I dressed like the bride of Dracula and spewed venom on anyone who tried to be nice to me. You changed my life."

Frances clasped my hands in hers. "The Valiant might be destroyed, but they'll never steal your memories. Thrifty Co. can't take away how that theater healed you or what it meant to your parents— to all of us. The Valiant will always live in you. It's not about the building. You're the Valiant, Katie." She squeezed our hands, tears streaming down her cheeks. "Be valiant. Live its legacy."

I shook my head, pressing my lips together to hold back the flood. "I don't think I can."

"You've got this. God brought you to us, to the Valiant all those years ago, knowing it would lead to this time in your life. The building might be destroyed, but what you put into it, what you gave to it never will be. I think the Valiant was just a starting point. Not just for you to turn your life around as a kid. But even now. You have the chance to turn it around again." She hugged me again. "I believe in you. I believe in you, Katie Parker."

The makeup would have to be reapplied. I was wrecked. It was all just too much. Frances's words, Charlie, my beloved theater being taken away forever, my best friend moving on in her life with a husband. All of it. *God, I can't do this. It's too hard.*

"Promise me you won't be one of those girls who gets married and leaves her old friends behind," I said. "I need you in my life."

She nodded and swiped the dampness from her cheeks with white tipped nails. "Nothing can separate us."

A knock sounded at the door, and Frances's dad peeked his dark head inside. Wonder filled his face at the sight of his beautiful daughter. Gone were the braids and pencils stuck in her hair. Gone were the Disney princess t-shirts and funny patterned socks.

She was ready to walk down the aisle to the rest of her life. Leaving behind the last remains of childhood.

I envied Frances for knowing what she wanted and who she wanted to experience it with.

"Mi vida." Mr. Vega tenderly held his daughter's face in his hands and kissed both cheeks. "You look so beautiful. I'm so proud of you."

"Thank you." She sniffed.

"It's time to go, mija," he said. "Your moment is here."

"Okay, Daddy."

He then spoke soft words to his daughter in Spanish, bringing more tears from both Frances and her mother. Frances nodded and grabbed a nearby tissue, blowing indelicately. I didn't know what he said, but just the way he said it had me nearly undone.

"Let's have a family prayer for Frances," Mr. Vega said.

I turned around, wanting to give them their time and busying myself with touching up my makeup.

"Katie." Mr. Vega held out his open hand. "We're waiting for you."

Oh, my word. How I loved these people.

"You are family." Mrs. Vega grabbed my hand and placed it over Frances's. "My sweet girls."

We bowed our heads, and Mr. Vega prayed for Frances and Joey, for God to bless them with many years and happy days. For health and wisdom and love.

"Amen." Mr. Vega gave his daughter her last kiss as a single woman. "Let's get this show on the road!"

The parents filed out, and I could hear the strains of an acoustic guitar. I slipped my feet into my high heels, and Frances and I exited the room and walked across the lobby to stand just outside the doors of the sanctuary. Charlie stood there, regal in his light gray three-piece suit and pink tie, like something out of a magazine. His parents stood beside him, and his little sister held a basket of rose petals, wearing a pink lacy dress.

"You look amazing," Charlie said to me.

A wintery frost settled into my voice. "Thank you."

The guitarist began the first notes of Frances's favorite love song, and Mr. Vega offered her his arm.

"Are you ready?" he asked.

Frances looked straight ahead. Nodded.

Mrs. Benson took the arm of the first usher, a high school friend of Joey's, as her husband followed them down the aisle. Another usher soon came for a beaming Mrs. Vega.

Sadie Benson went next, throwing petals and grinning like a future beauty queen.

Charlie gently took my hand and draped it over his forearm. Even through the layers of his suit, I could feel the warmth, the energy that only belonged to him.

The ushers opened the double doors again.

"This is us," Charlie said.

This is us.

Charlie and I slowly walked, following the path of coral petals. I tried to imagine myself taking this long walk as a bride. Ian had offered me the opportunity. But when I thought about who might be waiting for me at the front of the church, there was only one face I saw.

Charlie Benson's.

I smiled at some old high school friends and fellow church members. Sam and Maxine occupied the tenth row, and when we passed, my grandma looked Charlie up and down then gave me a discreet thumbs-up. Finally, we reached the altar, and Charlie's fingers slid over mine as he lifted my hand from his, and we took our places on opposite sides of the associate pastor. Joey and his brother hugged, bringing an unbidden smile to my lips.

The guitarist broke into the wedding march, and dresses swooshed as everyone stood to their feet for the bride.

Frances glided down the aisle, her father smiling, but losing his battle against tears.

I stole a glance at Joey, and my heart expanded in my chest.

His face said it all.

He loved her.

This man of few words loved her. Not a fawning, game-playing adoration that I'd witnessed in Ian, but an awe-struck, I'm-drunk-at-how-much-I-adore-you love. Joey's expression held joy and rapture, like he was seeing her for the first time. The same expression he would wear sixty years from now.

"Wait."

The room froze at that one word from the bride.

Oh, no.

Frances stood mid-aisle, her feet immobile, as if captured in cement. Her father spoke feverishly in her ear, but Frances just shook her head, her updo bobbing.

No.

Oh, no, no, no.

"I'm sorry," she cried. "I. . .I don't think I can do this."

A collective gasp nearly lifted the rafters.

"Frances?" Joey took a step toward his bride.

"No, please." She held up her hands to hold him off. "We rushed this. It's not right." And then the most horrid of horribles happened.

Because Frances Vega trained those dark brown eyes on her maid of honor.

"Joey and I have made a colossal mistake." She picked up the hem of her dress, a woman ready to run. "And Katie was right all along."

With that, Frances broke from her father's arms and sprinted as hard has her heels would allow, right out of the sanctuary.

Chapter Twenty-Eight

LIKE CINEMATIC SLOW-MOTION, two hundred heads swiveled toward me.

"What have you done?" Charlie's words rang like buckshot in my ears.

"I . . . I . . ." The gears in my brain stuttered and stopped. "I don't know. I can fix this. I'll talk to her."

"No—"

But it was too late. I took off down the aisle, only tripping once on the hem of my dress. Chatter swelled all around me. People pointed. Dirty looks were thrown. Frances's grandma flipped me double birds.

But I kept running.

As did Joey. He was right at my heels, and I feared he'd tackle me to the ground on his way to his bride.

The blur that was my best friend ran into the room we'd been in earlier and slammed the door.

"Frances, let me in." I pounded with the flat of my hand. "I mean it. I'll break this door down."

"You have the arms of a ten year old boy," she called. "Go away!"

"Open this door, or I'm telling that whole congregation about the time you skinny-dipped at science camp!"

The door flew open and Frances jerked me inside.

She looked like a fury.

"You need to take some deep breaths." I used the voice one employed to talk a jumper away from the ledge.

She tugged on the tight collar at her neck. "My gosh, I'm about to roast alive in this thing." Like a hamster, she walked in fast circles, her heels grinding into the carpet. "I'm hot, I'm sweaty, and I need to get out of here."

"You need to sit down."

"I don't want to sit."

"You need to get back out there."

"I don't want to get back out there!"

"You need some hard liquor and street drugs."

Frances stopped pacing.

And laughed.

My nerves had me giggling as well. "What in the world is going on?"

Frances sank into a Sunday school chair and let her head rest on the back, staring at the veined ceiling. "You were right. I don't know him. And Joey doesn't know me."

"I didn't say that."

"I can't even take my cat. I love Mango. We've been together through so much. My first heartbreak. His mange phase. And now I can't even eat a bowl of cereal in front of my soon-to-be husband. You *know* how I love my Toastie Oaties."

"I think you're taking the *intolerant* part of lactose intolerant a little too far. I'm sure Joey won't mind if you have some dairy."

"But what kind of wife would I be if I ate that in front of him?"

"One who's whole-grain satisfied?"

"I'm being serious. We can't even afford to be on our own. I'm terrified I'm going to be working so much, I'll flunk out of the PhD program."

"You've never flunked anything in your life." I grabbed a chair and pulled it right next to her. "And that's what really scares you. You've done everything so perfectly. Aced every school subject, every college class, anything you've ever put your mind to. But this marriage business is unchartered territory."

"It's absolutely frightening. I haven't slept in two weeks."

We both startled as the door shook and fists pounded the door. "Frances! Frances!"

Her eyes widened. "It's Joey. Don't let him in here."

"Frances!" he called.

"You've got to talk to him," I said.

"You go talk to him."

"Me?" I barely knew the guy.

"Yes. Go out there and tell him. . .tell him I just can't marry him."

"Frances, I don't think—"

She shoved me with the force of a WWE wrestler. "Tell him!"

I made my way to the door, praying for God to send a holy rapture. I was never going to live this day down.

I eased outside and shut the door behind me. "Hi." I swallowed and tried to think of profound things to say. "How are you?" Oh, geez. How was he? Joey looked like he'd just watched his life ripped away from him. His face was ashen, his eyes wide and rapidly blinking, as if hoping to see a new picture.

"I need to talk to her." Sweat beaded at Joey's temple. "I gotta get in there."

"That's not a good idea. She, um, she sent me out here to speak to you."

"What did she say?"

Oh, boy. "She said that. . ." I wanted to tell him anything but this. "She said she couldn't marry you."

"Why?"

"Frances thinks maybe you guys haven't had enough time to know one another."

"So what?"

"Well . . . maybe if you had a little more time to date."

"People get married quickly all the time. Her parents did and look how they turned out."

"True. But Frances is worried you two have some obstacles that might be hard to face together. Like money. Responsibilities."

"Katie, I love this woman so much." His pain was sharp enough to pierce the both of us. "She's my everything."

My guilt was boundless. "I believe you, Joey."

He fisted his hand and pounded on the door. "Please let me in so we can talk."

Silence was his only response, but Joey wasn't giving up.

"Frances, I know you think we don't know each other well enough, but that's not true. I know so much about you. I know that you're the most beautiful person I've ever met. And you're pretty on the outside, too. I know that you have a kindness that fills me up. You're the girl who visits lonely people at the nursing home and picks up stray puppies on the side of the road. You're the girl who never passes a street musician without dropping in change. You smile at the sun and find four-leaf clovers. And your laugh. My gosh, your laugh. When I hear that sound, I have to stop whatever I'm doing and just watch you." Joey leaned his head against the door. "I know your heart, how strongly it beats for the people you love. How fiercely you care for your family and your friends."

A scraping sound came from the other side, like Frances had dragged her chair closer.

Joey pressed his palms to the door, as if his hands could pass through the wood and reach her. "I know we're gonna be broke. And I don't have a handful of degrees like you. But I'm good with the cars, and I can pick up an extra job, work double shifts. We might not have cable TV and steak dinners for a while, but I promise you those years are coming. And I don't care if I have to eat beans and rice, as long as you're there with me. We might be poor in Massachusetts, but I'm a rich man as long as I'm with you."

"Any luck?" Charlie asked, joining us in the hall.

I shook my head no.

"Be my wife," Joey said. He had spoken more words in the past few minutes than I'd heard from him in the entire last month. "Be my wife, and I promise no matter what we lack in material things, I'll make up for it in fun, in memorable days, in all the ways I'm going to love you. You know me, Frances. Don't think you don't. I'm the guy who would slay dragons for you. The one who will be your biggest cheerleader. The one who will always be true, who lives to hold your hand. I want to hold that hand forever."

Joey's volume dropped. He was now speaking to an audience of one. "I don't know what's ahead for us. I can't promise you it's going to be easy and we won't have hard times. But I do promise to be faithful. To love you every day of my life. Let's do this thing together, Frances. You and me. Let's have an adventure and figure it out together. We're all we need."

I pulled a tissue from my strapless bra, a little trick Maxine taught me years ago. I dabbed my eyes then blew my nose.

A rustle came from the other side.

A sniff.

Then the door creaked open, and Frances took one step outside. "I love you, Joey." Her face was splotchy, her nose Rudolph red. "I seriously love you." She threw herself into his arms and kissed him like nobody was watching.

And only two hundred or so were.

Joey held her close, the color returning to his skin. "Will you marry me? I don't care when or where. But just say you'll be my wife."

"Today." Frances laughed, a soulful chuckle that indeed turned heads. "Let's get married today."

With her updo completely unraveled and her makeup in artful streaks down her cheeks, Frances walked down the aisle with her fiancé. They stood before the pastor, God, and those who loved them best, and exchanged vows. Promising to cherish each other in sickness and in health. For richer or poorer. With cats or butter and cream.

"I now pronounce you man and wife." Pastor Higgins closed his Bible, and his sigh of relief could be heard two blocks over. "You may now kiss your bride."

Family and friends jumped to their feet, cheering for the couple.

Joey tipped his wife over his arm and kissed her but good.

And I finally let out the breath I'd been holding.

Today love had won.

It beat out fear. And darkness. And doubt.

All because two people said yes.

Chapter Twenty-Nine

THE DINER WAS extra packed Monday morning. Locals wanted to get in for the blue plate special as many times as they could before Micky's closed. Though there were more people stuffed inside, including a line that went out the door, the volume was subdued and eerily hushed. Folks carried on conversations in a tone usually reserved for funeral visitations.

In Between was sad. The melancholy ribboned through every city street, bounced off the rooftops, and was stirred into coffee cups with the sugar and cream. No matter what side a person had been on, it was a loss. There would be no more cinnamon rolls made by Loretta's rough hands. No free coffee at the hardware store. No more haircuts whose prices varied by how much gossip you could bring to the chair.

Life moved on. It changed, it grew, it died, it threw out something new.

I realized I wasn't good with change, and since coming to live with James and Millie, security had become an obsession. My idol. Somehow I would adapt to life without the Valiant. Life without Charlie.

Though maybe not today.

The object of my anger and years of affection now sat with his little sister in table number twelve. My section.

I snagged Kourtney as she walked by. "Hey, can you get that—"

"Consider it done." Her tresses hung extra frizzy and limp today, as if in protest of her impending job loss. Kourtney adjusted the tray she carried. "Thanks for fighting for the diner."

"What will you do now?" I asked as the swell of cafe chatter swirled around us.

"I've been thinking about beauty college." She shrugged. "I think I have a gift."

I smiled at my summer friend. "I know you do."

I spent the next forty-five minutes hustling it 'til I wondered if my deodorant had given up. I had a pocket-full of tips, and the heart-felt condolences of most of my patrons. But my gaze kept roaming back to table twelve. Charlie sat close to his sister, and I don't think he moved that I didn't catch it. He colored the menu with her, smiled at everything she said, and help her cut her steaming waffles when they arrived. And when the little girl wanted to pour the syrup herself, he didn't say a word when she flooded her plate.

"Shug, if you keep pouring that coffee, we're gonna need some extra napkins."

"Oh!" I set the pot on the table and yanked a dry dishrag out of my back pocket. "Mrs. Dylan, I'm so sorry. Let me mop that up."

"It's okay, dear." Her veiny hand patted mine. "Why don't you go over and talk to that Benson boy?"

Mr. Dylan waggled his white eyebrows. "You know you want to."

"I'm very busy. And he looks busy. We're both quite busy."

"Men do stupid things." Mrs. Dylan lowered her voice out of the range of her husband's wailing hearing aids. "But forgiveness is the key. You'll find they make horrible mistakes and often make us angry. But if I broke it off with my Herman every time he acted the dolt, we wouldn't have made it past the fifth date. Now you go talk to your fiancé."

"He's not my fiancé."

Mr. Dylan set down his coffee mug. "There's another stupid thing to forgive him for."

I cleaned up the couple's table, brought them a complimentary hot cinnamon roll to share, then gave myself a pep talk all the way to Charlie's table.

I could talk to him.

I could be civil.

I would not try to rip out his larynx while his sister was present.

The closer I got to table twelve, the less I felt that white hot poker of anger. It was still there, but my bone-deep sorrow seemed to have dulled the sharp point. I still hated the situation, still held Charlie somehow partially responsible, but I had no energy left to yell or spit venom. And somehow my responsibility in Frances's wedding meltdown pressed on me until I knew I had to speak.

God help me.

"Hi," I said. All around us tables of In Betweenites pretended not to stare, some better than others. And if looks were bullets, half of the Garden Club would've had Charlie lying in a pool of his own blood on the floor.

"Hello." Charlie's eyes searched mine. It was little consolation that he looked just as tired as I felt. "I'd promised Sadie some breakfast before taking her to school."

"You were brave for coming in here."

He scanned the room, his eyes lighting on people he had known so well. "I think they hate me worse than they did Coach Gilroy after three straight losing seasons."

"They just need time."

"And you?"

"I put away my Charlie Benson voodoo doll just this morning." I twisted that dampened dish rang in my hands. "Charlie, I'm sorry for the wedding interruption. I know what you think, and you're probably right. I wasn't as supportive as I could've been."

He ran his finger around the rim of his coffee cup. "It ended well."

"But I didn't want you to think I tried to sabotage the wedding."

"Didn't you?"

It was a fair accusation. "At some point I might've tried to talk Frances out of marrying your brother. But in the end, I could see the writing on the wall. And I backed off. I did." Couldn't we give me credit for that? "As soon as the wedding started, I knew Joey truly cared for Frances. I guess the seeds of doubt had been planted, and it was too late. And I'm sorry. The last thing I wanted to do was hurt Frances and Joey or mess up their day."

He took his napkin and wiped his sister's chocolate milk mustache. "Love is messy. It's risky and scary, and sometimes it just doesn't make sense. It asks us to take a risk." He threw down his napkin and trained those hard eyes on me. "I'm glad Frances made the choice she did."

The choice I had walked away from. "No matter what it looked like Saturday night, I do want them to make it."

"Thank you," he said. "And. . .I'm sorry as well." He glanced at his sister, who was hanging onto his every word. "For everything."

"I wished things could be different." All of it—the theater, our relationship.

"I really hope you find what you want, Katie."

Sadie poked her brother in the shoulder. "Are you going to tell her goodbye?"

Goodbye? "You're leaving?"

"Yes." Charlie's face showed no expression. "Sooner than expected. I have some things that need taking care of back in Chicago."

"I thought you were staying here, helping the community transition." Unbelievable. The papers weren't even signed, and Thrifty Co. was already going against their word. "That's what your boss McKeever said at the town hall."

"Thrifty won't take over the properties for at least six months. Until then, I've asked to be relocated."

To someplace where I wasn't.

So this was goodbye. "You take care, Charlie."

His hand on mine stopped my retreat. "Katie." He swallowed and paused, as if needing a moment to rearrange his words. "I meant what I said at the Valiant."

That he loved me? That he wouldn't take my love on conditions? That I needed to get my life in order?

"Which part?" I heard myself ask.

"All of it."

"Let's go, Charlie." Sadie tugged on his shirt sleeve. "I'm gonna be late for school."

"Goodbye." My words came out hoarse, scratched. And so very final.

Charlie's warm hand squeezed mine.

Then he let me go.

Tears falling, I quickly made my escape to the bathroom, where I took a few moments to allow the fist around my heart loosen its grip.

When I returned to the diner floor, Charlie was gone.

"YOU JUST VOLUNTEERED to work a double?" Kourtney filled a cup of ice with soda an hour later and handed it to me. "You must be in a bad way."

I didn't want to go home. Didn't want to face the quiet and hear my own thoughts.

"I'm fine. Too much fun here to leave." I downed the cold liquid, letting the euphoric burn slide down my throat.

Kourtney took a long pull from her tea glass. "If you think this is fun, you should get out more. I could introduce you to my cousin Sean. He just got out of the pen and is probably pretty lonely. A good woman could totally turn him around."

"Tempting as that offer is, I'm gonna pass this time." I slid my drink beneath the counter.

"He was like number one in the prison rodeo circuit."

I peeked into the kitchen window to check for my orders. "I just don't think it would be fair to Sean to be my rebound guy."

Kourtney shrugged. "Maybe next week."

I grabbed three hamburger specials, two chicken-fried steaks, and a chef salad. "Loretta, look at me," I said as my boss stepped behind the counter. "I finally did it." The devastation of the last few days couldn't stop the bloom of my smile as I balanced three plates on each arm.

"That's great." She stuck a pen behind her ear and grabbed a bottle of ketchup. "You're a total pro now."

At least I was good at something.

"Oh, and Katie?"

I brushed past her, my proud arms beginning to quiver. "Yes?"

"You're fired."

I laughed as I rounded the counter. "Because I asked for a raise and a company car?"

"I'm serious."

I stopped so hard, I nearly dumped all six plates onto the floor. "What?"

She took three of the plates from me, and I followed her to a table of men in matching coaching shirts. "Here you go, gentlemen," she said.

I stood there in a stupor, so Loretta pulled the remaining plates from my grip and served them as well.

I followed Loretta back to the counter. "Are you seriously firing me?"

"Yes."

"Why? Am I doing something wrong? I haven't dropped a plate in a week."

"How long?"

"This morning was a bowl. Totally different."

Loretta grabbed a dish towel and wiped the counter down. "Did you know that at some point, a mama eagle pushes her babies out of the nest? She shoves them right out, and they have to fly to survive the fall."

"And if they don't fly?"

"I guess they don't buy her a Mother's Day present. The point is, you're using this waitressing gig as a security blanket, and I'm not going to be a part of it anymore."

"I'm using it as a means to make money. So you're going to fire me, and you think you can hire someone who'll want to take a job that will run out in a matter of months?"

"It won't be easy. But you need to move on. Katie, it's time to make some decisions."

"But I'm not ready. I don't know what I'm going to do." I hated that whiny catch in my voice.

"Now you have time to think about it." She punched some buttons in the cash register, and with a beep, the drawer popped out. Loretta reached in and grabbed five crisp one-hundred dollar bills, money that I knew hadn't been taken in payment today. "Here's your severance."

"I'm not accepting that."

"You're not getting any two weeks notice. I want you out of here today. And you will take this money. It's going to be my first investment as a wealthy woman. I don't care how you use it, but spend it wisely. Buy a nice interview outfit. Take some computer class. Use it to get yourself a plane ticket." At my look of horror she rolled her eyes. "Okay, maybe not a ticket. Maybe some therapy for your fear of flying."

"I don't need your money."

She grabbed my hand and closed my fingers around the cash. "Thirty years ago, your dad answered a knock on his door in the middle of the night from a frightened woman who had just left her mean husband. I had bruises all over my face, couldn't see out of a swollen right eye, and three scared kids were crammed into my single cab pickup. I had nowhere to go. James and Millie took me in. Got

CAN'T LET YOU GO

me some help and set me up in a little rental off of Sycamore. Not only did your dad pay for my legal fees to get that rabid skunk of a husband away from me, he and the police chief would do nightly drive-bys the first few months, just to make me feel safe. I'd worked at this diner for years, and when it came up for sale, I had no way of buying it because my credit was so bad. So your father co-signed, and I never missed a payment. I put my kids through college on scrambled eggs and the fluffiest pancakes this side of Dixie. I know you don't need this money. But you're gonna take it anyway. And I want it spent on your new direction."

Tears gathered on my lower lashes. "I don't have a new direction. The Valiant was my back-up plan."

"Hon, back-up plans won't make you any happier than your last resort. When the time is right, you'll know what to do with the money." She gave me a wink that crinkled her skin. "And your life."

Chapter Thirty

THE NEXT WEEK I picked James and Millie up at the airport. They hugged me immediately, and I promptly burst into tears. The kind that involved snot. And those noises that sound like part-giggle, part-asphyxiation.

"I think we'll just redo the wood floor in the whole house," Millie said as she made her green smoothie the next morning. "It will be a great excuse to finally get that darker shade I've been eyeing."

Maxine had pedaled over on her bicycle and sat at the breakfast nook table, hot pink helmet still on, now sipping a cup of coffee. "We worked our tails off after that leak. Katie was a total slouch, but Charlie and I picked up the slack."

I knew Maxine was baiting me for a comeback, but at the mention of Charlie's name, I just deflated. I had dreamed of him every night since our giant fight. I wondered when he would ever be exorcised from my soul.

James sat beside Maxine, a half-eaten bowl of oatmeal next to him, and thumbed through the stack of mail that had piled up in his absence. "Already got a check from insurance. That was quick. Here's a letter from Maxine's sister in Arkansas. A *Seventeen* magazine?" James tried to hand it to me.

"It's not mine."

Maxine plucked it from his fingers. "I'll take that."

The doorbell rang, and James hopped up to answer it.

"Girls, I'm going to a yoga class later if anyone wants to join me," Millie said as she chopped some strawberries.

"Oh, yeah." Maxine snorted. "Nothing I love better than getting all bendy."

Millie opened the refrigerator door. "It's good for the digestion and peace of mind."

"So is Maalox and a trip to the mall." My foster grandmother clicked her polished fingernails on the table and watched her son-in-law return to the kitchen. "Whatcha got there?"

James held up a white box. "No return address, but it came from a Chicago post office. I had to sign for it."

An Alaskan shiver slid along my spine. Was it from Charlie?

Maxine pulled James's oatmeal her way. "Who's it to?"

"The Scott family." My dad grabbed a pocketknife and sliced through the tape. Even Millie stopped her kale tearing to see what was inside.

James set the mystery box on the table. "Files. Some paperwork." He laid it on the table. "Some photos? Is this. . .the mayor?" He held the picture to the light, and I looked over his shoulder.

"It's the mayor and that McKeever from Thrifty Co." I grabbed another picture. "Who's this with the man from the special commission?"

"That's Charlie's uncle," Millie said. "The one who works for Thrifty."

James rustled through the box, as if he were hunting something in particular. He would read a page, then pick up another, scanning as fast as he could. "Here it is." He shook his head. "I'll be darned."

"What is it, James?" Millie asked.

"What we have here is documentation of a payoff from Thrifty to certain community members, local government, and at least one member of that impartial commission." In his fingers, he held a flash drive. "I'm betting we'll find even more here."

Chairs slid across the floor, as we raced one another to James's office. He fired up his Mac, and inserted the drive. James clicked on the new icon and a menu appeared.

Millie put her hands on her husband's chair and leaned in. "There are hundreds of files there."

Maxine, Millie, and I stood unmoving for the next hour as James opened every file. More photos, scanned bank drafts, grainy images of deposit slips, even ten voice recordings of illicit meetings.

"Thrifty paid their way into this town," James finally concluded. "And I don't mean the big fat checks they were ready to hand to us."

By the time we had sorted through it all, we had enough information to thoroughly ruin our mayor, three city council members, and two members of that special commission.

James grabbed me by the shoulders and gave my cheek a loud kiss. "I think we're saved." He laughed and hugged me to him. "I think the Valiant is saved."

BY EIGHT O'CLOCK that evening, the news was all over town. The local media camped up and down our street, our phones had been ringing like the world was ending, and friends and strangers alike stopped by for visits. The Thrifty deal had been rescinded, and multiple people had lost their jobs.

I needed some peace and quiet, and only one place would do.

The sun was still at full scorch when I pulled into the Valiant parking lot. Rehearsals for the summer musical were already over, and I knew I'd have the place to myself. Unlocking the doors, I went inside, inhaling deep of the familiar, comforting scent. My cheeks tugged with my smile, and I took a moment to look all around the lobby. It was like hugging an old friend. It was all I could do not to drop to my knees and kiss the floor.

Thank you, God.

I could hardly walk straight for being drunk on the gratefulness and relief.

My legs carried me into the theater, and I ran my hand across some of the names on the rows. I kissed my fingers and pressed them to the chair that held the names of the Scotts. All of us.

I went in the back and climbed the steps, walking onstage, past the set that would make the hills come alive next week. I stood center stage, imagined the spotlight on my face, the crowd waiting in anticipation. I settled onto the floor and lay on my back, closing my eyes and listening to all the subtle sounds of an old theater settling in.

Now that the theater was saved, I would take over in the fall. James had already approved it.

I would be the one handling the accounting, organizing the events, maintaining the facility.

It would be business.

No more spotlight on my skin. No more standing ovations or bringing a crowd to tears or raucous laughter.

Thanks to some anonymous whistleblower, I had gotten exactly what I wanted.

My future was set.

My job, secure.

"Be valiant," Frances had said. "*You're* the Valiant."

I startled at the footfalls coming down the carpeted aisle and lifted my head.

"You know," Maxine said. "For a girl who just got her wish, I expected to see a big, fat smile on your face."

"I'm meditating on my happiness."

She found her way onstage. "Aren't you going to get up out of respect for your elder?"

"No."

"So be it." My grandmother plopped herself down beside me and rested her body on the floor. "This is quite nice," she said after a long moment. "I assume my white sweater is getting dirty business all over it, but still, not a bad spot to rest in."

"What are you doing here?"

"I had to get out of that zoo of a house. So I hopped on Ginger Rogers and here I am." It wasn't age that kept Maxine away from the steering wheel of a car, but her horrible driving skills. Her bicycle, Ginger Rogers, had gotten the two of us into many adventures. "I assume you told the Valiant she's saved."

"I did. She's very happy."

"And are you?" Maxine turned her head to study me. "Are you happy?"

"Yes, of course. We got a Hail Mary of a miracle, and my theater is saved."

She watched me so closely, I knew something profound was about to leave her lips. "You need some lipstick on."

I laughed. "I love you, Maxine."

She laughed too, then closed her eyes, took some deep stage breaths, then went quiet. We laid there like that for a long stretch of time, Maxine with her thoughts, and me with mine.

Until her fingers reached for my hand.

"It was nineteen sixty-something," she said, piercing the silence. "I was young, skinny, and I could dance better than any girl in Vegas. A man came in every Friday night to watch my show. You could find me front and center in the final kick line, and he always sat in the second row, middle seat. After months of watching, he approached me one night. I figured he wanted a date. The boys liked them some Maxine, you know what I mean? I had a reputation for showing them a *real* good time."

"Am I old enough for this story?"

"Poker, you nitwit. I was a mean poker player with the gentlemen after the show. Few could beat me."

"Because you cheated?"

"That offends me."

"You still keep the occasional ace in your bra."

"You'd be surprised how often it comes in handy. Anyway, Edward Bridgerton was his name. He handed me his card. Said he was a director and wanted to talk to me about a role in this movie he was doing. Mr. Bridgerton told me he saw star power in me, and if I was interested, he had a small part for me in a little movie. He asked me to join him for dinner that night."

"And were you interested?"

"Boy, was I. It would've been a dream come true. The life of a showgirl was fun, but it wasn't easy, and I knew it had a big fat expiration date on it. But Mr. Bridgerton wasn't my only regular customer. Because a man named Davis Simmons had also been coming in to see our show. Twice a week he got the steak buffet, a water with no ice, then came in and watched us dance. He was in construction and there on business for the summer, so I knew he was just passing through. Asked me to meet him for dinner at the Sands that same evening."

"And you did."

"A smart girl leading with her head would've met that fancy director. But my heart said . . . go out with the quiet fellow who blushed and stared at his shoes when he asked to buy you a meal. So I told Mr. Bridgerton I was sorry, and I had surf and turf with the man I'd marry before the Christmas season."

"And what became of Mr. Bridgerton?"

"A few years later that movie came out, and I bought myself a ticket to see what I had missed. And let me tell you, it was a dandy. So good I saw it twice. My part would've been pretty small, but it would've surely led to other things, like it did for many of its stars."

"Did you regret it?"

"I suffered the occasional days of *what if*, but I was always happy with my decision. I was blessed with a happy marriage to a wonderful man, and we had a beautiful family." Maxine lifted my hand to her mouth and left her lipstick pucker on my skin. "And that includes you. He would've been crazy about you."

"How did you know that was the right thing to do?"

"I never knew until I jumped. That was part of the fun." Her blue eyes seemed to look right to my withered heart. "Honey, when you get to be my age, you realize your regrets in life aren't the things you did, so much as they're the things you didn't. The chances you let go by. You have to ask yourself what is it that just won't leave you alone?"

"My grandmother."

"What else?" she asked with a sly smile. "That relentless thing that consumes you. You think about it when you wake up, and it's the last thing on your mind when you go to bed."

"Charlie." There. I'd said it. "I still think about Charlie."

"*O teach me how I should forget to think*," quoted Maxine.

"What?"

"It's a line from your very first play. Recognize it?"

I thought I might. "Did Romeo say that?"

"He did indeed. 'O teach me how I should forget to think,'" she repeated. "Sweet Pea, sometimes thinking is the last thing we should do. Logic doesn't always lead us down the right path. Logic tells us not to take chances. Not to chase after that risk. To ignore the what ifs. I guess part of growing up is deciding when to listen to your head . . . and when to listen to your heart."

"I want to be valiant." My whispered admission sounded like a trumpet blast to my ears.

Maxine drew herself up to a seated position and eased to her feet. With a tug on my hand, she pulled me up. "Then do it, honey." She held a fierce grip on my shoulders. "Be valiant."

"What if I fail? What if I go all the way to New York and don't make it?"

"Then we'll eat lots of pie and decide what to do then. But for now, take that chance. You have a gift, and Sweet Pea, life is waiting for you to pick it back up."

I took another long look at the theater—my home for so many years, my sanctuary and place of safety. "I'm really scared."

She gave my cheek a gentle pat. "Sounds like the first line to what will become a remarkable story. One I can't wait to see you write."

We walked off the stage hand-in-hand, my grandmother humming a catchy little ditty, and me with my whirling thoughts. The next few weeks and months would be terrifying, but I was ready to take that first step. If I fell on my face, I had a wonderful family to pick me right back up.

"Oh, Maxine." I flipped off the lights over the stairs. "The part that director offered you. You didn't tell me what movie it was for."

She glanced at the Austrian hills behind her and gave a winsome smile. "It was called the *Sound of Music*."

Chapter Thirty-One

T HE PLANE SHOOK and shimmied like a cart on a roller coaster. My fingernails made slivered indentions on the chair arms, and the woman beside me sent a curious look in my direction more than once.

What? Was it not normal for one to cry out the Twenty-third Psalm during takeoff? And was it totally weird to sing "Jesus Take the Wheel" during landing? I had survived two hours and fifteen minutes of this calamity we called air travel, and I didn't want any more of it. Maxine had slipped me something she called a "calming Tic-Tac," and James and Millie had prayed over me before I went through security. I had a bladder full of three diet sodas, and I had accidentally shredded my *People* instead of reading it.

"We're just about there," the woman said. She looked to be a little older than Millie, and now regarded me with kind eyes. "I take it you don't fly much."

"Not if I can help it. I had a horrible flight last month, and this is my first time up in the air since."

"It must be something important that's got you on a plane then."

"It is," I said. "My whole life is waiting for me." I hoped. I prayed. I wished.

With way too much tilt than I thought necessary, the pilot brought that bird down. And when we filed out to exit, I nearly rushed the open cabin and kissed the crew in my gratitude.

I didn't expect to find my bags waiting for me, but when the conveyer belt chugged to life thirty minutes later, there they were. I'd cried less at funerals.

Sitting in the taxi, my heart still running a sprint, I pulled my directions up on my phone. Grateful to be on land, I didn't care that the driver spoke no English and operated his car like we were trying to gain on the lead in Talladega.

"Here. Out. You go." The driver put it in drive and held out his hand. "Money. Me."

"Okay, sure." I dug in my purse and pulled out some twenties. "Money, you." I placed the cash in his hands, then let a uniformed man from the hotel handle the luggage.

Ten excruciatingly long minutes later, I had checked in, touched up my makeup, said a prayer, and eaten two candy bars.

This was it.

My appointment with destiny. I was as ready and prepared as I could possibly be.

I checked the address I'd been given, then walked the five blocks.

Which turned into ten.

Which turned into fifteen.

And then it started raining.

I was lost.

Totally turned around, and my navigation on my phone didn't even pretend to care.

"Excuse me." Rain pouring on my head, I flagged down a passing walker smartly holding an umbrella. "Can you tell me where this is?" I showed her the address.

She pointed back the opposite direction. "Five blocks that way. Then take a left by the bus stop."

"Thank you!" I ran the rest of the way, my silver flats, once a sensible traveling choice, now eating into the back of my heels. My breath came in heaves, and my hair, which had been styled into glorious waves, now hung so far over my face, I nearly missed that left turn.

But there it was.

My first appointment in town.

The building loomed in front of me, dark and scowling. But I walked through the doors, dripped all over the lobby, and climbed the stairs.

When I reached the fourteenth floor, I was sucking air worse than Maxine blowing out her birthday candles. I stumbled my way past three doors, until I finally found the right one. I was soaked through, my hair had since formed Medusa-like knots, and the pain in my side had me doubling over, my hands planted on my knees, dragging in sweet oxygen.

Until the door opened.

I saw shoes. Two running shoes connected to legs.

"Are you okay?"

I held up a finger. "Gimme just . . . just a minute." Should I be seeing spots? Did that mean I had hurt some brain cells? Or that I needed another candy bar?

"I'm. . .I'm here to see you." I finally managed to lift my head.

And looked into the disbelieving face of Charlie Benson.

"Katie." My name on his lips sounded like a prayer. "What are you doing?"

"Shivering. And sweating." I rubbed my runny nose with the back of my hand. "It's a weird combination." And then I sniffled and my lip quivered. "I wanted to look hot for you."

Charlie took a slow inspection of my form. "You look like you just walked through a hurricane."

I attempted to toss my hair over my shoulder, but it just stuck to my hand. "Yes, well, here I am. In Chicago. Are you going to let me in or not?" *Because this vision could be all yours.*

He stepped back and held open the door, and as I limped by, I held my head high. I was a Scott. I had dignity.

I also had something really vile stuck to my sole.

Charlie closed the door and led me to his small living room. "Can I get you a change of clothes?"

"No." Luxurious as that sounded, I wanted to get straight to business.

"Did you drive here?" he asked.

"I flew." Loretta would be proud of how I'd spent her severance.

"You flew." At that he almost smiled. "By yourself?"

"Yes, and it was perfectly terrible. But I only had to breathe in the little baggie twice."

He went to the couch and clicked the remote to silence the TV before sitting down. "Must be something important if you got on a plane."

"It is." Good heavens, I smelled like a dumpster. "I can't help but notice you're not at work today."

Charlie wore faded jeans and a gray t-shirt, and he clearly hadn't shaved in a few days. He stretched his arm across the back of the couch and shrugged. "I told you I can work anywhere my laptop is."

I settled onto the edge of a worn leather chair and felt the water squish in my sagging underwear. My powers of seduction had been lost miles ago. "I've been calling you for the last twenty-four hours. You didn't want to pick up the phone?"

"Had to get a new number. My work phone got . . . misplaced."

"I see." Rain droplets slid down the side of my face.

"I don't believe we established why you happen to be in my neighborhood."

"I just wanted to talk. Catch up with an old friend." I craned my neck and saw moving boxes stacked in the floor of the kitchen. "We got quite the shock back home." I watched his expression for any reaction, but the man probably had an ace in his shirt as well. It was a poker face Maxine would certainly be proud of. "Seems your Thrifty Co. paid some people off to support the buyouts. The mayor, two of the guys on the special commission, some city dignitaries."

"Really?" He sounded bored.

"Someone leaked the information. I hear it was an internal source at Thrifty."

Charlie shifted on the couch and picked at the skin on his thumb. "Is that right?"

"Yes. Lots of evidence. It appears this informant had probably been building his case for quite a while."

While Charlie continued to exercise his right to remain silent, I got up from the chair and sloshed across the carpet to sit on the opposite end of the couch. "I wonder what will happen to that informant?" I asked casually.

"I hear he was fired immediately." The poker face was gone, and Charlie looked me dead in the eye.

I slid the rest of the way down the couch until my damp jeans pressed against his dry legs. "Why didn't you tell me?"

"I couldn't." He leaned back and let his head hit the cushion. "Nobody could know until it was over."

"Are you okay?"

He rubbed a hand over his face. "No."

"Maxine said the bank fired your dad."

He nodded gravely. "There's also an investigation to see if criminal charges need to be pursued."

"That's what you meant when you wanted the wedding to be perfect for your mother. You knew this was coming."

"I was able to break the news to my mom before it went public. She's devastated. But not surprised." His mother had been the one to tell me how to find Charlie.

"And your dad?"

"I can't even talk about it. Not yet." Charlie propped his feet on the coffee table, crossing at the ankles. "He was furious. No matter how in the wrong my dad is, I betrayed him. His own son. My mom kicked him out, so he's in some hotel outside of town. Sadie doesn't understand any of it. How do you explain to a kid that her daddy's a criminal?"

"I'm sorry. I can't imagine how difficult this was."

"It was the right thing to do. I started seeing red flags late last year . . . so I started documenting. As much as I wanted your theater to survive, I didn't want my corruption suspicions to be true."

"Does Joey know?"

"Mom was going to tell him when he got back from his honeymoon." Charlie looked as soul-weary as I'd felt the day I left London. "So the Valiant's safe?"

"Yes. And Thrifty's lawyers have offered to cover all the legal costs and some large shut-up money not to sue." James was going to use his to build that new wing on the church. "So the people who wanted to retire get to do that and keep their businesses, and the Valiant will live many more years."

"I guess that means you'll be taking over soon?"

I stood up and walked to the window and watched the rain puddle in the street. "I'm not going to be the Valiant manager. This week I realized my heart is on the stage—not behind it. So I've got some auditions here and in New York. Small parts, but I have to start somewhere."

"That's great." Charlie walked up behind me, and I could see his reflection in the glass. "Did that heart happen to tell you anything else?"

I turned then, painfully aware of how close we stood. "It told me that I had walked away from a boy one too many times. Because I love this boy."

Charlie rubbed a smudge of something off my cheek, his finger gliding over my skin. "Anyone I know?"

"A very brave informant. I don't expect him to believe this isn't tied to the saving of the Valiant, but it's not. I've loved him since I was sixteen. It just took me a while to get it straight in my head. To realize that fear was holding me back—on my career, on letting go and completely falling in love with my whole heart. It's pretty scary," I admitted.

"Maybe that guy's scared too. He might be a mess."

I reached for Charlie's hand and reveled in the texture, the heat. "Be my mess."

He smiled at that, revealing one sigh-worthy dimple. "I'm gonna love you fiercely, Katie Parker Scott. Are you sure you're up for that?"

"Yes," I said. "I think I finally am. I love you, Charlie. And I'm sorry for everything. For letting you go, for all the things I said, for the stuff I said to Frances about—"

"Katie"—He put his fingers to my mouth, rubbing his thumb across my bottom lip—"You got on a plane for me."

"A shaky, wobbly plane."

"I think you really might love me." His lips lingered a breath away from mine. "I've lost a lot this week, but nothing tore me apart like losing you."

I slipped my hands around his neck, my fingers touching the ends of his hair. "We can deal with the rest of it together."

"You sure about this?"

I pulled his face to mine and kissed Charlie with all that I had. My smelly, soggy body against his, I poured everything into that kiss—my hopes, my fears, my insecurities, and my love for a boy who seven years ago fished me out of a pool. If Charlie had only known what he'd really caught. A girl with tangled thoughts in her head, hesitant feet that were now ready to walk toward those new things, and a passion for him that was as relentless as it was consuming.

Arms holding this gorgeous man, I leaned back and smiled. "So this informant. What do you think he'll do now?"

Charlie kissed my temple and smiled. "Drive a beautiful girl to some auditions in town. Then hold her hand on a flight to New York. He's going to watch her dreams come true." My knees nearly buckled at the wonder in his face. "And beg her to love him."

"For how long?"

"Forever," Charlie said. "He's going to love her forever."

The Scott family theater would go on, and I would always adore it. It had been my salvation, the place where I had found my life's purpose. It had taken my adolescent anger, my tears, and my laughter, and given me memories of a lifetime and set me on the path of a destiny bigger than my dreams.

I would carry that theater of mine in my heart always.

And with Charlie by my side, I would push through the fears. I would be brave. I would be bold.

I would be valiant.

If you enjoyed this book, please consider leaving a review at your online retailer and Goodreads.

Acknowledgements

With much gratefulness, I would like to thank:

Erin Valentine, my sweet friend and awesome editor

Christa Allan, Kristin Billerbeck, and Sibella Giorello, for getting it, being my support system the past few years, and speaking my native tongue of sass and sarcasm. The best is ahead.

Lizann Tollett, prayer warrior and my buddy in the trenches of life

Kelli Standish, for your incredible encouragement, your fighting spirit, and the million things you do for authors.

Beverly Jones, for pool Sundays

My school family, for laughs, encouragement, and Sonic runs. Oh, and educating children.

My much adored readers, for every email, comment, review, and happy thought you've sent my way. Thank you for loving my In Between family. You're total Sweet Peas.

About the Author

Four-time Carol award-winning author Jenny B. Jones writes romance with equal parts wit, sass, and Southern charm. Since she has very little free time, she believes in spending her spare hours in meaningful, intellectual pursuits, such as watching bad TV, Tweeting deep thoughts to the world, and writing her name in the dust on her furniture. She is the author of romantic comedies for women such as RITA finalist *Save the Date*, as well as books for teens, like her *Katie Parker Production* series. You can find her at **www.JennyBJones.com** or standing in the Ben and Jerry's cooler.

Visit Jenny's Website
http://www.jennybjones.com/

Join Jenny on Facebook
https://www.facebook.com/jennybjones

Follow Jenny on Twitter
https://twitter.com/JenBJones

Sign up for Updates on Upcoming Books
http://www.jennybjones.com/news/